PRIVATE
CAPTAIN

A STORY OF GETTYSBURG

MARTY CRISP

SCHOLASTIC INC.

New York   Toronto   London   Auckland   Sydney
Mexico City   New Delhi   Hong Kong   Buenos Aires

ISBN 0-439-56543-X

Copyright © 2001 by Marty Crisp. All rights reserved.
Published by Scholastic Inc., 557 Broadway, New York, NY 10012,
by arrangement with Puffin Books, a member of Penguin Group (USA) Inc.
SCHOLASTIC and associated logos are trademarks
and/or registered trademarks of Scholastic Inc.

12 11 10 9 8 7 6 5 4   4 5 6 7 8/0

Printed in the U.S.A.   40

First Scholastic printing, October 2003

To my Civil War ancestors

I come from Maryland, a border state between the North and South during the War Between the States, 1861–1865. This history was traced back through my father, Charles Morris Tibbels, and my grandmother Etta Beall Tibbels for my son, Joshua Mark Crisp, who is an avid student of this fateful 19th-century American conflict. Our roots trace to:

- my great-grandfather *William Henry Beall,* who worked as a civilian carpenter for the Union Army, repairing bridges;

- my great-great-uncle *Lemuel Hancock Beall,* a private in the 20th Pennsylvania Cavalry, Company K;

- and my great-great-uncle *Benjamin Franklin Beall,* a private in the 7th Maryland Volunteer Infantry, Company C.

These three brothers survived.

- The fourth brother, my great-great-uncle *John Wesley Beall,* according to family tradition, joined the Confederate Army and was killed in action.

ACKNOWLEDGMENTS

The writing of this story would have been impossible without the generous help of:

- *John W. W. Loose,* Lancaster's premiere historian;
- *Larry Alexander,* a fellow newspaper reporter and a reenactor, who is a captain in the 30th Pennsylvania Volunteers, Company E;
- *John Valori,* a high school social studies teacher and a sergeant in the 6th Louisiana and 14th Indiana Volunteers (both Company G);
- *P. G. Simmons,* a very special friend who always finds time to read and critique every manuscript;
- my son, *Joshua Mark Crisp,* who inspired this story in the first place;
- and my husband, *George B. Crisp,* who somehow makes my computer do what it needs to do, instead of what (I truly believe) it wants to, and is my very best friend besides.

Any factual errors in this story are the author's, and the author's alone.

Patricia Lee Gauch, editor

Table of Contents

CHAPTER 1

June 28, 1863

Ben awoke suddenly, with something tickling his ear.

He couldn't remember where he was. There was a stifling pillow laid over his head, and he was sticky with sweat. Captain's snout was pushed under the pillow, his wet tongue slurping across Ben's cheek and ear.

Ben shook off both pillow and tongue.

"Yeah, yeah, leave off," he whispered to the big, yellow dog, his voice sounding loud in the dark room. Ben had no idea how late it might be. He couldn't believe he'd fallen asleep. Not tonight, of all nights.

Here he was, supposed to be gone, halfway to finding Reuben. How could he fall asleep at a time like this?

Ben turned his head and looked straight into Captain's eyes. In the faint moonlight that crept around the edges of the window shade, they shone like polished coals. He remembered it all now. He remembered jamming the pillow over his head to escape Danny's droning voice. His pesky cousin was sleeping in Reuben's bed tonight after his family had fled Hanover and the Reb invasion.

Ben swung his legs to the floor and tiptoed over to check on his cousin.

Danny lay on his back, a soft, whistling snore coming with every breath, his head propped up on three pillows. Aunt Mavis always said her little Danny needed to keep his head above the "congesting sleep vapors" that came at night.

Ben had an urge to shove a pillow over Danny's head and see if that didn't congest him good and proper.

Except he had more important things to do. He let himself out into the hall without another sound and opened the glass face on the grandfather clock at the top of the landing. He could feel the hands, pointing straight up and at a right angle. Three o'clock. Three o'clock in the morning!

Ben couldn't believe he'd overslept by so much. He hurried down the steps to the kitchen and pulled his flour sack, filled with food and supplies, from the spot where he'd stashed it behind the big iron stove.

As he swung around, his bare foot clunked against a wooden case full of tonic bottles, making them rattle. He closed his eyes, half holding his breath. Danny's dadblame "Turlington's Balsam of Life"—Aunt Mavis gave the runt a tablespoon of the foul-smelling stuff every night. Maybe she thought it would make her only child start to grow. It sure enough smelled like the manure Lancaster County farmers spread on their fields to make their corn grow tall.

Ben opened his eyes and allowed himself one long, deep breath. No one in the darkened house seemed to be stirring. He unrolled his ball of clothes, shed his night-shirt, and pulled on his cotton drawers, his old, gray wool pants, and Reuben's hand-me-down muslin shirt. Ben lifted the white web suspenders over his shoulders and slipped his arms into Pa's brown wool work jacket, rolling the sleeves up twice. He carried his shoes and socks in the crook of one finger. Captain had padded down the stairs behind him, but the dog slipped under the long trestle table. Ben couldn't even make out his shadow now, despite the fact that Captain's fur was such a pale yellow, it was nigh onto white. Maybe the dog had fallen asleep under there. Which was just as well.

There was no way he could take a dog with him. It'd be quicker to travel alone, and he didn't have room to cart along food for a blame-fool dog. Besides, Captain was Reuben's dog. He wasn't likely to go trotting along at Ben's heels. Never had before, anyroad, and Ben suspected he never would.

Ben lifted the latch on the back door, trying not to make a sound. He thought he heard a muffled thud on the floor overhead, and he paused, waiting.

No. There was no other noise, except the distant, faint ticking of the grandfather clock. Captain was still invisible under the table.

Ben closed the door so gently, it made only a soft

*click-click*ing. He walked in his bare feet down the wooden staircase, into the yard behind the dry goods store, nudging a lump of chewed turnip over the edge of the bottom step as he passed. The dog must have stolen the crunchy tuber from the bushel basket under the steps. Captain was the vegetable-eatingest dog Ben had ever seen.

Ben waited until he was out front on the brick sidewalk, half a block down from the store, before he pulled on his black wool socks and heavy leather brogans. The moon was barely visible, a sliver of silver overhead. It was the kind of moon they showed in the pictures in nursery rhyme books, with a cow jumping over it.

The *Farmer's Almanac* said there was only a quarter of a new moon tonight, and that was fine by Ben. The darker the better. He was bent over, lacing up the rawhide ties, when something brushed against him, almost knocking him over.

Ben made a strangled sound deep in his throat. It was a wordless, choking noise, and it surprised him, even though he was the one making it. It was the sound of fear. Ben hadn't let himself even think about being afraid, all the days he'd been planning this. But he couldn't deny that he'd made the sound.

Ben raised his head and saw the yellow dog's long, wavy coat, shining like pale gold in the oily glow of the streetlamp.

"Get away. Go back," Ben whispered, clucking his

tongue softly and waving his arms at Captain. How had the dog gotten out, anyroad? Ben was sure he'd closed the door tight.

Captain sat down in front of Ben, watching him tie his shoelaces. Ben considered grabbing the dog's old leather collar and dragging him back to the house. But what if Captain barked? What if all the kerosene lamps blazed on in the parlor and Aunt Mavis came out and caught him by the ear, like she always did, and his mother came out in her soft, blue flannel gown, and looked at him with those pale blue eyes of hers, with the same unbearable hurt in them as when they'd got word about Pa dying?

No. He couldn't think about Pa tonight. And he couldn't risk going back.

Ben got to his feet and shifted his sack to a more comfortable position under his arm. "Suit yourself," he told the dog. "But if we run into Rebs, you remember. You didn't listen when I told you to go home."

Ignoring the dog, Ben began to lope down Lime Street, toward the intersection with Orange. He had a lot of time to make up. He was already three hours late, and he'd just started.

The street was deserted, lit in an eerie, flickering way by the iron streetlamps' dim glow. Nothing looked real. The looming brick houses. The marble front stoops. Ben knew they would look ordinary as toast in daylight, but in the shadowed darkness, they looked spooky and threatening. Ben shivered, despite the warm June air.

The houses were dark, except for a single lamp burning in the front parlor of the Owens' house. It was strange to see a parlor light burning at three in the morning, but the Widow Owen didn't sleep much anymore. Ben had heard Mama talking about it to Aunt Mavis.

Henry Owen was fourteen, only two years older than Ben, but he'd up and joined the militia a week ago. Ben figured Henry's mother was sittin' up again tonight, worrying about old Henry.

She oughta worry, in Ben's opinion. Henry couldn't lob a pebble into a washtub at two paces. His aim was awful. It was hard enough to picture Henry, with his glasses pinching his nose, shooting at attacking Rebel soldiers. It was impossible to picture him *hitting* them.

Ben trotted along quickly, putting distance between himself and Reynolds & Sons Dry Goods. He knew where the roots grew up through the bricks in the sidewalk along here, so he didn't stumble. Captain had disappeared in front of him, or maybe behind. But Ben couldn't be worrying about a dadblame dog. There was too much else to worry about.

Like getting caught and hauled back home. Or not finding Reuben in time, before the big battle everybody said was sure to come any day now. He had to find his brother *before* the battle. Ben had stood at the courthouse door, reading the casualty lists after Antietam and Bull Run. He had to find Reuben before they posted another list. *After* the battle might be too late.

Ben broke into a run. He wanted to get out of the city as quick as he could. Even though Lime Street was deserted, too many people were up and about on other streets, what with the Rebs so close. There were home guard soldiers at the barricades every few blocks along King Street. Some of them had bonfires going, flickering in the distance, sending the shadows of the tall, crowded-together buildings into an uneasy dance.

Ben could smell the sharp tang of roasting hickory wood, and it made him think of autumn and Reuben's last visit home. His big brother had looked like a general in his blue wool uniform, though he'd been only a lieutenant then. They'd joked about Captain being the only senior officer in the family. But no longer. Reuben had made the rank of captain in April. He'd said so in his last letter. The last letter they'd gotten, anyroad. Letters were so slow these days, Aunt Mavis said a body could die and be buried before you even got word he was sick.

That's why Ben couldn't write Reuben a letter. He had to tell him about Pa in person, and bring him home to help run the store and be a comfort to Ma. Somebody sure had to help her. Ben was no good at keeping the store's inventory straight, and he was no good at saying the right thing when Ma's face clouded up, the way it did every day now.

But this he could do. He just had to hurry. He probably ought to run even faster, but it was too dark for real speed.

Besides, he felt a little sick. His stomach had been twisted up with excitement all day, ever since he'd decided to go, and now he felt like he'd swallowed one of the bricks underfoot and it was bumping against his insides with every step.

Ben breathed deeply and concentrated on moving through the darkness, skirting the pools of dim light cast by the oil burning in the tall, iron streetlamps.

Captain had run off. The dog couldn't know Ben was going after Reuben. It had no reason to stick around. Probably run off to dig up a fresh turnip.

Something exploded with a bang behind Ben and whistled through the air over his right shoulder, making the hairs on the nape of his neck stand on end. It whacked loudly into a corner of the house Ben was passing, spitting splinters of brick that sounded like a shower of straight pins onto the sidewalk.

"I *meant* to miss you that time, boy, but if you don't throw down your gun and turn around slowly, the next one will be aimed right between your shoulders." The words sounded more like the growl of a mean dog than the voice of a human being. Ben turned, very slowly, his hands spread wide, palms up. He backed up a step as he turned, the way you'd face a porcupine who was bristling at you.

"I don't have a gun, mister," Ben said, wishing his voice didn't always crack when he got nervous. He could make out a white mane of hair, and a ragged, red-and-blue frock coat in the glow of the streetlamp.

"That's far enough." The growl stopped him, and Ben wondered how he'd managed to stumble into the war quite so soon. He could see the long barrel of an old-fashioned blunderbuss pointing squarely at his chest.

"Speak up, lad."

Ben couldn't quite make out the craggy face, hidden under the shadowing brim of a tricornered hat.

"One wrong word, you Rebel spy, and I'll shoot you for the cowardly dog you are."

CHAPTER 2

West to the War

I'm no spy, mister. I'm Ben Reynolds, from right up the street here. My pa . . ." He felt his breath catch, like it did every time he mentioned Pa. "My ma runs the dry goods store."

"Reynolds? Step closer, lad. Let me get a sight of your face."

Ben started to take a step forward and almost tripped over the silent form of Captain. Apparently the dog had circled back to see what was keeping him. Now he had taken up a guard position just in front of Ben's feet. Ben sidestepped and started forward again, with Captain crowding beside him. The presence of the big, yellow dog made Ben feel safer, somehow, even with a gun aimed right at him.

"Ah, yes. I recognize you now, lad. Sorry if I frightened you, but we can't be too careful these days." The gun lowered, and Ben realized he was looking at Colonel Martin P. Martin Junior, the eighty-seven-year-old gentleman who lived with his spinster daughter in the big house on the corner of Orange and Queen.

At least, folks called him "Colonel," although Ben didn't think he'd ever fought in a real army. He was dressed in long black stockings, black wool knee britches, a white shirt, and a tattered, red-and-blue Revolutionary War frock coat. People said the Colonel's pa had been a minuteman in the Battle of Lexington and Concord.

Ben wondered if the old man in front of him was as loony as the boys at school said he was. The man had taken a shot at him, right here in the middle of Lancaster. Times were tense, but still. . . .

"So, where are you off to, lad? Going to fight the Redcoats, are you? Wish I could go along with you, but I've been charged with guarding this street for the Queen," the Colonel said with a low chuckle. "Queen Street, don't you know. But I see you have a companion. I could use a fine dog like that one there to help me patrol. If you could see your way clear to sell him to me, I'd give you . . ." The old man rummaged around in the pocket of his coat and Ben could hear something jingling. ". . . shall we say, two bits and some coppers?"

Martin P. Martin was definitely crazy if he was offering thirty cents for a prime hound dog who had Chesapeake Bay retriever blood in him. Ben wagered Captain was one of the finest hunting dogs in the eastern U.S. Reuben said he had the best nose in three counties. A dog worth at least a full dollar, Ben was sure of it.

He looked down at Captain's funny pink nose. The

dog's nose was edged with black, like maybe it had started out the color of a lump of coal, but had been scraped and worried until the black wore clean off.

"He's not my dog," Ben told the Colonel flatly. "He belongs to my brother, Reuben, who's away fighting the Rebs. Reuben's in the 106th Pennsylvania, Company A."

"Ah, Reuben Reynolds. Well, it's good you got home on leave, lad. I'm sure your mother needs you after the sad news about your pa." The Colonel came closer and knelt down with an audible creak to pet Captain. "I heard about the unfortunate business at Camp Curtin in Harrisburg. Measles is no small peril to a soldier, but I take it hard that it killed a fine man like your pa. So, you say you're on your way home, to comfort your poor mother? It's good you could get away from the battle."

Ben's right hand clutched Pa's pocket watch deep in his front pants pocket. Ben could almost feel it ticking, right through the round gold case.

"I'm not Reuben, Colonel. Reuben is my brother with the 106th. I'm Ben. I'm the one who's trying to *find* Reuben. I aim to bring him home to help Ma with the store. But I gotta hurry. I'm heading for Columbia tonight."

"Ah, yes, we must defend Columbia. If the Redcoats cross the bridge there, it'll be hell to pay for Lancaster. Now get on with you, lad. Hurry to our western border and defend our fair commonwealth from these cowardly invaders. I've got this street covered. You cover the bridge."

Ben nodded and turned to go, wondering how anyone—even someone as muddled as this old man—could believe it was the British Redcoats coming, instead of the Confederate Graycoats. He felt a hand on his shoulder and turned back, only to be pulled into the Colonel's surprisingly firm embrace. The old man kissed Ben on both cheeks and thumped him on the back.

"You go out there for the both of us, Reuben Reynolds. And when you see your brother-in-arms, General John Reynolds, tell him Martin P. Martin sends felicitations. But watch close that the Reb spies don't cut your throat on the way. They're everywhere."

Ben nodded again, eager to get away. General John Reynolds was Lancaster's favorite son in this war, and distant kin to Ben to boot—maybe a third or fourth cousin. But Ben didn't plan to meet up with any generals, relatives or not. Captain had disappeared around a nearby corner, and Ben set out at a fast trot to follow the dog. He could hear the Colonel shouting after him, something about "death to the infidels," and only hoped the growly voice wouldn't wake up all of Lime Street, all the way back to his mother and Aunt Mavis.

Ben crossed Penn Square, dodging the barricade fires and hugging the darkness around the shop buildings. It was the middle of the night, but people seemed to be up and about all over the city. Ben stopped on the corner of King and Prince, a block past the makeshift barricade in the square, and looked back. It wasn't a proper wall at all, just piles of hay bales, old tables and chairs, stacked lumber, and upended wagons. In the dark glass of a shop window, Ben could see the reflection of the torches the men guarding it carried. Most carried torches in one hand and Enfield rifles in the other.

Ben looked north, up Prince Street. It was much darker up that way, away from the barricade's flickering torches and bonfires. He could make out the imposing front of Fulton Hall. Captain sat on the sidewalk in front of the long row of doors. The dog had apparently detoured a street rather than pass the bustling barricade. He'd had the right idea.

Ben hurried past the hall and the carriage lot beside it, where he and Henry used to play chuck-a-luck before the war started and things like boys playing dice games stopped. But he wouldn't think about that now. Too much thinking could slow a body down.

Ben detoured northward, walking rapidly past houses with their windows open and unshuttered in the late June heat. The city smelled vaguely sour, as if all the backyard privies were overflowing and the horse plops, invisible in the warm darkness, were steaming in the street.

Now that he was away from the bonfires and streetlamps

in the main part of the city, Ben's eyes were starting to adjust to the darkness. He followed the railroad tracks, angling west and cutting over to James Street. From there, it was only two blocks to the campus of Franklin & Marshall College.

The college buildings were silent and deserted. Crossing the quadrangle gave Ben the eerie feeling of walking through a cemetery. He'd been out here just yesterday, watching the students drill and shoot. They must have already gone out to make a stand with the home guard at the bridge in Columbia.

Ben had to get there. He broke into a flat-out run, straining his eyes to avoid stumbling over low bushes in the darkness. What if something happened before he could get across that bridge? What would he do then? He had to get there while there was still time.

Captain must have felt the same urgency because the dog was running around him in wide circles now, like a sheepdog trying to nip his woolly flock along.

Ben tried to run faster than the circling dog, but Captain's easy lope, tail waving high like a regimental flag, was impossible to beat. Captain barked for the first time that night, a joyful sound, as if running was what he'd had in mind all along.

Ben cut cross-country. His detour of the barricades in the city had taken him north of the Columbia Pike, and now he began to move south again, toward it. The Pike led

directly to the little river town of Columbia, with its mag-
nificent mile-long covered bridge over the Susquehanna
River. The bridge ran between Columbia in Lancaster
County and Wrightsville, directly across the river in York
County. If a body was heading west, it was the only bridge
for thirty miles up or down the broad barrier of the mighty
Susquehanna. And Ben aimed to cross it by mid-morning,
even if he had to walk all night.

It was so quiet in the fields and woods that he wondered
if he was the only human being awake and moving outside
the city. It was a spooky feeling. He wished he'd brought
along the tintype in the parlor, the little square picture of
Reuben, in his black felt derby, sitting with the polished
barrel of his rifle across his knees. Ben himself had been
the photographer for that portrait, taken in Reuben's little
studio in the attic above the store.

'Course, Reuben had talked him through every step.
When to pull the lens cap off. How long to let the light hit
the delicate emulsion Reuben had painted on the glass
plate. Truth was, Ben wouldn't have known the hole you
put your eye to from the hole that took the picture if
Reuben hadn't taught him.

But there was no way Ben could've brung along the tintype in the little gold picture frame. It was in the parlor,
and his mother was sleeping on the parlor settee, having
given up her room to Aunt Mavis and Uncle Elliott. They
were part of the flood of refugees fleeing east through

Lancaster. Danny's family had packed up a wagon and fled Hanover two days ago, and Ben had been plagued ever since by his eleven-year-old cousin—bragging on how he had single-handedly taken on the Rebs.

When Ben reached Brubaker's Run, he stopped and filled the tin flask he'd borrowed from the rosewood display cabinet in the store. Captain walked straight into the cold, clear water, thrusting his muzzle deep in the bubbling current as he drank.

When Ben stood up, the dog bounded back out of the stream and shook himself vigorously, aiming the spray, it seemed to Ben, in his direction. "I didn't invite you along, you dumb dog." Ben didn't want to admit it, but the splattered water felt good on his hot skin. At least the company of the yellow dog made the countryside seem less lonely.

Ben knotted the flour sack across his chest and over his shoulder and stuck out both arms for balance. He jumped to a rock in midstream and, from there, to the opposite bank. Captain splashed back into the water after him and out the other side. This time, the dog didn't bother to shake. He ran ahead, disappearing into the darkness. Ben ran his hand along his flour sack, feeling for the shape of the candle he'd packed—it was so dark out here, he could barely see his own feet. He pulled his tin of kitchen matches out of his shirt pocket and held them uncertainly. No, they'd attract attention, flaring up in the darkness. Ben put them back reluctantly. He hadn't expected it to be *this* dark. It was never this dark in the city. There was always light coming from somewhere. But not out here.

Ben took a deep breath and kept walking, more slowly now, in the direction Captain had gone. He felt like a blind man, feeling his way along with his feet and his arms. He hoped he didn't get lost. It had looked so easy on Pa's map of the state. It didn't even look that far to York County. Reuben and the whole Union army would be following the Rebs, and the Rebs were nigh on close enough to march into Wrightsville. Surely he'd catch up with Reuben tomorrow. He'd cross the bridge into Wrightsville, and find his brother there waiting for him. He would.

Crickets seemed to be all around him, filling the darkness with a chirring chorus that had no melody. There was no sign of Captain. Dadblame bootlicker dog.

"I don't plan on looking out for *you* the whole way. If ya get lost, you'll stay lost." Hearing his own voice made Ben feel better.

He trotted across an open field and took what he hoped was a shortcut through the woods. He had to watch his feet carefully in the faint starlight, to keep from stepping in a hole or tripping over a root. The quarter moon was worthless, already setting, just when he needed it most.

He passed Baer's Distillery and didn't even have to look up to know it. The smell of hops and barley was so strong, he felt like he could get drunk just by breathing the air.

A quick bark ahead made Ben look up, and a root

grabbed the toe of his shoe and sent him sprawling onto both knees in a soft carpet of pine needles and leaf mulch. Ben reached down and ran his fingers over the wool of his pants knees. No rips. He stood up, brushing himself off, and caught his first glimpse of the brightly lit Farmer-and-Drover's Inn. He was nearer to the Columbia Pike than he'd thought. Despite the late hour, lanterns hung from every outdoor post and bracket. Candle glow spilled from every window, and Ben could hear the distant rumble of voices. Indeed, he could see wagons and carriages of every description pulled up near the stables out back.

Ben dropped to a crouch. He scooted around the glow cast by the tavern, scurrying like a crab, keeping his head down. He didn't stand up straight until he felt his feet hit the solidly packed dirt of the pike beyond the inn.

He could see better in the open expanse of the road. It was still dark, but without the trees all around him, he could make out his feet and even see Captain, sitting about ten feet in front of him, on the side of the road.

Ben pulled the Union cap out of his waistband. He put it on, tilting it forward like he'd seen real soldiers do. He trotted briskly, his long legs pounding along in an easy rhythm, and he hummed softly as he went. It made him feel good to hum the chorus from "Battle Hymn of the Republic." He even threw a mock salute at a passing possum that scurried across the road in front of him. Maybe the truth really was marching on, like the song said.

Captain ignored the possum and ghosted through the darkness beside Ben for a long time before disappearing again. Ben didn't call the dog this time or try to whistle him back. Captain could do whatever he wanted.

This was Ben's journey, and he knew exactly where he was going. He was going west to find the War. When he found the War, he'd find Reuben. He was on his way now, and the whole Confederate Army couldn't stop him.

CHAPTER 3

His Brother's Dog's Keeper

The sound of something moving behind the roadside bushes sent a prickle of fear down Ben's back. Captain appeared out of the blackness ahead, growling softly. The back of Ben's neck tingled. Someone was out there sneaking around in the dark, watching him. Maybe it was a Rebel spy. Maybe the old Colonel wasn't crazy after all.

Captain growled again, low in his throat. Ben thought he could see the leafy branches of a nearby honeysuckle bush in the dim grayness of the starlit summer night, swaying. He grabbed Captain's leather collar before the dog could lunge at their hidden company, and hung on to it, straining to hear anything in the predawn silence.

"Is somebody there?"

Ben winced at the sound of his own voice. He sounded like a girl. His voice had just started to deepen, but whenever he got excited, it got all high-pitched and funny-sounding. Ben dropped his chin and concentrated on talking low. He kept his voice matter-of-fact.

"If somebody's out there, you better show yourself. Or I'll let go of this killer dog, and he'll tear you to pieces."

Ben waited, gripping Captain's collar so tightly his fingers were going numb. They were at least two miles out of town, and Ben hadn't seen a soul since they'd left the city behind. He could clearly hear his own ragged breathing and feel the thump of his heartbeat pulsing behind his sweaty forehead. The sweet smell of honeysuckle usually made Ben's mouth water, but right now his mouth was as dry as a bonfire's ashes.

Ben waited for the bloodcurdling Rebel yell he felt sure was coming. The boom of a cannon. The whistle of a minié ball burying itself between his eyes.

Captain growled.

Ben waited, listening.

The unseen presence behind the honeysuckle bush suddenly giggled. "Reuben's dog wouldn't bite *me*," it said, and then it giggled nervously again, ending with a hiccup. "I'm the one who let Captain out when he was scratching at the door after you. He likes me."

Ben blinked, not quite believing his ears.

"That better *not* be you, Danny Seldomridge."

Captain growled softly, but Ben noticed that the dog's yellow fur hadn't bristled up, and his tail swung slowly back and forth in a halfhearted wag.

"Who *else* would it be?" Danny thrashed his way through the tangling branches of the sweet-smelling bush and tripped down the short slope into the road, clattering like a tinker's wagon loaded with pots and pans. He was dressed in Uncle Elliott's black canvas jacket and Aunt Mavis's beat-up straw hat.

Under the open jacket, Ben could see a canteen tied to one belt loop and a tin cup tied to the other. A large ax was stuffed into Danny's waistband, and a big, iron skeleton key was visible between the buttons of his shirt, on a string around his neck. One of Aunt Mavis's fancy pierced-tin lanterns hung around Danny's neck from a rawhide cord and a blanket hung over his shoulder, dragging on the ground.

"I knew I'd catch you up, if I ran," said Danny in a well-pleased but breathless voice. "I just knew you'd be somewhere along the Columbia Pike."

"How come I didn't hear you?" Ben demanded angrily. "You're making as much noise as the Gypsy who comes around with bells on her ankles and tells fortunes at the fair. I should have heard you a mile away."

"I had this here blanket wrapped around me," Danny told him, the pride of the plan obvious in his voice. "Wrapped tight, too, so I wouldn't rattle."

"Well then, tell me what in tarnation you're doing here." Ben loosened his death grip on Captain's collar, and the dog trotted over to explore Danny's legs with his pink nose, lingering at the crotch and again at the skinned knee, where Danny's brown wool pants were freshly torn.

"I'm coming with you. That's what I'm doing!" Danny sang out the words. "Want me to light my lantern, Ben, so we can see where we're going?"

"Don't you dare." Ben's voice was clipped. "I'm doing this by myself. I know where I'm going, and you're *not* going with me."

"Sure I am. I'm coming with you, just like Captain. We're gonna find the army, right? And then we can join up and fight the Rebs and get this durn war won."

"*I'm* gonna find the army," agreed Ben, moving close to his cousin so that he loomed over the smaller boy. "And *I'm* gonna bring Reuben home. And you're gonna turn right around, right now, and get on back to the city before Aunt Mavis misses you."

"No. I'm not." Danny shook his head. "I'm coming with you. We can go to my house in Hanover and get supplies. I have the key." His words were pleading, and he held up the skeleton key on the string around his neck as proof. Then he hiccuped. Ben savored the momentary hesitation he could hear in his cousin's voice. It was clear that, for the first time in all his eleven years, Danny Seldomridge understood that Aunt Mavis wasn't around to protect him. This time, Danny's bossy mother couldn't force Ben to take his cousin along.

"I'm not takin' you," Ben said quietly. "I can't be responsible for you when I got to think about finding Reuben."

"I can be responsible for myself, Ben Herr Reynolds," Danny shot back, using Ben's full name just like his ma did when she was angry. "The Rebs are right here in Pennsylvania, you know." Ah, there went Danny, displaying his greatest talent—his talent for stating the obvious. "So now it's my war, too."

Ben snorted with laughter. "You don't care about this war." He turned his back and began to walk away, tossing a few parting words over his shoulder. "You don't even understand why we're fighting."

"I understand good as you," Danny challenged, catching Ben's elbow and trying to swing him around. "We're fighting to make the Southern states do what we want and not let them make their own country on our American land."

Ben snorted again. "That sounds like something a kid would say." He turned slowly and faced Danny, his hands on his hips. "This war is about slavery and states' rights." He tapped Danny's shoulder with one finger and Danny backed up a step. "It's about important *issues*. My pa said so. And it said so in the newspapers, too."

"It's about whatever you say, Ben." Danny had never sounded so agreeable before. "Just take me with you. I promise you won't be sorry."

The hard-packed dirt road suddenly vibrated under Ben's feet as a fast-moving spring wagon rounded the far bend and raced toward them. It was closely followed by a carriage and a two-wheeled cart. All three vehicles carried heavy loads of furniture and supplies, tied together with ropes. The loads jounced noisily as the wooden wheels bounced over the rutted road. Ben could just make out the outlines of a few things in the glow of the lanterns that bobbed on poles jutting from the front corners of the wagons and the cart like dancing fireflies. A lone, wooden rocking chair rode atop the mound roped to the spring wagon.

"Hi-ay!" one driver shouted at the snorting, wild-eyed horses harnessed to his wagon. Ben jumped as the cart driver cracked a whip over a pair of scrawny mules.

Ben and Danny scrambled up the road berm and dived into the honeysuckle bush. But Captain dashed directly into the road, dodging around the lead horses.

"Come back here, you fool dog," shouted Ben, not sure whether Captain was trying to protect him or trying to get him into trouble. Ben was conscious of his heart drumming loudly in his ears. He pulled Reuben's tin clicker hurriedly from his pocket and used it to call Captain. The dog instantly left off chasing around in the road and came over to the bush where Ben was crouching. Reuben had taught him well.

Reuben was a good teacher. Fifteen years older than Ben, and more like a father than a brother really. He was the one who taught Ben to swim in the Conestoga Creek. Reuben was the one who covered for him when he wanted to go off and play chuck-a-luck with the other boys instead of working in the store the way Pa wanted him to.

Ben clicked the tin frog again, and Captain came right up to him. The dog rested a paw on Ben's knee. He wasn't sure why he'd stuck the old clicker in his pocket with Pa's watch. He was amazed it still worked on the dog. Cap had been barely a year old when Reuben went off to the war. There'd been no training since then. Ben reached out and scratched gently under Cap's whiskery chin. The dog tilted his head, as if he wanted Ben to keep it up.

But there was no time for such foolishness. Pa had warned him to keep his distance from the dog. He said it would jinx Reuben if anybody else got too attached.

Ben managed to stand up despite the honeysuckle vines. He slid back down the short slope to the road, bringing Captain with him, keeping hold of the collar this time.

The cart and spring wagon had already rattled past, but the carriage driver slowed down and pulled up beside Ben.

"Ho there, boy," hailed the driver. Ben could now make her out to be a dark-haired woman with her hair in a tight bun on top of her head. Her frowning face looked sharp and beaky in the beams of the carriage lamps. "Do you need a ride?"

"No, ma'am." Ben took off his Union cap and nodded politely. "But thank you kindly for the offer. I'm headed in the opposite direction." Captain sat quietly at Ben's feet, staring intently up as if trying to read Ben's face in the murky light of the oncoming dawn. "I'm bound for Columbia and the bridge."

The old lady touched the reins so her horses pulled her several inches closer to where Ben stood. There was enough light for him to make out a treadle sewing machine, a rolled mattress tick, and a spinning wheel jammed on top of the bulky black mass filling the interior of the carriage.

"Are you daft, boy? The Rebs have been spotted on the other side of the river. I saw 'em myself when I crossed the bridge from Wrightsville to Columbia not an hour ago. Everybody's fleeing east. At least, everybody who can. You gotta run, lad. We all do. We gotta get to Lancaster. Or Philadelphia. Someplace safe."

Ben tried to be polite. This woman looked like she was probably somebody's mother. But she wasn't his. "I just came from Lancaster," he told her. "I'm going west to find my brother. He's with the 106th Pennsylvania, Company A. They're probably close behind the Rebs. So I gotta get going."

The carriage driver leaned forward in her seat to get a better look at Ben. "It's not much of a plan to head west. You'd be heading right into the arms of them Rebs.

"*The Rebs*, understand? Nigh on to the whole Confederate Army. They's burning and killing and stealing whatever they can find. Leastwise, that's what folks are saying. So get up here on this seat beside me, boy, and move along smartly. You need a ride, and I could use the protection of a strong lad and his dog."

"He's not my dog," answered Ben quickly, pausing as though that fact alone should explain to the woman why he couldn't go with her. "He's my brother's dog."

"And I'm his cousin," said Danny, suddenly popping up in the middle of the honeysuckle bush. The horses snorted nervously and stamped their feet. The driver gaped at Danny as if she thought she was seeing the ghost of old Robert E. himself.

"We're going to find the army and join up," Danny announced. Ben winced. Danny sounded awful cocky for a fella standing in the middle of a honeysuckle bush. "Ben and me'll push the Graycoats right outta Pennsylvania."

"Aren't you two a little young for soldiering?" The lady's eyebrows met in a hairy V as she frowned. "Do your mamas know what you're up to?"

Ben didn't answer. Danny tripped over a trailing honeysuckle vine and rolled down the sloping berm into the road, clattering all the way. Ben reached down and lifted his cousin, a little roughly, to his feet.

"You'd be doing me a big favor, ma'am, if you'd take my cousin here back to Lancaster with you."

But Danny squirted like a handful of new butter right out of Ben's hands and danced down the road a piece, making sure he was out of reach. "I'm not going back," he chanted. "I'm not, I'm not."

Ben shook his head impatiently. "I gotta find the Union Army." He shrugged at Danny, turning his back on his cousin. "I gotta go west."

"Jus' where do you expect to find the Union Army?" asked the woman in the carriage.

"I'm headed for York County. I'll cross the bridge today and go on from there."

The driver laughed as if Ben had said something funny. "Well, you better get a move on if you're planning to cross that bridge. It was pert near cut off by the Rebs when I left. The home troops are still fighting a rear guard. But if the Rebs try to take it—and I'd bet a fistful of silver dollars they will—our militia boys will blow it up for sure. They already got the dynamite charges laid."

Ben could hardly believe what he was hearing. That bridge was the pride of Lancaster County—a full mile long with one side for trains and the other for wagons. If there was talk of dynamiting it, things must be more of a mess than he'd thought.

"But the Rebs could jus' swim across," objected Danny, coming two steps closer. "Blowing the bridge won't stop 'em."

"Trying to swim the Susquehanna would make them easy targets for our sharpshooters in the breastworks along the riverbank. No." The woman paused, twisted in her seat, and leaned over to glance behind the carriage.

Ben could feel the vibrations in the leather soles of his brogans. More wagons were coming.

"No." She lifted her reins. "The bridge is the key. And if you don't have enough sense to come with me, you boys better hurry yourselves along. Otherwise you might not have a bridge left to cross." With that, she nodded her head, flicked the reins, and yelled "Gee up" at her horses as she hurried to join the other wagons on their way toward Lancaster.

Ben realized with a shivery feeling that he and Danny and Captain were the only travelers on the whole Lancaster and Columbia Turnpike heading in the other direction.

CHAPTER 4

Milking It

It was like trying to paddle a canoe upstream when every keelboat, every paddle wheel, and every barge in the whole world was coming at you from the opposite direction.

Sunrise had come and gone as Ben and Captain trudged in a tired line, single file, at the edge of the wide, dirt road. Danny trailed close behind. There were backups of wagons and riders at every tollhouse they passed, even though the poles across the busy road had all been raised and left up to keep the crowd of refugees moving. Half the time it was easier to weave a path between the hemlock trees along the road, ducking under the long-needled pines, than to try and walk on the more level surface of the pike.

The dust from the passing wagons and carriages was choking in the hot summer sun, and the sense of fear and panic in the air was even thicker than the dust. Ben thought several times about giving up, turning around, and going home. Each time he dismissed the thought immediately.

The fact that Danny Seldomridge was following him was enough, all by itself, to keep Ben heading forward. It was unthinkable to let Danny see his fear. He wished for the hundredth time that he was completely on his own, the way he'd planned. But telling Danny to go home hadn't worked, and trying to shove his cousin in the other direction only made Ben feel like a bully.

He'd tried yelling. He'd even tried leaving Danny beside the road, running ahead when his cousin stooped to root a pebble out of his shoe.

Danny would hang his head and look like he was about to cry. Or he'd scream out in fear and start chasing Ben, barefoot, until he tripped and fell. And Ben would always give in.

At home, Aunt Mavis insisted Ben include Danny in everything he did. Every game of stickball, even though Danny couldn't hit and always dropped the ball. Every splash in the Conestoga, even though his cousin couldn't swim. Danny wore a big, loose shirt to wade in, looking like a girl in a billowy dress and making all Ben's friends hoot with laughter.

But Aunt Mavis wasn't here now. Truth was, she was probably frantic wondering where her dear little boy had gotten off to.

Maybe that was why Ben kept letting Danny follow him. Maybe it was to spite Aunt Mavis.

Trouble was, Ben felt too tired right now to spite

anybody. It was more like dragging Danny along was something that was his to do. Pa told him there would be things in life that didn't seem fair and didn't seem right, but they happened, and somebody had to shoulder them. That's how Ben felt about Danny.

He didn't know how he felt about Captain. Was the dog his to do, too? And what about Pa's jinx? Fact was, last time he was home, Pa'd said Captain should be sitting at home, wagging his tail, waiting for Reuben after the war was through. 'Course, the war had already been going on for what felt like forever, with no end in sight. How long could a dog wait, anyroad? Dogs didn't live that long.

Ben had to quit all this thinking. It was starting to make his head hurt. He looked down at Captain, who was trotting beside him again. The dog was like his personal scout, ranging ahead, checking behind, or staying at his heels. In the morning light, Captain was the color of one of Ma's perfect griddle cakes, the ones Pa liked to eat in a big stack of a Saturday evening, a light gold with patches of darker yellow that looked like streaks of melted butter dripping down his flanks. His head was wide and flat with ears that hung down like a hound's ears, but only half as far. They flopped most of the time. Ben reached down without even thinking about it and rested a hand on Cap's broad head. The dog's tail whacked against his legs as they trudged on.

They stopped in a grove of cherry trees to rest and eat a little something. Ben was still in a hurry, but Reuben always said it was better to stop on your own hook than to flat-out fall over 'cause you pushed too hard. Ben had a vague hope that the traffic on the Columbia Pike would clear out some while they rested and make the last mile to the river go easier. Peach and apple trees lined both sides of the road in orderly orchards, scattered among corn and wheat fields stretching back as far as the eye could see. But only the cherries were close to ripe. The fruit, not fully red, was still edible and slightly crunchy.

Danny and Ben picked fat fistfuls of cherries, eating four or five at a time, and making a contest of spitting the pits at a knothole in a nearby oak. Captain made wild leaps, trying to catch the flying seeds. The dog brought his captured trophies back and proudly dropped them, in all their slobbery glory, in Ben's lap.

After stuffing themselves with cherries, both boys drank water out of Ben's flask. Ben filled his cupped hands with the water that was left so Captain could share a swallow.

"Want one?" asked Danny, holding out a golden lemon drop.

Ben was amazed at the offer. Danny usually hoarded his favorite candy, just like he did everything else he owned. Ma said it was because Danny was an only child. He wasn't used to sharing.

"Sure." Ben reached out and took a hard, round, yellow candy from the twisted piece of brown paper Danny produced from the front pocket of his canvas jacket. "Thanks."

Ben was still sitting under a gnarled cherry tree, suck-ing on the sugary lemon sweetness and thinking about the first thing he'd say to Reuben once he found him, when he heard the roar. Actually, it was more of a bellow. A loud, drawn-out howl of frustration and pain.

Danny, who was lying down beside Ben, half asleep in the shade of the cherry trees, shot up, scrambling to his feet and pulling out his ax at the same time. "What was that?"

Ben got up, too, more slowly, swiveling his head in all directions, holding one hand to shade his eyes so he could see past the trees into the sunshine of the road. Could the Rebs be here already? Was that sound the famous Rebel yell that every returning soldier talked about—the blood-curdling battle cry that could make brave men turn tail and run?

The bellow repeated itself slightly closer, and Ben shiv-ered, despite his wool pants, and the sweat beaded on his forehead. The sound wasn't human.

He took a step in the direction of the road, pushing his thick, sandy-blond hair back where it fell into his eyes. He was squinting now, trying to see . . . trying to see what?

His mind flashed on a lithograph he'd seen in *Leslie's Illustrated*. It showed a long, scaly monster—an alligator, it was called—that lived in the deep South and had jaws as long as your arm, lined with rows of big, pointy teeth. The article said gators roared and bellowed in their Southern swamps.

Ben was suddenly sure that the Rebs were close, and they'd brought their gators with them. "You best find a stout tree and climb it," Ben advised Danny grimly. "I'm gonna scout around."

But Danny started laughing, and that sound bothered Ben more than the roar of the unknown animal.

"Look over yonder," Danny called, trotting off at a diagonal to the road.

Ben followed Danny, irritated at his cousin's know-it-all attitude, but grateful that he wouldn't have to wrestle an alligator all by himself. He wished he had Pa's rifle. But the gun hadn't been returned with his father's other effects from Camp Curtin, and all Ben had was the mumblety-peg knife Reuben had given him before he went off to war. Ben rooted around in his flour sack until he found the knife, the blade wrapped in an extra pair of socks. He put the sack down and walked on in a crouch, the knife held in front of him like a saber.

From around the next tree came a heavy tramp, and then a wild-eyed, brown Jersey cow appeared, pulled along by Captain. The dog had the cow's frayed rope halter firmly gripped in his teeth.

"By the great horn spoon!" Ben sagged against the nearest tree, his knees weak with relief. He stuck the knife in his belt, and hoped his voice didn't sound as shaky as he felt. "I didn't know an old cow could bellow like that. She must be sick or something."

Danny had already caught hold of the halter that ran behind the bug-eyed creature's twitching ears. The lead rope was frayed on one end, like maybe it had broken. Ben had seen plenty of cows before, but he'd never seen one that looked—or sounded—quite like this unhappy creature.

Danny bent over, running a practiced hand over the cow's bulging sides. Danny, Ben suddenly remembered, milked the Seldomridge family cow in the little barn behind Uncle Elliott's general store in Hanover. Aunt Mavis didn't make him do it. Uncle Elliott did. Every morning and every afternoon. So it was possible Danny really did know something about cows. Ben was glad he hadn't said anything out loud about the wild gator.

Captain was licking at the cow's obviously swollen udders, running his pink tongue up the full-to-bursting skin and looking over at Ben as if to say, "Do something."

"This 'un needs milking as much as any cow I've *ever* seen," Danny said, turning and handing the rope halter to Ben. "It must have gotten loose from one of those wagons heading east. Guess they didn't have time to milk it this morning. It's gonna bust if we don't do something."

"We?" Ben asked. Danny used the word "we," but it was obvious he expected Ben, as the leader, to do the "something" he was recommending.

"We don't have a bucket," Ben objected. The words sounded lame, even to his own ears. But it was all he could think of. "We've got nowhere to put the milk."

Danny patted his stomach and grinned. "I don't think it matters much to the cow, as long as it don't have to carry it." The creature bellowed again, rolling its eyes as if urging Ben to get on with it.

Ben knelt beside the stricken creature. Captain stood at his shoulder, watching. He'd milked a cow once or twice, at a friend's farm, but he'd never been very good at it. At home they got their milk out of big redware crocks stored in the cold cellar. But he'd be hornswoggled if he was going to let Danny Seldomridge see that he didn't know how it was done.

Ben began to pull on one hanging nipple and then the other. Nothing happened. The cow moved restlessly, skittering sideways, making Ben walk on his knees to keep up with her. He was getting a little trickle of white liquid, and he tried to tilt the nipple up and shoot it into his mouth, the way he'd seen Uncle Elliott do with the Seldomridge cow.

The cow stamped, snorted, and let out a moan, so low and long, it sounded like a rumble of thunder from a faraway storm. The cow moved again. This time Ben fell over, still clutching a long nipple in each hand, and about a cup of thin, white milk squirted out on the ground.

"Here, let me try it." Danny was kneeling beside Ben, pushing his fingers aside. Ben rolled out of the way without protest and was surprised that, as he lay on his back, a blast of warm milk suddenly hit him on the chin. "Open your mouth," Danny instructed. "And say when."

Danny's skill with the distraught Jersey was impressive. He shot milk at Ben and at Captain, who danced and twisted and swallowed noisily as if they had just invented a wonderful new game. He even squirted milk into his own mouth, gulping and swallowing, and generally getting most of the milk down the front of both his shirt and Ben's. The skittish cow seemed a little calmer as Danny began to dig a hole in the weedy dirt with forceful squirts of milk, filling it with a miniature white lake.

"This cow was a gone coon. Good thing Cap found it and brought it to us," Danny said, giving a final pull and squeeze, and straightening up. "Now what do we do with it?"

Danny and Captain were both looking at Ben as if they expected him to have an answer. How he got elected leader of their little war party, Ben didn't know, but he wasn't comfortable in the position. "How should I know? You're the cow expert," Ben said sarcastically. "What do *you* think we oughta do with it?"

Danny answered thoughtfully, as if it had been a serious question. "Well, I guess we have to take it with us. If we leave it loose, it'll just get the same way again."

"Take a cow with us?" Ben asked incredulously. "Are you out of your mind?"

"We'll have fresh milk every day," Danny offered, sounding less sure of himself now. "Till we get where we're going. Where *are* we going, anyroad, Ben?"

Ben stared at Danny, furious at his cousin, both for being there and for asking questions Ben couldn't answer.

"We'll take it," Ben said suddenly. Reuben wasn't here. Danny was an idiot. Captain was a dog. Obviously, everything was up to him. "We'll take it into Columbia and see if somebody there needs a cow. Somebody'll want it. And then we'll cross the bridge and find Reuben."

Danny was stroking the animal's velvety nose. Captain was licking the baggy udder. Ben felt a momentary pang of jealousy that a dumb old Jersey cow got so much sympathy, but he himself was expected to make decisions and know what to do and nobody cared how he felt. Danny acted like there was some big plan, when the truth was, Ben hadn't thought any further ahead than sneaking away and heading west. He'd figured he'd cross the bridge and keep going west till he found the armies. Then he'd get Reuben out of there before the big battle.

After that, the plan got pretty vague.

Danny began to laugh as he turned back to Ben. "I thought it was some kind of horrible monster making that noise at first. Maybe even a Rebel attack." Danny shrugged good-naturedly. "Good thing you and Cap weren't scared. Guess you knew it was a cow 'fore Cap even brought it over."

Ben didn't deny it. Instead, he grabbed the halter and began to lead the cow back to the turnpike. He wondered if the pioneers had felt like this when they walked beside their brace of oxen pulling their Conestoga wagons, heading into the great unknown. Of course, the pioneers didn't have to mess with a nuisance like Danny Seldomridge or take along a dog who wouldn't stay put.

They cut due west off the road to follow the Reading and Columbia Railroad line, skirting schools, churches, and businesses in the small river town. For all the people who had fled eastward, the town of Columbia still seemed overflowing with people headed toward the river, just like Ben and Danny. Nobody wanted to miss the show if a battle broke out. Those Southerners had been keeping the war all to themselves for two whole years, and it was about time Northerners had a crack at the action.

Captain ran far ahead of the boys, then circled back as if trying to give them a report.

"Hey, mister! Where's everybody going?" Danny called to a passing stranger before Ben could stop him. Ben didn't want to call attention to themselves or their disheveled appearance. They'd been up most of last night, and walked over ten miles to boot. A vision of Aunt Mavis coming up behind them, grabbing Ben by the ear and Danny by the shoulder, and dragging both of them back to Lancaster played through Ben's head. "What's going on?" Danny repeated, and Ben punched his cousin in the arm, causing Danny to yell "ouch," and spin around.

The gray-haired gentleman striding along Second Street seemed distracted, but he called back an answer.

"The Rebs are shooting at us from the Wrightsville side." Instantly, Ben realized that the distant popping sound he kept hearing was the echo of gunfire, more than a mile away across the wide Susquehanna in neighboring York County. "The home boys are in retreat. But there's talk they might set fire to the bridge, and most folks want to see it, if they do."

Ben could smell the wet, musty odor of the river, and something else, like the faintest hint of Chinese firecrackers set off on the Fourth of July. Captain was out of sight again, having rounded the bend where the railroad tracks paralleled Front Street next to the river.

"Wait up," whined Danny, as Ben began to run. But he didn't slow down. What if they were too late? What if the bridge was already blown? The cow trotted along behind Ben, mooing a protest at the uneven surface of the rail ties and the cinders in between. But she kept up. Then Ben spotted Captain on a rise of land beside the river. The dog's feet were spread, its pinkish-black nose pointed westward as if to show the way.

The report of a cannon flattened Ben's stomach, and he found he couldn't tell whether it had been fired from the Columbia side or the Wrightsville side. The boom seemed to bounce back and forth across the choppy gray water of the river. But there it was! The bridge, less than a block away, just sitting there all normal-like; not in the least blown up.

Ben dropped the cow's halter and ran, flat out, until he reached Captain at the river's edge. He was so out of breath, he bent over and leaned his hands against his knees as he gulped in air. Danny ran behind, yelling, "Wait up, wait up."

A massive boom, even louder than the cannon blasts, rumbled toward him, making his whole body vibrate. A thick curl of black smoke rose into the late-afternoon air, hanging in the blue sky like a question mark. It must be the bridge. They'd blown up the bridge.

Men were running and shouting. People were climbing onto the roof of the railway station to get a better view. Several of the ladies standing on the railroad platform beside the station were crying. A few screamed. One fainted.

Ben couldn't seem to get his brain to think in a straight line.

But as the smoke cleared a little, it looked to Ben as if the bridge was still standing. All of it, still there, with just a hole in the roof.

Maybe it wasn't too late.

CHAPTER 5

Crossing That Bridge When He Comes to It

Ben didn't linger on the rise beside the river. He started running again in the direction of the bridge. He paid no attention to Danny, who was pulling the cow and yelling at Ben from some distance behind. The crowds were thicker now. Captain wove between legs, gaining ground. Ben, trying politely to push his way through, fell behind.

"Did you see my husband?"

A woman in a pink dress, her apron twisted in one hand, grabbed Ben by his elbow, spinning him around. Her eyes stared straight at him, but Ben felt sure she didn't really see him. Her eyes were puffy and Ben could see tear streaks on her cheeks. "Did he make it across before they blew the bridge?"

"The bridge *isn't* blown. Look, lady. It's right there."

Ben could hear shouting voices, but he couldn't quite make out the words. He heard someone yell "oil," and saw half a dozen young militia men roll wooden barrels into the dark mouth of the covered bridge. One of the men turned and said something to the boy behind him, and Ben caught a glimpse of a familiar face. It was Henry! Henry Owen, right here in Columbia, fighting with the militia. Ben waved and shouted, but Henry didn't see him. He seemed pretty busy with whatever was going on down there at the bridge.

"Our boys're gonna burn it now, fer sure," drawled an old man leaning on a gnarled black cane. "Them explosives the rear guard planted didn't make a dent."

"Boy oh boy!" squealed a youngster jumping up and down and clapping his hands. "Burn it! Burn it!"

A second woman came up beside the first and wrested her clutching hand away from Ben's shirt. "You have to calm down, dear. You'll give yourself the vapors."

" 'Bout time you waited up," Danny said, squeezing in between Ben and the women. "Cows don't gallop like horses, you know. I tied ours up to that tree yonder. It's gettin' a mite skittish."

"Lookee there! Our boys are off the bridge!" hollered the old man with the cane, slapping Ben on the back. "Them Rebs didn't reckon on Yankee ingenuity. Our boys've drenched the floorboards with coal oil. If we can't stop Johnny Reb one way, we can sure stop him t'other."

"FIRE!" screamed a distant voice. Sure enough, Ben could see angry red tongues of flame licking through the roof of the covered bridge out near the middle of the river. Thick gray smoke poured into the clear blue sky. It smelled like a boiler fire in a railroad engine, channeled and funneled and oily.

The woman with the missing husband was clutching Danny's shoulder now instead of Ben's as she stared at the smoke billowing from the covered bridge. She didn't blink or make a sound. She just, all of a sudden, fell over.

She landed limply against Danny, who stumbled under her weight and fell against Ben. Ben managed to keep his feet. The woman's eyes were closed and her face was ghostly white.

"She fainted," Danny grunted, with his usual talent for stating the obvious. He squirmed out from under so all the woman's considerable weight lay on Ben.

"Sal! Sal!" The second woman grabbed the limp figure by the waistband of her gingham skirt and slapped at one of the lady's pale cheeks. Then she pulled a gray wool cap out of the front pocket of her white apron and began to fan the one she'd called "Sal" with it.

"Help me, boy," she commanded Ben. "Let's drag her clear of these folks so she can breathe."

Ben looked around. She couldn't be talking to him. He didn't have time to be helping some fainting stranger. He had to get across that bridge before the fire took it.

But the woman with the gray hair and gray eyes was looking right at him in the same no-nonsense way Aunt Mavis always did. As she took one of the fainting woman's arms, Ben grabbed the other. Danny managed to get his hand under one foot, but the other foot dragged along the ground as they heaved her higher up the slope, over to the willow tree where Danny had tied up the cow. It was shady there and a bit cooler under the drooping branches. But the sharp tang of smoke reached through the greenery. Even under the leafy tent made by the ground-sweeping branches, Ben could hear a great, distant roar as the fire gobbled up more and more of the oil-soaked bridge.

"I'm Mrs. Hopkins. Grace Hopkins," said the woman still fanning with the gray cap. "There's water at the pump beside the livery yonder. Run and fetch me some. Hurry, boy." This time she was looking at Danny.

Danny took off as if the fire were right under his feet. Ben had the fainting lady's head against his shoulder. He tried to hitch her up into more of a sitting position against the trunk of the tree.

"Lord a mercy," Mrs. Hopkins whispered, staring distractedly out through the slender, green leaves of the willow at a distant slice of slate gray river. Ben stood up and looked over her shoulder. Between the branches, he could see a span of the burning bridge plummet into the river below. Steam rose with a sizzle from the cold water, and burning timbers floated on the surface like little rafts with cargoes of orange flame.

The crowd had grown quiet. Ben could hear several women sobbing, but even that sound was soft and sort of reverent. Ben just stared at the licking flames burning up what little plan he'd had.

"You're watching history being made, boys," Mrs. Hopkins said, almost whispering. "I s'pose they had to do it. But I never thought I'd live to see the day we'd burn our own bridge."

Danny returned, panting heavily and sloshing water out of a mossy, wooden bucket. The cow mooed in protest, apparently upset that water was being delivered but not to her. She lowered her brown head and fidgeted back and forth, from foot to foot. That was a lot of fidgeting, when a body had four feet.

Danny pulled on Ben's arm. "What are we gonna do? Huh? What are we gonna do now?"

There he went, assuming Ben would know exactly what to do next.

"Give that cow some water," Ben directed Danny. He turned to the gray-haired woman, the one who hadn't fainted all over him. Maybe *she'd* know another way across the river.

"Is there another bridge around here somewhere? Maybe a little footbridge upriver? Or downriver?"

"Don't you fret, lad. There's not another bridge all the way to Harrisburg. The Rebs'll never get us now. And they don't dare set foot on the ford. Colonel Frick has cannons aimed right at it. He'll blow 'em all back to Dixie if they stick a toe in the water."

Ben's hand slipped into his pocket and he fingered Pa's watch. He couldn't stop staring at the fire. It was like a hungry animal, gobbling its way from stone pier to stone pier, sending a cascade of flaming wood into the churning river below. Sections of the bridge looked like a blackened skeleton and smoke not only rose like a signal flag above the fire, but puffed in a gray cloud from the two openings at the Columbia end, where trains had once entered the covered structure on one side and wagons on the other.

Sunset was coming on fast, but the blaze from the bridge was like a giant lantern. It made it seem bright as midday. The flames jumped from span to span, heading straight toward the Columbia side. Men were lined up and waiting with buckets and a pumper cart with its hoses dipped in the river. But before it reached them, Ben felt a cool breeze against the back of his neck. The wind was shifting. The breeze swirled the branches of the willow and the flames turned and raced back on themselves. A continuous rain of burning planks fell into the water below, hissing as they hit.

Now the flames were headed toward the Confederates, a roaring beast that looked as if it could burn all the Rebs right out of Pennsylvania and back to Dixie. There was a cheer from the Columbia bucket brigade and some scattered applause from the crowd. But most onlookers stood grim-faced, watching the destruction of the bridge that had meant a livelihood for every mule driver, railroad worker, and merchant in town.

Burning timbers floated down the river like a flotilla of ancient funeral pyres. Every now and again a rifle popped, the noise of its crackling shot bouncing back and forth across the water until Ben couldn't tell if the shots came from this side of the river or the far bank.

Not that it mattered.

Even the best sharpshooter in the world couldn't hit a target a mile away.

It was getting dark now, but the fire on the river gave an eerie glow to the gathering dusk.

"Oh my! Lookee there! It looks like this one got too close to the fire!" The old man was chuckling and thumping his cane on the ground.

Mrs. Hopkins and Ben looked down at Captain, who came trotting up to the willow tree from the direction of the bridge. The dog's yellow coat was streaked with soot. It was obvious Captain had reconnoitered the bridge. Mrs. Hopkins looked at Ben curiously. "That your dog?"

"He's not my dog," Ben replied automatically, adding, "he belongs to my brother, Reuben. Reuben's with the 106th Pennsylvania, Company A."

"This *is* my cow," Danny proclaimed, untying the Jersey from the tree. "I'm going to call it Honest Abe."

"It's not your cow," Ben corrected. "We found it loose on the Columbia Pike. Do you ladies need a good milker?"

"No, lads." Mrs. Hopkins smiled and patted Ben's

shoulder. "We can't take a cow. It's a most generous offer, but we'd have to put it in the spare bedroom, and that's already filled to bursting with a family of six from Hanover."

"I'm from Hanover," Danny piped up.

Mrs. Hopkins gave him a sympathetic look. "Well, at least you escaped to safety, lad. That's what's important."

"We're going back there now," Danny announced. "Me and Ben and Captain and Honest Abe." Both women looked at Danny with alarm.

"You can't go back to Hanover," Mrs. Hopkins declared. "The whole of York County is Reb territory now. It's not safe to the west or the south. Besides, there's no bridge anymore. No way to get there."

"You said there was a ford, somewhere upstream." Ben surprised himself with the calmness of his voice. "Can you tell me where?"

"You *can't* ford that river. It's practically dark. And you're toting a cow. And a dog. I've seen full-grown men ford it, but never after dark. Besides, all those Reb cannons will be pointing right at you. You'd likely be killed."

Ben met the woman's eyes steadily. The old man with the cane had ducked into a shed at the end of the nearest street and came back with a small kerosene lantern in one hand. He spoke up suddenly.

"Iffen it's battle souvenirs you're lookin' for—here." He grabbed the gray wool cap Mrs. Hopkins had been using as a fan and shoved it into Ben's hands. It was a Confederate infantry cap.

"A friend and me picked that up this afternoon over to Wrightsville. There was a skirmish, and we found it in the grass. I don't even want it. I hate anything them Rebs touched."

"Uh. Thanks." Ben already had his Union cap stuffed in one pocket. Now he reached down to jam the Reb cap into the other. But Pa's watch was already there. Ben pulled out the pocket watch, snapping open the gold case. In the glow of the lantern, he could just make out the hands pointing to the Roman numerals VIII and XII.

It was eight o'clock. Far later than Ben had thought.

"We gotta get moving," Ben said, but before he could click the lid shut, Danny's hand shot out and grabbed the watch.

"Let me see it." Danny cradled the open pocket watch in both hands. "You never let me see it."

Ben tried to grab it back, but Danny spun around and ducked behind the lady in pink. The man with the cane raised his lantern and looked over Danny's shoulder.

"That's a mighty fine timepiece, son."

"It's my pa's." Ben stopped trying to grab it back, afraid his slippery cousin would drop it if he jostled his arm. "It's a Swiss watch—came here all the way from Switzerland. See. The case is genuine gold plate, and Pa said it has a jewel setting." Ben couldn't keep the pride out of his voice.

He would never show the watch off on purpose, but if people wanted to admire it, who was Ben to stop them? The lantern light made the enamel painting inside the lid shine. It was an American eagle with a banner in its claws. The banner was red, white, and blue, and there were words on it, engraved in Latin.

"What does 'Tem-pory Om-nee Rebel-at' mean, any-road?" Danny asked.

"It's *Tempus Omnia Revelat*," Ben corrected his cousin. It wasn't that he could read Latin any better than Danny, he'd just heard Pa say the phrase so many times it was stuck in his head. Pa would push his chair back from the dinner table, pat his belly, and say, "Many a man coulda made a meal out of that." It was Pa's little joke, and Ma always laughed at it. Then he'd pull the watch out of his vest pocket and snap it open to check the time. " '*Tempus Omnia Revelat*,' son. Time will show you what's yours to do."

"What does it mean?" prodded Danny.

"Pa said it means 'time will reveal everything.' He said each man finds out what he's got inside, if he just gives it time."

"Your pa sounds like a right smart man." The white-haired old man with the cane took the watch reverently from Danny's open palms and handed it back to Ben, snapping it shut. "How'd he come to give you such a valuable watch?"

"He's dead," Danny offered, as if Ben's pa were no more to him than a faceless soldier killed in battle.

"He died at Camp Curtin a month ago," Ben explained, and when nobody said anything, he added one more word.

"Measles."

Before he could avoid it, the lady in pink had her arms around him and was sobbing against his neck.

"Poor boy. The war done made you an orphan. Them dirty Rebs."

Ben patted her gingerly on the back. The Rebs really hadn't had anything to do with Pa dying. Ben could hardly hold them accountable when Pa had never even been as close to a Reb as he himself was now. Besides, much as he tried to deny it, he only missed Pa a little. Pa'd always been so busy clerking in the store, or doing inventory, or going out to a political meeting. It was Reuben Ben really missed.

Ben slipped out of the fainting lady's smothering embrace. He pulled the gray cap out of his pocket and buttoned the watch fob onto the leather strap behind the brim. Then he put the cap firmly on his head. The watch bounced against the brim like a fancy decoration on a lady's straw bonnet.

"I have to find my brother, Reuben. He's with the 106th Pennsylvania right now, but our ma needs him at home.

I'll cross this river any way I can, long as I can get to Reuben."

Ben nodded his head sharply to emphasize his determination, and the watch slid to the side and clunked against his cheek. It might not be the most comfortable way to carry it, but Ben figured it would be high out of the water if he was walking or paddling or swimming to get across.

"Now, come on if you're coming, Danny. We have to go."

"But I'm hungry," Danny whined. "We didn't have anything but cherries all day. It's not too late for supper yet, is it?"

Mrs. Hopkins put an arm around Danny's shoulders. All around them, the streets were emptying out as people hurried home, whispering about what they had seen and what it would mean when they all woke up tomorrow without their precious bridge.

"You boys come on up to the house, and I'll fix you plates of sausages and boiled potatoes. We might even find some apple schnitz pie if we look hard. What do you say to that?"

"I say, let's eat!" shouted Danny, jumping up on a protruding root and vaulting from there to the cow's back. The cow continued chewing her cud placidly, standing motionless as Danny settled himself between her bony shoulders. Captain barked and circled around them in excitement.

"Get down off that cow," Ben commanded.

Danny ignored him.

"I'm gonna ride it," he announced, grinning at Ben with the same challenging grin he always used whenever Aunt Mavis was around to make Ben agree. "Honest Abe is gonna carry me all the way."

The old man chuckled and shook his head. "Can't call a cow by a man's name, boy," he told Danny. "Not the right side of the bloomers."

"Yeah. It's stupid to name a cow. Almost as stupid as it is to ride one," Ben huffed. "You can't do it."

"Can so," Danny argued.

Mrs. Hopkins shooed the lot of them out from under the willow tree and up a narrow street that led from the riverbank into the town. Her chin jutted out in a determined way, and she didn't turn, even once, to look at the smoking ruins.

"I had a cow when I was a girl," she said, silencing their bickering with her soft voice. "I called it Mavis. Mavis is a very nice name for a cow."

Ben started to laugh. "Mavis sure would be a good name for that cow." Ben looked at Danny, waiting for the tantrum that was sure to come.

"Mavis is my ma's name." Danny's voice was more reflective than upset. He seemed to be in the process of making up his mind. "Mavis *is* a very good name for a cow."

Ben couldn't believe his ears. Was it possible his cousin actually had a sense of humor?

The air was still thick with a whitish-gray smoke that looked like dry fog in the darkness. "You boys could spend the night on our parlor floor," Mrs. Hopkins urged. "We got a braided rug, and I believe I could hunt up another blanket or two."

Danny turned to Ben eagerly, but Ben was already shaking his head no. Danny's shoulders sagged. This would be their second night without sleep. It would be Danny's first night without his daily dose of Turlington's Balsam of Life. But Danny would have to get used to the rough life if he was so all-fired set on tagging along.

"We need to be on our way, ma'am," Ben insisted.

"What you *need* to do is go home," countered the gray-haired woman who was leading the way. "If you got brothers away in the war, it's cruel to make your mamas grieve for two more."

How could his mother miss someone who filled in the inventory ledger upside down? Someone who sliced off a whole-pound slab of soap but only charged for a half?

Ben didn't know how to answer Mrs. Hopkins. He was no good to his mother at all. But when he brought Reuben home, then she would stop grieving and everything would be fine.

Mrs. Hopkins sighed. "But you ain't my boys. So, if you won't listen, at least get a good meal in your bellies before you head off. That dog of yours looks pert near hungry enough to eat that cow. Better give *him* something, even if you don't think you need it yourself."

"He likes vegetables," Danny said. "Especially turnips and radishes."

"Why, that's the dangdest thing I ever heard of." The old man sounded downright jolly, as if nothing had happened. He acted as if a pall of smoke didn't hang like a shroud over this quiet little river town. His dim lantern barely showed the ruts in the dirt street. "A vegetable-eating dog, you say? At least you got a dog to look out for you." He paused and then asked, "You got any guns, boy?"

Ben shook his head.

"Just Captain," Danny said, leaning so far forward on the neck of the plodding cow he practically tumbled over her head. "He's good protection."

"They're better off without guns," Mrs. Hopkins said, herding them all toward a little stone house with green shutters and a green door. "Guns are killing a heap of people in this sorry war."

"Not us!" Danny crowed. "They won't get us."

For once, Ben hoped Danny was right.

CHAPTER 6

Tempus Omnia Revelat

W hat time is it?"

Danny's voice leapt out of the darkness behind Ben, making him jump. Danny was riding Mavis along the riverbank, following Ben as he ducked under low-hanging sycamores and between trailing honeysuckle bushes. The small, borrowed kerosene lantern, half shaded with the gray Confederate cap, didn't cast much light. The quarter moon looked about as big as the night before, but it gave less light, barely penetrating the pall of wood smoke that shrouded the river. The tiny sliver Ben could see when he squinted up at the black sky still reminded him of the nursery rhyme about cows jumping over the moon. But Mavis plodded heavily along behind him without, apparently, any thought of jumping over anything.

Ben's hand went to the watch hanging from the brim of the gray cap. He didn't click open the lid. It was too dark to see the hands. The lantern wick was turned as low as it would go without going out completely, and Ben could see maybe two feet in front of him by the lamp's yellow light.

"I don't *know* the time." Ben knew his voice was sharp. "It's dark, that's all. Dark enough to cross without anybody seeing us. Doesn't matter what time it is." Mrs. Hopkins had said the crossing was almost a mile upriver. Surely they had walked a mile.

"I think it's *real* late. Not as late as last night, but after midnight, mebbe. That's what I think."

"I think you talk too much."

The thick undergrowth that lined the riverbank was giving way to a clearing. There was a sign up ahead. It was a board nailed between two trees, but it was too dark to read it. Mrs. Hopkins had said there was a crossing sign. Was this the right place? A dragonfly buzzed across the small circle of light cast by the lantern. Its silvery wings shimmered in the glow. Captain and his nose could help, but Captain was nowhere to be seen.

That blame-fool bootlicker dog was always way ahead or way behind. He never walked in front, leading the way, as he'd surely do for Reuben.

At least the slow cow wasn't breaking twigs and kicking rocks on the grassy verge. The cow was so close behind him, Ben could feel her warm, moist breath on his neck.

"Shhh," Ben cautioned. He tiptoed out into the open, beyond the trees. Was this still the path? His eyes hadn't quite adjusted to the darkness, and he tripped on a jutting rock as high as his knee, half-buried in grass and weeds.

"Ouff!" The rock jammed into Ben's shin, and he

sprawled clumsily on the ground. He dropped the lantern, snuffing it out. Mavis's splayed hoof came down directly on the back of his left leg.

"Watch it!" Ben whispered, wishing he could holler. That really hurt. The cow stepped back almost daintily. Her square muzzle dropped curiously and nudged at the back of Ben's head, as if she were apologizing for stepping on him. For a dumb old cow, Mavis was pretty smart.

Ben scrambled to his knees. As he turned to look at the cow, he felt something new on his face. There was a cold, moist pressure against his cheek. A pair of darkly gleaming eyes stared into Ben's, and a rough tongue slurped soundlessly over Ben's mouth and nose.

Captain.

"Yeah, yeah, leave off," Ben whispered, rocking up on his knees and attempting to brush himself off. He swiped a hand across his wet cheek and took the piece of rope the old man with the cane had given him out of his pocket. He needed to tie it to Captain's collar before the dog got away again.

The big dog, his yellow fur a ghostly glow in the faint starlight, stood perfectly still. He gave no sign of bolting.

"It's a good thing you came back." Ben kept his voice low, but firm. "You scouted up ahead. Now you can show us the fording place."

Ben's eyes were finally getting used to the darkness, and he could make out the dog's face staring back at him. He hoped Captain's questing nose could smell all the folks who'd forded at this crossing before. How long did a smell last, anyroad? Danny had wasted too much time at Mrs. Hopkins's, eating everything in sight. Yet, the wet charcoal odor of the burned bridge clung to the darkness with no sign of fading. Ben only hoped the burn stink wouldn't cover every other smell around. He really needed Captain's nose to find the way. With the mile-wide Susquehanna in front of them, there wasn't any room for mistakes.

"What're you doing?" Danny asked, speaking in a normal conversational voice that sounded to Ben like a shout in the stillness of the night.

"Sshhh!" Ben whispered, whirling to punch his cousin on the leg, which made Danny's cup and lantern rattle and Mavis moo. Ben grabbed hold of the cow's rope halter with one hand, cupping his other hand over her velvety muzzle. She snorted softly into the curve of his palm.

"Sshhh," he repeated urgently. "If anybody hears us, we're done for!" A crossing—if this *was* the crossing—went two ways. With the bridge out, who knew if some stray Rebs might decide to try fording the river themselves.

Ben pressed on, placing his feet with care a pace behind Captain, trying not to make a sound. A few dozen yards beyond where Ben had spotted the sign board, the path turned left and made its way toward the edge of the black water. Captain trotted along confidently, stopping at a wide dip in the shoreline. With no trees to block the sky here, what light there was reflected in watery ripples of gray. Dark gray. Light gray. Sparkling, liquid, shimmering gray. There was something unreal about being here, and Ben wondered, for the hundredth time, if he was really home in bed, dreaming he was standing here on the shore of the mighty Susquehanna in the middle of the night, with Yanks behind and Rebs ahead and a cow right at his shoulder.

But it wasn't a dream. He was really here.

"This is it," Ben announced softly, trying to sound like he was sure. Danny seemed so certain Ben knew exactly where they were going and how to get there. He'd found the bridge, hadn't he? Only now, there was no bridge. Just the ripple and splash of water, stretching in front of them in the dark. Lucky it hadn't rained lately, to make the water swell and swirl between its wooded banks.

Ben shook his head, shaking such thoughts away. If finding Reuben had been a good idea last night—and he was sure it had been—it was still a good idea tonight. He put the darkened lantern on the spongy grass, hoping Mrs. Hopkins would find it again someday. He almost wished the big, bossy woman was here with her disapproving frown, forbidding him to go on.

Ben bent and flicked at the leather laces of his brogans, untying them, then tying the shoes together and slinging them around his neck. Captain whined softly, but he didn't bark. Ben stuffed one wool sock in each shoe.

"Get down off Mavis and take your shoes off," Ben commanded. "And be quiet about it."

Danny's answer was *very* quiet.

"No."

"What do you mean, 'no'? Get down, Danny, and take your shoes off. You lead the cow. I'll lead Captain."

Somehow at this moment, when the most sensible thing they could do was to leave the cow behind, and maybe the dog, too, the idea didn't even occur to Ben. They were all going. They were going together. It wasn't time for discussions or refusals. Danny must do as he was told.

"No," Danny repeated. "I'm gonna ride across on Mavis."

"What?" Ben sputtered. "That's the dumbest thing I—"

"I can't swim, remember?" Danny interrupted.

Ben opened his mouth to reply. Then he closed it. He had no idea whether cows could swim or not. He'd seen big, placid Guernseys standing in water, cooling off in a farm pond on a hot summer's day. He'd seen Holsteins crowded together under a tree in a rainy downpour. But he'd never actually seen a Jersey—or any other kind of cow, for that matter—swimming.

Well, as Aunt Mavis liked to say, no time like now to find out. Besides, this was a ford. It couldn't be deep here.

Ben sighed, wondering if he could manage to rescue both Danny and the cow if he needed to. What if he had to decide which one was more important?

Ben grinned and stuck one toe in the water. He shivered at the coldness. Eeny-meeny-miny-mo. Danny or Mavis? The cow or his cousin? What a choice that would be.

Ben looked out at the water stretching in front of him forever. There had to be a shore on the opposite side with a thin strip of pebbly beach like this one where they could climb out. But he could see no sign of it. Ben shivered again. He suddenly understood how those old-time sailors felt when they worried about sailing off the edge of a flat earth, never to be seen again.

He took two steps out from the bank, his feet picking their way along on the rocky surface hidden by the dark water. It was mainly round pebbles, with a sharp rock jutting up here and there, just to make a body stumble. Ben's feet were just starting to get their summer calluses. He'd only gone barefoot since school let out last month, so the bottoms of his feet weren't as tough as he needed them to be.

He tried to set his feet down gently, probing for sharp edges with his toes, and wiggling his heels down between rocks when he could. The water rose to his ankles and then to his knees. The river was running low, and the rocky ridge of the ford should be downright easy to cross for anyone as had a mind to—anyone who wasn't scared of meeting enemy soldiers on the other side. Besides, if Mrs. Hopkins was right, the ford should come out a little north of Wrightsville and the Rebs.

He could hear the cow behind him, splashing patiently along, even when the cold water rose to her soft, pink udder. She did, however, give a snort of displeasure when Danny thumped his feet into her sides.

"What're ya doing back there?" Ben called softly.

"This is fun!" Danny answered, almost shouting.

"Sshhh." Ben turned and looked back at his cousin, surprised to see they hadn't come all that far from shore. Funny, but it *was* sort of fun. Cold and wet, maybe, but something to tell the fellas at home about.

If he ever got back home.

Ben tried to lift his feet higher and move faster at the same time. But the two things didn't go together. He felt for his flour sack, hanging around his neck with his shoes. It was nice and dry. The pocket watch hung high out of the water, swinging from its fob beside the brim of his cap. The cold metal watch case hung down beside his face, tapping against his cheek with every step.

Ben reached up to touch it, just as the flat rock under his foot shifted. He threw his arms out wildly, trying to keep his balance. Then the rock tilted, spilling his foot onto the muddy bottom. His ankle twisted a little, but the water was too numbingly cold to feel pain. Ben fell forward, throwing one leg out in front to catch himself as the water closed up to his chest. Windmilling his arms, he dropped Captain's lead, and the dog went on without him, not even looking back.

Somehow, Ben got his feet under him again.

Ben stood there in what he figured was the middle of the river. He was scared to go forward. He was ashamed to go back. The water was almost up to his waist. He reached up to straighten the gray wool cap on his head, where one of his windmilling arms had knocked it sideways. The sleeve of his shirt clung wetly to his arm. He could feel his collar clinging to his neck. Everything below his neck was wet. Ben tilted both shoes, and a bucket of water cascaded out of them and back into the river.

"Tarnation," Ben swore, keeping his voice low. Wet pants had been tolerable, but being wet all over made him cold. His teeth were starting to chatter. Ben beat his arms together, hugging himself to try and stop the shivering. He started moving again, putting one foot in front of the other.

There was really no choice but to go on.

It felt a little better on his feet now. Instead of rocks, there was mud underfoot. Ben took another step. The river was suddenly up to his chest.

In one step.

The current was tugging on him strongly like a live thing, trying to carry him downstream to where the blackened skeleton of the Columbia-Wrightsville bridge jutted from the water. He couldn't see it in the darkness, but he knew it was there, its sooty piers and charcoaled timbers marching across the river in a grim reminder of the bridge that had once been.

"You still back there?" Ben managed to call in a loud whisper.

There was no answer for what seemed like forever, and then Ben heard Danny's thin voice a long way back, whining for Ben to come back and help him.

"Mavis doesn't like this, Ben. She doesn't like it one bit. She's not moving unless I keep kickin' at her. Come back and get us, Ben! Please, Ben! "

Ben sighed again and turned back, fighting his way through the steady push of the chilly water until he reached the cow. Sure enough, Mavis stood stock-still in water almost up to her back, snuffling at Ben unhappily as if to say, "What did you get me into?" Ben lunged angrily forward, grabbing at the cow's rope halter.

It was the wrong move.

He slipped on the muddy bottom, falling again and this time going all the way under, head and all.

He came up gasping and sputtering. Ben rubbed a water-wrinkled hand across his eyes, trying to clear them of water. Dumb cow. Dumb Danny. He felt for the hat and watch. They were still there.

Ben got a good grip on the rope halter and started forward again. There were more rocks here, and he set his feet gingerly, trying hard not to lose his balance. He wasn't sure if the water was still getting deeper, but they were way out now, more than halfway across. Ben was so tired, he felt like sitting down right here in the water and resting a spell. Only it would be over his head.

So Ben kept moving, one foot in front of the other, leaning forward against the dark, insistent current. He concentrated on going in a straight line.

The rocks underfoot were getting farther apart. It was plain old river bottom here. Mud squished between his toes. How many hours had they been crossing this river, anyroad? It felt like they'd been at it all night. It sure didn't take this long to go a mile on dry land.

Captain nosed against Ben's shoulder. The dog had been so far ahead, Ben figured he'd swum all the way across and climbed out the other side. But here he came, out of the night, just when Ben had given up on him.

Ben reached out and grabbed Captain's leather collar. The choppy water was easily up to Ben's chest now, and the current was like a bully pushing on him, trying to push him over sideways.

The cow's lead rope jerked in Ben's hand, pulling free.

Ben turned to see Mavis flat out swimming past him. She was right beside him, not paying him any mind, her head stretched out in front as Danny clung to her neck. Ben flailed an arm in her direction, trying to catch her tail as she passed.

He missed.

The water was up to his neck, even when he was standing straight up on his toes. It was too deep. This couldn't be the ford.

Ben flapped his arms, awkwardly trying to tread water. He felt weighed down, like an anchor was about to pull him under.

This was all wrong.

Of course! It came to him when a particularly desperate splash of his own arms showered his head with water. The mud had been a dead giveaway, and he hadn't even thought of it. The ford should be on top of rocks. The current! Mud underfoot meant the current had pushed Ben downstream, to the deeper part of the river.

"I don't like this, Ben," Danny shouted back from his perch atop Mavis. Ben could see his cousin climbing higher on the cow's neck, resting his head on top of the cow's head. "I don't like this at all," Danny yelled as the cow floated downstream, past Ben.

"Do you think I do?" Ben yelled back, flailing at the water with the hand that didn't have a stranglehold on Captain's collar.

Ben tried to relax enough to let himself float behind the dog. His breath came in gasps, and he kept swallowing mouthfuls of the muddy water and coughing it up, making retching sounds the Rebs would surely hear a mile away.

But he didn't care about that. He didn't care about anything except not losing hold of Captain. He didn't know which way the shore was. He must have been walking crooked to lose the ford. But Cap must know.

Ben turned on his side and floated, trying to get his mouth out of the water and catch his breath. His head went under and bobbed back up. His feet kicked and his right arm moved in rhythm, but most of his forward motion came from Cap's powerful doggie paddle. Ben tried to concentrate on a strong, steady stroke. But he seemed to be moving downriver a lot faster than he was moving across it. His arms felt like blocks of wood, cold and stiff and numb with a tiredness he couldn't remember ever feeling before.

The sodden flour sack and the water-filled brogans hung like great heavy stones from his neck. He could slip them off. It would be easier to keep his head above water without them. But how could he expect to find his brother if he didn't have any shoes to walk in?

Still kicking, he reached up to push the gray wool cap more firmly down on his head. He didn't want to lose—

Ben's fingers touched his wet hair.

The hat was gone. The hat and Pa's pocket watch with it.

A strangled sob broke through the splashing noises. Ben wasn't sure where the sound came from. It could've been from his own throat, except that was filled with a lump as big as a great doughy dumpling.

Ben felt something moving beside him, knocking into him. He felt Captain's wet nose on his cheek. His fingers were still locked around the dog's collar, but he had lost track of his arm. He didn't feel connected to his body. Captain nosed him again, as if he was checking on Ben and urging him on.

He thought he heard someone crying off to his left, but with all the river water sloshing in his ears, he couldn't be sure. He kept swallowing mouthfuls of the ashy stuff and spitting it out again. It coated Ben's tongue with grit.

Drowning would be a stupid way to go. He kicked harder. He should be saving Danny. His bratty little cousin was his responsibility now. He could almost hear Aunt Mavis, right beside him in the water, telling him to save Danny. But who was going to save Ben?

He brought his head up as high as he could, blinking water out of his eyes, trying to see what was ahead. There was only darkness and water. Moving water. Water that knew where it was going a lot better than Ben did.

Ben noticed with surprise that he wasn't shivering so hard anymore. He flailed at the water, but his arm didn't break the surface. There was no strength in it. He felt an almost pleasant warmth spreading through his chest, and he had to fight to keep his eyes from closing. He was so tired.

He didn't know how Captain could keep going. The current pulled at them. It seemed determined to keep them going downstream forever. Ben's eyes fixed on his own hand, clamped around the dog's collar in a grip that seemed disconnected from the rest of his body. His fingers looked white and stiff in the starlight—like Pa's fingers when he was lying in his coffin in the front parlor. If his fingers were already dead, soon, he'd have to let go. Soon. . . .

He felt something thud against his hip. A big fish? A spent Confederate cannonball?

His body bumped into several more hard things under the surface. Ben stopped paddling with his right arm and reached down.

Rocks!

He was bumping over rocks. It was shallow here. So shallow, Captain was standing on the bottom, the water only up to his broad chest. The dog set up a barrage of barking. Ben couldn't imagine why. It wasn't like Cap to be so all-fired noisy.

"Ssss." Ben tried to make the "sssh" sound, but his frozen lips wouldn't pucker. "They'll—hear—you." Ben's word were halting, his voice no louder than a whisper.

He had to put his feet down. He had to stand up and walk on out of this dadblame river. But his legs were still fluttering in the water behind him, as if they weren't getting any orders from his brain.

"Reuben?" Ben blinked as he croaked the word. A phantom apparition of his brother seemed to float in front of him. He blinked again, clearing more water from his dripping eyelashes. He could see his brother's uniform. It was all gray shadows in the dim light that came every morning, just before the dawn. It looked like Reuben's uniform. The gold buttons. The wool pants. The cap.

Wait. The cap was wrong.

Reuben would wear his derby, not a cap.

He could hear a voice close by. It was right here in the river, somewhere above him. A voice from above. Did God have a Southern drawl?

"Here's another one, Curtis. You got that one?" The voice was coming from the apparition.

Another voice shouted back. "Yeah, Jim, I got the kid and the cow."

Captain had stopped barking. He growled softly, but stood still as gentle fingers pried Ben's grip from his collar and closed around Ben's wrist.

"Come on now, boy," the apparition said. "Put your feet down. Your dog's dragging you through about a foot and a half of water here."

Hands reached out and pulled Ben up. Strong arms held him. They weren't Reuben's arms at all. The voice wasn't Reuben's either. His brother would never call Captain Ben's dog.

Ben blinked at the soldier who grinned down into his face. A soldier with a yellow mustache, the same color as Captain's fur. The mustache's thin ends dangled below the man's chin.

Ben gasped as the river mists bit into him. The delicious warmth he'd started to feel in the water left him in an instant. Ben began to shiver violently as the dank chill of his river-soaked clothes hit him. He tried to keep his eyes open. But it was impossible.

He wanted to ask: Are you really an honest-to-God Reb?

But he couldn't get the words out before the world faded to black.

CHAPTER 7

June 29

Ben opened his eyes slowly. There was a flicker of fire-light. Not from the burning bridge. From a campfire. He heard people talking around him. He'd been aware of the sound for several minutes, but with his eyes shut, he could deny what his ears told him.

The voices were Southern, their words drawn out in a mellow, almost sleepy way. Ben closed his eyes again, trying to think.

"What we gonna do with 'em, Jim? I never seen no soldiers like this afore. If them two's spies, then I'm Abe Lincoln."

"Wait! Lookee here!" A second voice sounded triumphant. "See this hat? They swum that there river to git to us. To git to safety. They escaped from the dirty Yanks. That's what they done."

That was when Ben had to open his eyes, to see who would say such a thing. He really didn't need the light from the fire. The sky was beginning to lighten, hinting at a new day.

A tall, blond man loomed over Ben. The man wore gray wool pants and a gray wool vest, unbuttoned and hanging open over an unbleached muslin shirt. In one hand, he held a soggy Confederate cap. A cap with a pocket watch swinging from the leather band above its brim. The fella's sleeves were rolled up over his elbows, and his hairy forearms dripped water, one drop falling on Ben's forehead and making him blink.

"Hey! He's awake, Jim. He's got his eyes open." A second head appeared beside the first. This one looked to belong to a boy barely older than Ben himself.

"Well now, young fella." The blond man knelt down beside Ben. He put his arm under Ben's shoulders and pulled him easily into a sitting position. "Curtis, get the boy a drop of that elixir Williams is always bragging on. It'll warm his insides, and the fire will take care of his outsides."

Without meaning to, Ben glanced downriver toward the bridge. Sure enough, it was almost full day, probably nigh on to five o'clock in the morning, and the blackened bridge pillars were clearly visible. The current had brought him right back down to the bridge. Or what had been the bridge. Only a couple of charcoal timbers hung from the blackened stone piers to prove there had been a bridge there yesterday. Funny how much could change in a single day.

Ben wondered if he'd passed out, or maybe these dirty

Rebs had given him a dose of swamp water to make him lose his mind. Ben lay there, staring at the spot where the bridge should be, and the blond man started to laugh.

"Staring won't bring it back, son."

Ben didn't see what was so funny. Dirty Rebs, going around burning other folks' bridges. Ben blinked, suddenly remembering that the Rebs hadn't burned it.

The home guard had done that.

Jim's laugh was a big man laugh, deep and throaty, kind of like Reuben's. Jim even looked a bit like his older brother. Same heavy eyebrows. Same droopy mustache and the same square chin.

The color of the eyes was different, though. It was light enough now to make out a sparkle of brown glints. Reuben's eyes were dark blue, like the sky at home right before a thunderstorm, whereas this Reb's were sort of yellowish-brown, like porridge with pats of butter floating in it. What's more, this man wore a wide-brimmed straw hat, not a black felt derby like Reuben.

Ben stared into those eyes, confused and a little numb. A blanket had been wrapped around his shoulders and another covered his legs.

"Come on, boy. Take a swig of this. It'll bring you right around."

Ben accepted the blue glass bottle from the Rebel. He looked around at a small campfire, a half dozen men still sleeping on blankets or flat out on the ground, using their ragged haversacks as pillows. The cow was tied to the branch of a sycamore tree, munching contentedly on thick grass. Her udder hung loose beneath her. Ben glanced up at the boy, who hadn't bothered to wipe off his milk mustache. The Reb boy's face was smooth and pink and clear of any trace of a beard. He couldn't have been more than two or three years older than Ben at most.

Ben frowned at the bottle in his hand, not quite able to sort it all out. Danny lay beside him, also wrapped in blankets and apparently sleeping soundly.

Danny was here, then. The cow was accounted for. But where was Captain?

The blue bottle in Ben's hand was labeled "Turlington's Balsam of Life," the same stuff Aunt Mavis always gave Danny. Ben glanced around apprehensively, suddenly more afraid that Aunt Mavis might be here than he was of the Rebs.

And these *were* Rebs. He was sitting here with men of the Confederate Army. Invaders. The enemy.

The same men who'd be shooting at Reuben soon as the big battle came along. Dirty killers.

So how come they carried Aunt Mavis's favorite tonic?

"Here." The blond man took the bottle out of Ben's hand, removed the cork with his teeth, wiped off the glass lip on the front of his shirt, and handed it back to Ben. "Go ahead now. Drink up."

Ben pinched his nose shut, tilted his head back, and

swallowed. Two gulps, and he began to gag. He could still smell it, and it smelled like Pa's bottle of medicinal whiskey at home. It tasted like fish that had been left out in the sun too long, and it burned all the way down. Ben lowered the bottle, coughing and snorting. Captain suddenly appeared beside him, licking at the open bottle like it was the best stuff he'd ever tasted.

After the dog finished licking the bottle, he reached over with his wet tongue and started licking around Ben's mouth. He just kept licking and licking. Ben wanted to throw his arms around the dog, but he resisted. It wouldn't be right to make a scene in front of these Rebs.

Either Cap liked the taste, or he was glad to see Ben awake.

It was the taste, Ben decided quickly.

It had to be the taste.

"That'll set you to rights!" the big Reb exclaimed, reaching down to scratch the dog between its floppy ears. "It'll burn all that river water you swallowed right outta you! So now, what have you got to say for yourself, young fella? Who are you? Where you going?"

Ben cleared his throat, stalling for time. His brain didn't seem to be working right. His mouth opened, then closed, then opened again. He looked down at his hands. One of his sleeves had a piece of brown river weed still hanging from it. The sleeve was brown, too. He was wearing Pa's brown wool jacket. Almost butternut brown—like the Rebs.

"Where am I?" Ben asked, stalling.

"Lord a mercy, boy, you and your dog and your cow and this other boy here done swum the river to get to us, all the way from over yonder." The Reb boy waved his hand vaguely toward the Columbia side.

The man held up the Rebel cap, the same one the old man with the cane had given Ben so long ago, all the way back yesterday under the willow tree, when the bridge was burning. Captain wagged his tail approvingly. "We found this in the water with you. Well, your dog found it. We spotted you as you was getting close. Curtis was all for using his rifle and picking you off, but I seen you was jus' kids. I thought you might not make it, the way you was a-goin'. Might not a neither, if it wasn't for this good ole dog a yourn."

"He's not my dog," Ben responded automatically. He immediately wished he could swallow the words.

"Well, whose dog is he then? He ain't no stray, that's for sure."

Ben didn't dare bring up Reuben. He'd already said too much.

"He's . . . he's Danny's dog." Ben pointed at his sleeping cousin, hoping his voice wasn't cracking with fear like he thought it was. If these soldiers thought even for a minute that he was a true and loyal Union son, Ben didn't know what they'd do.

Ben could suddenly hear Danny's whining voice inside his head: "Them Rebs would as soon shoot you as look at you. They eat babies. They chop off fingers and string 'em on necklaces." Ben swallowed hard.

The blond man didn't seem to notice. "That might be, but I swan, the dog favors *you*, boy. He's a friendly cuss, in't he? Reminds me jus' a lick of Curtis's old yella coon hound, Ripley."

Danny chose that moment to roll over, groaning, and open his eyes. He looked straight at the Reb and screamed. He would have kept screaming, maybe forever, except Ben grabbed him and slipped his hand quickly over his cousin's big mouth. Ben smiled apologetically.

"He has nightmares. Wakes up like this all the time. It used to drive our ma crazy."

"Where is your mama, anyroad?" the blond man asked.

It was just like Pa said. One lie led to another, till you could hardly stop lying.

"She's dead." It popped out, just as if Ben had been planning to say it all along. Danny finally stopped screaming and staring at the Reb. Now he stared at Ben. Ben turned him loose, ignoring the fact that Danny's jaw was slack, his mouth hanging open in amazement.

"Yeah," Ben continued, hoping he didn't sound as desperate as he felt. He needed a story that would cover everything so thoroughly, not even Danny could mess it up. "We got sent to relatives up north here. We're really from Maryland." They didn't have Southern accents in Maryland, did they?

"We got sent up here to stay with our aunt Mavis and uncle Elliott." A bit of truth, for effect. Reuben always said a lie worked better if it had a bit of truth mixed in. "We picked up the cow on the road." More truth. "And my little brother here . . ." Ben still had Danny in a partial headlock and now he playfully pinched his cousin's cheeks. Ben didn't even flinch as Danny caught the pinching fingers in his teeth and bit down. "My brother, Danny, is addlepated from all the shooting, and from losing Ma and all. He's as like to talk crazy as not."

Danny managed to tilt his head and get a better grip on Ben's little finger. He bit down hard and Ben released him, shaking his hand.

"Feisty little thing, ain't he?" The boy spoke this time. He wore a Confederate uniform identical to the one worn by the blond man, but a mite newer looking. He sounded amused.

"You can't believe half of what he says," Ben added.

"These are Rebs, Ben," Danny whispered loudly, as though the whispering would keep them from hearing. "The Rebs have got us."

Danny hiccuped.

"Yeah. Ain't it wonderful?" Ben responded, talking a little too loud.

"They's Rebs, Ben. REBS!" Danny hiccuped again.

"Just like us," Ben hissed.

"Like who?" Another hiccup.

"See, I told you he was addlepated." Ben smiled apologetically at Jim.

"Don't worry about it, boy. I've seen plenty like that."

The sun was fully up now, and warm enough on his back that Ben shrugged out of his blankets.

"Well, boys, I'm Jim," offered the blond man, "and this here is my little brother, Curtis."

"I ain't 'little,' " Curtis protested. "I'm fifteen and a half, and a private in this here army."

Jim shook his head indulgently. "I can offer you some hardtack stew, boys. Curtis here butchered us one of the local hogs, so we got fresh ham, too. Even real honest-to-God coffee for a change. The mayor of York insisted we take it from his own stores." The blond man winked at Ben as if he were letting him in on a joke.

Danny had finally stopped hiccuping. "I'm hungry enough to eat a gator!" he exclaimed. He seemed to have forgotten everything that had gone before. Danny turned to Curtis. "Do you fellas really have gators with you? 'Cause that's what I heard."

"Oh sure." Jim picked up a tin pot and poured out a mug full of steaming coffee. "Pet gators. They pull our supply wagons."

"Really?" Danny was obviously in awe.

"Well son, if you believe the Confederate Army travels with alligators, I'm surprised you don't believe we eat babies and string kids' fingers on our necklaces."

Danny had fallen silent, frowning.

"Them's all Yankee lies," Curtis announced. "We's the good side."

"Oh. Yeah." For once, Danny sounded as if he didn't know where to take the discussion.

"We're sure glad you found us," Ben broke in. There was more than a bit of truth in that one. "I'm Ben, and the crazy one here is Danny."

"You gonna stay here?" piped up Danny excitedly. "In Pennsylvania, I mean? In a permanent camp with breast-works and cannons and all? They got cannons across the river."

"Much as we'd like to finish what we started here, we can't." Jim's voice was steeped in regret, but he was smiling cheerfully. "Word is, General Lee's calling us back. Seems like there's gonna be a *real* battle soon, right here on Yankee land. We gotta move out so we don't miss it. We're gonna give them Blue Boys a taste of their own medicine this time and fight 'em on their own home ground."

"You're leaving?" Ben wasn't sure if he was pleased or disappointed. The frying ham smelled delicious, and even the bitter black coffee tasted good. The hardtack stew, like Aunt Mavis's oatmeal, lay heavy in his stomach, and Ben hadn't eaten much of it, though Danny finished off the pot.

"If *you're* leavin', what are *we* gonna do?" Danny asked. It was an obvious question, although one Ben hadn't thought of yet.

Jim scratched his chin, studying on the problem. "We could take 'em with us," Curtis offered. "Otherroad, when we pull out, the Yanks'll get 'em."

"You're right, little brother." Ben was surprised to hear Jim's reply. In a way, he was relieved, too.

"We'll put 'em on the supply train to York. They'll be safe there. York's our city now."

"But we're going to Hanover," Danny said firmly. "That's where I live."

For a fleeting instant, Ben pictured throwing his cousin back into the river.

"That's where you *used* to live," Ben corrected, thinking fast. "Afore the family moved to Maryland in '61."

"The track's tore up thataway." Jim didn't seem to question their destination. "But I can get you part of the way. I'm pretty sure we hold Hanover, too. It should be safe enough."

Hanover was more than twenty miles to the southwest. At least they'd still be moving in the right direction, Ben thought. But it would be quicker to follow Jim and Curtis directly to the battle. That had been his plan—to find the fighting. Surely he'd find Reuben wherever the fighting was.

"You can ride with this here dog on the train to York if

I can find you a space. You just hang on, boys. In a coupla days, all of Pennsylvania will be ours, and your way back to Maryland will be free and clear. Now tell me what's your last name, so I can tell the engineer."

"Seldomridge," Danny announced before Ben could open his mouth and say "Reynolds." "Danny and Ben Seldomridge. And we have to take our cow, too. We captured her from the Yanks."

"Good enough." Jim rose, laughing, and Captain was right by the Reb's side. "We'll look for space in a freight car for the whole bunch of ya. Now, call your dog, boy."

"Yeah," Ben repeated, poking Danny with his elbow. "Call *your* dog."

Danny clapped his hands and managed one weak whistle. "Come on, Captain. Come here," he called. The dog looked at Danny and allowed his tail to twitch once, but he didn't move in the boy's direction.

Ben put down the watch and Rebel cap Jim had handed him and fished Reuben's tin clicker, the one Reuben used to train Captain, out of his flour sack. "Here," Ben urged Danny. "Use this."

Jim was looking at Danny, doubt in his eyes. But at the sound of the green, frog-shaped clicker, Captain bounded up to Danny and sat watching the boy expectantly, waiting for an order.

Curtis trotted after Captain and reached down, holding a hand out for the clicker. "Can I see that?" For once in his life, Danny didn't argue. "Well now, that's really somethin'. I sure would admire to have me a thing like that."

He clicked it twice, and Captain shifted to face him and held his paw out to "shake." "Will you look at that?" Jim drawled. "Be nice if you could teach old Ripley to behave so fine."

"Would ya swap me for it?" Curtis blurted.

"What ya got?" Danny asked, ignoring the fact that the clicker didn't belong to him.

Ben tried to catch his cousin's eye. Dadblame fool. If Danny traded away Reuben's tin clicker, Ben wouldn't have any power over Captain at all. The dog would probably run off on his own and never return.

"Tell ya what." Curtis's eyes danced with some secret he was keeping. "I got me a souvenir y'all might like." He walked over to his own neatly tied bedroll and opened it out. Ben could see a Union cap, a tin penny whistle, a harmonica, a wooden comb, and a tintype in a small oval frame. Curtis picked up the blue cap. That's when Ben noticed the hole in the peak.

"This was worn by some fool Yank trying to keep us offen that old bridge." Curtis stuck a finger through the hole. It looked like a wriggling white worm coming up through an apple. "Picked it up yesterday when those Yank cowards was on the run. We tried to put the fire out, but the folks here in Wrightsville claimed they had no buckets. Can you believe it? Danged if buckets didn't show up aplenty when the wind blew the fire this way and their houses started going up. General Gordon said to help 'em, despite the fib they told us about them buckets. He said we're only fightin' soldiers—not women and kids. And dang if a little town girl didn't bring me this hat and drop a pretty little curtsy after we helped them save her house. She was about the same age as Jim's little girl, Abigail. Not quite as pretty, but real polite." Curtis stopped talking and examined the clicker, clicking it several times as Captain sat expectantly at his feet.

"I'll trade you even-steven, boy. That hat's almost as good as a Yankee scalp."

"See? I told you they scalped people," Danny whispered, under his breath this time. Ben said nothing. He couldn't tear his eyes away from Curtis's fingers, still wriggling in that hole in the cap's peak. There was no sign of blood, but the dark blue of the wool could be hiding that. There was no question a Union head had been inside that cap when some Reb put a hole in it. A Union head like Reuben's.

"So you really want my clicker, huh?" Danny broke the silence. "Ya got any candy?"

"That's not your clicker," Ben whispered fiercely, his head turned so no one but Danny could hear. "It's mine and you know it."

"My dog. That's what *you* said. My dog. My clicker." Danny's voice was smug.

"I'll get you for this," Ben hissed under his breath.

He felt his throat getting all lumpy. Reuben had made that clicker, and now a Johnny Reb had it in his hand.

"I got me some fresh honeycomb I'll throw in," Curtis agreed. He pulled a shiny yellow oilcloth packet from his haversack and removed a hunk of gooey honeycomb, breaking the waxy comb in half.

Danny passed the blue cap to Ben and shrugged. "What else can we do?" he asked in a low voice as he eagerly took the sweet yellow stuff and began chewing on a sticky corner. "They have big guns."

Ben turned away and stuffed the cap into his flour sack. The one person who would never, ever see him cry was Danny Seldomridge.

"Well, that's right kindly of you," Jim said, moseying over and taking the tin toy from his brother to test its clicking. "Abbie'll sure love this thing. You did good, Curtis."

Jim kept clicking the frog as he turned and went off in search of a train. Captain followed the Confederate soldier as if the dog had decided to change sides.

"Well, that's that." Ben knew he sounded defeated. He felt defeated. "Cap's gone. He'll follow whoever has that clicker." Ben felt his anger rising. "Who said we were going to Hanover, anyroad? I sure didn't, and I don't want to." Ben punched at his flour sack angrily. Going to Hanover felt like going backward, even if it was to the west. Hanover was southwest. Ben felt sure they should go due west, like these Rebs. That would be fastest, and he had to find Reuben fast. There was a battle coming for sure now. Even the Rebs said so.

"If we go along with these Rebs, we'd catch up with Bobby Lee. A battle, Jim said. If there's a real battle, Reuben's sure to be there."

"Stop your bellyachin'." Danny looked so confident, Ben wanted to strangle him. "Captain will follow you any- where you go. You don't need no clicker. And at Hanover, we'll get supplies. I lost my lantern and my hatchet and purty near everything else when we crossed that river. We'll just go to the storeroom behind the store and get whatever we need. Who knows?" Danny paused for effect. "We might even find the battle before these Graycoats do. It might be in Hanover. You don't know. We'll have us a fine old brotherly reunion, you and me and Reuben."

"You're *not* my brother," Ben whispered through gritted teeth, poking Danny sharply with his elbow.

"Yeah, and Captain's *not* your dog," Danny shot back, laughing and dodging. "Not much, Ben *Seldomridge*!"

CHAPTER 8

June 30

Ben couldn't remember ever being this tired before. Not even after staying up all night back in 1861 to get a glimpse of President Abraham Lincoln when he came to Lancaster.

Of course he hadn't really slept at all last night and not much more than that the night before. The train didn't leave Wrightsville till almost noon and took about two hours to get to York. It was pretty slow for a train, with sentries posted on the engine's jutting cowcatcher, checking the tracks for any sign of sabotage.

It was strange. Ben felt like he was in enemy territory. But the Rebs clearly felt the same way.

The four were standing on the platform at the train station in York. Jim and Curtis would be marching off with General Gordon's men, west toward Chambersburg to meet General Lee. Ben and Danny would be striking out on foot, heading toward Hanover to the south. No one could take the train any farther because the Rebs had torn up the tracks to the west and south a few days earlier.

Jim had gotten them all aboard—even Mavis and

Captain—with some fancy talking. He'd made up a story about their sick grandma who'd likely die without milk. The transport sergeant looked at him like he'd gone coon crazy, but he let Mavis in the freight car with the artillery mules.

During the ride, Curtis said they should cross their fingers that some hungry officer didn't turn Mavis into spare ribs, and Danny got so mad, he wrestled the Reb boy in the aisle of the passenger car until everybody was laughing so hard, Ben nearly forgot there were Rebel soldiers with guns in every seat.

Here on the platform of the bustling York station, soldiers everywhere, Jim wished them luck as he hefted his ragged rucksack on the torn shoulder of his mud-stained jacket. Curtis solemnly offered small pieces of his remaining honeycomb to both Ben and Danny. Ben ignored the lint and hair clinging to his piece and sucked on one corner. Danny popped the whole piece into his mouth at once and nearly choked to death.

Ben waved as his new friends marched away. Even though they were Rebels, and the enemy, he wished he could've gone with them. Funny that the color of that one fool gray cap could make the difference between being friends and blood enemies.

Captain liked them, too, it was easy to see. Ben couldn't tell if it was the tin clicker they'd traded or the cherry tobacco smell from Jim's little corncob pipe, which smelled so much like the tobacco Reuben used in his own burled walnut pipe. The first time Jim'd lit his pipe on the train, Cap took to whining and Ben himself swiveled around to check if maybe Reuben had just strolled up behind him.

The way that dog took to the two Georgia boys, Ben thought, it was almost as if they were the ones he'd been lookin' for all along. It was a relief when the dog made no move to follow them. Captain came with him and Danny, even without the clicker. Danny had been right.

Ben felt the square muzzle and wet nose tickling his own hand again and again as it swung at his side during the endless walk to Hanover. They headed out in the afternoon, not walking too fast in the muggy June heat. It was easier to just go than to listen to Danny's endless whining and complaining if they didn't. Danny was probably right about needing supplies, too. They could use some food and mebbe another blanket.

Ben walked fast, almost trotting, trying to get this detour over quickly. There were no armies out here in the middle of nowhere. Just mile after empty mile of wheat fields and apple orchards, fragrant honeysuckle bushes and bushy-tailed squirrels that flashed up and down the trunks of oak trees. There were no cows grazing in the grassy meadows. No wagons or riders on the empty roads.

The late-June sun was so hot overhead, it made Ben's feet squish with sweat in his wool socks after only a few miles. Danny climbed back up on the bony back of the plodding, good-natured Mavis, bouncing with every step. He bent over and clung to her neck to keep his seat.

Ben kept wiggling his toes in his brogans, readjusting them where the leather pinched. He thought he might be getting a blister. Too bad the Rebs ripped up all the tracks. Ben wished they were riding on a train right now. What if the Rebs actually won the war, the way Jim and Curtis were so sure they would? Heck, they'd just have to rebuild everything they'd torn up, and nobody would like 'em because they'd made such a mess in the first place.

They'd started walking to Hanover before supper. Danny said he knew the way, but they'd taken wrong turns twice.

It seemed like years since they had left the Rebs on that crowded railroad platform in York. Right now, Ben couldn't think of anything except putting one foot in front of the other. Fifteen miles to Hanover. Most of it seemed to be uphill. Still, Ben hadn't allowed any stops except for short rests.

He wasn't sure what time it was. The watch didn't look any the worse for its dunk in the Susquehanna, but it wasn't ticking anymore, no matter how much Ben shook it. The hands just kept pointing at xii and v.

The sun went down, and they kept on walking. The crickets came out, making the road come alive with their chirping. The darkness felt like a weight, pressing down on him. To keep himself going, Ben started singing, too. He sang his brother Reuben's all-time favorite song: "We Are Climbing Jacob's Ladder."

"Every rung goes—higher—higher. . . ."

The hooting of a barn owl made Ben stop to listen. There was no sound of approaching voices, no sound of soldiers' feet scuffing wearily along the deserted road. There was nothing to be afraid of. Ben bent to retie the laces of his brogan where they had come undone.

He hummed the next verse. ". . . sinner, have you seen my Jesus?"

Ben straightened up and trudged on. He let his voice ring out, ignoring the skittering of rabbits and squirrels in the surrounding trees and bushes.

"We are climbing—Jacob's Ladder, we are climbing— Jacob's Ladder, we are climbing—Jacob's Ladder—soldiers of the cross."

Ben kept on singing for what felt like miles and miles, until his throat got too scratchy to go on.

They had to get to Hanover soon. It was definitely a blister there on his little toe. Maybe he could sit down under one of the shadowy trees beside the road and just rest for a minute. Close his eyes, just for a minute.

But that wasn't the plan. The plan. He couldn't seem to remember the plan. His tired eyes felt stiff when he tried to blink them. He had to blink to clear away the little white wraiths that darted across the road every now and again, like ghosts. Reuben had told him once that a fella could start seeing things that weren't really there, if he let himself get too tired. Ben had thought that was just his brother's way of getting him to go on up to bed. He should have known better. Reuben might be a whole lot older, but he wasn't like other adults. You could trust what Reuben said.

Ben couldn't stop thinking about sitting down, once the idea took him. He'd just sit for a minute with his back to the smooth bark of a birch tree. He would close his eyes, for three blinks, just to rest them. That would feel so good. Danny lay on Mavis's back as she plodded along, his arms locked around her neck, snoring softly. Ben hated his cousin more than ever.

The cow was moving so slowly now, a crawling baby could have passed her. Ben had to pull on her rope lead to keep her going. Captain circled the two of them, cow and boy, nudging, encouraging, driving them like a tiny flock of misfit sheep, onward ever onward.

It was false dawn as they finally came to the edge of the darkened town. Most of the stars had disappeared as the sky lightened to the east and the world was bathed in a thousand shades of gray. No lanterns showed on the street. Ben stopped trying to stifle his yawns and let a big one out. At least there wouldn't be soldiers in Hanover. Despite what Jim and Curtis had said about holding York County, Ben had a better source. The Graycoats had been here and gone: That's what Aunt Mavis had said. Hanover was an unimportant place with its smelly tannery and its railroad junction torn up by the Rebs. Not much left, really, except a few people lying low.

Still, there was something in the air that sent a chill down Ben's neck.

"Hey, Danny." Ben reached back and shoved roughly at his sleeping cousin. "We're here. I hope you're satisfied."

Danny came instantly awake and slid from Mavis's back, thumping the cow affectionately on her side. "I'm home! I'm finally home!" he exclaimed, sounding loud in the eerie predawn silence. "That wasn't so bad," he said to Ben. "My feet don't even hurt."

Ben thought about slugging Danny, but that would take too much energy.

Danny started trotting toward the town square, and Ben did his best to keep up. Mavis reluctantly yielded to Danny's insistent tug on her halter and quickened her pace, her hooves beating against the hard-packed dirt like an accelerating drumroll before a battle.

"It's still there!" Danny was practically shouting as they came abreast of Seldomridge Emporium, a two-story wooden building with a wide porch across the front. "Look, Ben! Look!"

The store's dark bulk loomed like a familiar landmark in a strange gray world. The big front windows were empty of merchandise and the door had a padlock on it.

"Shhh," Ben cautioned.

But it was too late.

A swinging lantern appeared in the window of the tidy brick house next door.

"Who's out there?" called a querulous woman's voice. "I got a gun here."

"Hey, Mrs. Hupert," Danny answered. "How's your lumbago? It's me. It's Danny Seldomridge."

There was a sharp intake of breath, and the lantern was shoved farther out the window and held high to cast a wider circle of light.

"My stars and garters! Is that really you, Danny? Where are your ma and pa? I thought you all went east to stay with relatives. Is Mavis all right?"

Ben wondered tiredly how the lady in the window knew about their cow. It took him a minute to realize she was talking about *Aunt* Mavis.

"That's just what we did, Widow Hupert. We went to Lancaster to stay with my cousin Ben and his ma. This is him, ma'am, right here beside me. This is Ben."

Boy, Danny sure could be charming when he wanted to be. Which wasn't often. Ben suddenly remembered the gray hat on his head and snatched it off.

"Get on in here, boys." Mrs. Hupert's commanding voice brooked no argument. "'Tain't a safe night out there for man or beast."

The lantern disappeared, reappearing a moment later in the widow's front doorway.

"Get outta that road afore someone shoots you."

The old lady, in a long nightgown and shawl, wore a ruffled nightcap tied under her chin. She held her front door wide open, peering around into the darkness as if she suspected Rebs were lurking in her rhododendron bushes. Danny approached with Mavis in tow. Ben and Captain followed.

"I swan, boy! You got a cow with you? Where'd you get a cow? The Rebs took everything with fur or feather around and ate it. They took all the cows. All the chickens. Even my prize rooster."

"This here is Mavis," Danny offered. "We found her on the road."

The widow stood blocking her door. "And that red-eyed creature?" She shifted her lantern. "Is that a wolf?" Her words were whispery, as if she were afraid to speak in a regular voice.

Captain was sniffing at the porch post. He lifted a leg, keeping it politely cocked away from his onlookers.

"That's Captain. He came along with Ben and me."

"Is that your dog then?" Mrs. Hupert asked Ben, eyeing Captain suspiciously.

"It's not my dog," Ben answered automatically. "He belongs to my brother, Reuben, who's in the 106th Pennsylvania. We're on our way to find him."

He wanted to sit down on the top step, lean against the porch post Cap had just marked, and go to sleep. His legs felt like logs, so stiff and heavy they weren't so much car- rying him as dragging him down.

Mrs. Hupert snorted. "The whole place crawling with Rebs and Yanks, and you expect to find one solitary soldier?"

Both boys nodded. Danny took another step toward her door. The porch steps creaked under Mavis's weight as the cow put a hoof on the first plank. Mrs. Hupert barred Danny's way, her arms spread wide, a look of horror on her wrinkled face.

"You're not bringing any livestock into my home," she announced indignantly. "No cows. No dogs. Why, the very idea."

"We were fixin' to stop at Danny's house for supplies," Ben offered. He didn't want to make small talk with an old lady in a nightcap. He wanted to find a quiet corner someplace and curl up and sleep. He wanted to rest his head on Captain's back, and sleep and sleep and sleep, maybe until the war was over.

"Well, it's pert near five o'clock in the morning," the widow said.

Ben reached automatically into his front pocket where Pa's old watch now lay. He pulled it out and clicked it open. Dadblast if she wasn't right. Five o'clock. Big hand on the xii. Little hand on the v. It was a miracle. The watch was working again. Ben held it to his ear. It wasn't ticking.

"You go ahead home, Danny Seldomridge. Go on and take your cousin and your animals next door to your house, and I'll bring you both some breakfast." Mrs. Hupert waved a brusque hand at them. Captain moved forward and swiped his tongue over the widow's dangling fingers, flopping down and turning belly-up, inviting a tummy rub. Mrs. Hupert chuckled softly and bent down.

"Now don't you have a way with the ladies, you handsome old hound." She rubbed in circles as Captain beat his tail in a rapid tattoo against the boards of her porch. "Oh, all right, you furry charmer. I'll bring you some breakfast, too. I might even be able to find a cup of oatmeal for your bovine friend, there."

Captain wagged his tail again and got up. He was like that. He could make nice with anyone. Young Rebs. Old Yankee widows. It was just that the only one who really counted with him was Reuben. Captain came over and sat on Ben's foot. Ben looked down and wiggled his foot out from under the dog's furry rump. Reuben had said: "Take care of my dog, Ben," when he went off to war.

He'd never said, "*Take* my dog."

Ben had been so careful for so long. He'd made sure there wasn't too much petting. He'd kept a certain gruffness in his tone. He'd tried hard not to get too attached to this dog. He'd be betraying Reuben if he did.

"Hey."

Danny's bony elbow hit Ben's chest, startling him so much he almost fell. Captain was at his feet and seemed to brace Ben's knees before they could give way.

"I never saw nobody sleep standing up before." Danny smirked. " 'Cept an old horse we had once, just before Pa shot him."

Ben dragged along behind Danny to the back door of the Seldomridge shop and house. Like his own family, Danny and his ma and pa lived in the same building as their business, but they lived on the floor below their store, while Ben and his ma lived on the two floors above theirs.

Danny produced the big, iron skeleton key that hung on a cord around his neck and led Ben inside.

"Lucky I didn't lose *this* in the river," Danny whispered. Why was he whispering now? It felt like there was no one awake in all of Hanover, except Mrs. Hupert next door.

Ben was too tired to worry much about Rebs hiding in the darkness of the empty house, jumping them as they entered. But he did think of the possibility.

"Be careful," he warned, realizing as he said the words that he didn't know what he wanted Danny to be careful of. Still, there was something. Captain whined and sniffed the dusty air. Ben was certain the dog felt it, too.

Danny led Mavis directly into his mother's ground-floor kitchen. The cow's hooves clattered on the brick floor and her tail twitched against a punched-tin lantern on a stand near the door, knocking it off with a crash.

Danny didn't seem to notice. He tied the cow to a rung of a ladderback chair and headed over to the pump to get Mavis some water. The cow turned and followed Danny, dragging the chair, *bumpity-bump,* across the uneven brick floor. The cow slurped eagerly at the priming pitcher as Danny poured it over the pump to help the gush of water get started. She licked the iron base of the pump all the way up to the spout, curling her tongue around the stream of water so it sprayed in her face before she gulped more of it in noisy bliss.

Ben sat down on a narrow cot, wedged between the pie cabinet and the back stairs. He collapsed onto it, more than sat. Danny said something, but Ben didn't hear him. Captain settled on the floor beside the cot, circling a spot until he could plop down, curled up with his nose under his tail.

Ben was already asleep, with one hand dangling down to rest on the dog's back.

CHAPTER 9

The Blue-Gray Day

Ben didn't remember closing his eyes. He woke with a start into faint daylight. Had he heard a noise?

Where was he?

He lay quite still, trying to remember. He could see a grandfather clock in a tall, wooden case just opposite where he lay. In the silence, he could hear its loud ticking. Ben drifted, half asleep. The long, black arrow of the second hand blurred as it ticked its endless way around the round, white clock face. The fancy scrolled hands pointed to the roman numeral x.

But was it ten o'clock at night, or ten in the morning?

Ben was so tired, it was hard to keep his eyes open. They were drooping again when the second shot rang out, not too far away. This time, memory flooded back.

Hanover. Seldomridge Emporium. The pop of a distant rifle had awakened him. Now he could hear Danny's bare feet slapping down the wooden stairs that led up to the store. The cow moved restlessly somewhere across the room, knocking over a copper pot that rattled against the brick floor with such a clatter, Captain began to bark.

Danny appeared, still fully dressed, and grabbed at his cousin's hand. Ben could hear horses galloping by up on the street.

"The Rebs! It's the Rebs, Ben. They're chasing our boys through the square, right out front. I went up to look when I heard the first shot."

The kitchen door slammed open so suddenly, both boys yelled. Captain growled. A large, caped figure loomed in the doorway, silhouetted against the bright daylight outside. "Wake up, boys," came Mrs. Hupert's frantic voice. "The Rebs are back. They're all over town again. The 18th Pennsylvania Cavalry came in this morning at daybreak and now the Rebs show up. They say ole Jeb Stuart himself is headed this way." The words came fast, and the old woman kept glancing over her shoulder, like maybe she expected a Reb to come up on her from behind.

A boom reverberated across the ceiling pot-rack, making every fry pan and kettle in the kitchen clank and shake.

"And now they're shelling us!" Mrs. Hupert screamed. The old lady was wearing a brown cotton dress and a red apron with a cape thrown over her shoulders. But on her head, she still wore her white nightcap. She'd obviously forgotten about it in her flight. A loaf of fresh-baked brown bread, warm from her oven, a jug of apple cider, and a crock of butter swung in a small basket over her arm. Rebs or not, Ben was ravenously hungry.

He jumped up to take the basket from her. A few hours of sleep would have to do. He and Danny ate quickly, sharing out the bread and butter with Mavis and Captain, while Mrs. Hupert paced the room, twisting her apron into a knot and complaining that the shelling had already made her second batch of bread fall. Ben wolfed down a piece of bread and thick, brown apple butter. They needed to get going and find Reuben. But wait. Could Reuben be here, right now? Could this be *the* battle?

Ben choked on his last bite of crust when something thundered above his head. First it made a whistling sound. Then it crashed with a resounding boom that made Ben's newly full stomach flip over. He somehow managed to gag down the bread in his mouth as wood splintered, glass shattered, and something huge thumped onto the floor above them and rolled across the room.

"We've been hit!" Danny exclaimed, clutching his chest as if he himself had taken the full impact. Mrs. Hupert had already gathered her full skirt and started climbing the stairs to the main room of the Seldomridge Emporium. The general store was cut into a rise like a bank barn, giving it two first floors. One, where the family lived, was on the lower side of the hill. The floor above opened out onto the street, on the upper side.

"Lay low, boys," Mrs. Hupert shouted bravely. "I'll see what those Rebs are up to."

Ben and Captain ignored her instructions and crowded behind her up the stairs. Danny followed more slowly.

"Saints preserve us," screamed Widow Hupert from the top step.

Ben pushed her from behind so he could see for himself. His mother would have called this rude. But Ben had already decided that manners didn't count in a battle.

A gaping hole in the front of the house let light and air into the unlit interior of the locked store. A table, once stacked with canned goods, was missing a leg. It lay on its side with cans rolling in every direction. Sparkling splinters of glass from the shattered display window gleamed across the floor like tiny crystals. White wool socks and white cotton handkerchiefs lay like snowdrifts across the plank floor, and the globe lamp with its dangling prisms had been blown right off the counter. Its icicle-size pieces added to the illusion that a late-June blizzard had just gusted in from the North Pole. All in all, it was a scene that made Ben shiver despite the blanket of warm humidity spread thickly over the town.

A low-hanging, oval portrait of Grandpa Reynolds on the far wall still hung on a partition in the middle of the room, but it had no face anymore. The cannonball had gone right through it. The thing must have run out of steam as it got to the Emporium. After shattering the window and ruining the portrait, it had dropped to the floor and rolled to the back wall. Now it sat there, a round, black ball looking for all the world like something you'd use to knock pins down if you fancied bowling on the green on a fair summer's evening.

Ben had never seen a cannonball this close before.

A pounding on the front door made Captain bark and leap right up on the counter. The dog raced around the L of the oak countertop and jumped down, barking a warning at the door. Mrs. Hupert hurried forward, picking her way around the litter on the floor. She threw the door open in an act that seemed to Ben to be either very brave—or very stupid.

It was a man in blue.

"Thank heavens!" she gasped.

"Is anyone hurt in here?" the man in uniform asked briskly. "We're setting up a field hospital by the railroad station. We'll treat any injured. There're quite a few of you civilians still in town."

"No, no. We're just shaken up, General." Mrs. Hupert fanned herself with a clump of black feathers from a broken feather duster she'd picked up off the floor. She pointed to the devastated interior of the store. "But just look at the damage! Those dirty Rebs! Are they gone for good now?"

"I'm just a sergeant, ma'am, and I'm sorry to say, the

Rebs are still very much in this. But they've pulled out of town for now. It's not their main army. Just their cavalry."

"Lord a mercy," the widow gasped.

If that didn't beat all. Ben shook his head in wonder. Here he'd thought they were detouring away from the fighting, and the fighting was right here in Hanover.

"The fighting's a quarter mile south of town at the Forney farm. We're gonna catch J. E. B. Stuart himself, I 'spect. We could use some help barricading the streets, though. Whaddaya say, boys? Ole Kilpatrick set up his headquarters at the Central Hotel over there." He gestured out at the now bustling square. "We need all the boxes and barrels and boards we can get to block this part of town."

Despite Widow Hupert's protests—she seemed to think she was responsible for their safety now that they'd eaten her bread—Ben and Danny eagerly followed to help. The widow stayed behind to sweep up broken glass, but Captain came with them as they grabbed a brand-new chest of drawers from a corner of the showroom and toted it out to the barricade. Ben could almost picture Aunt Mavis having apoplexy when she found the chest was missing. Ben chuckled as he thought of it. It might be war, but right now, it felt more like a grand adventure.

Wagons, hay bales, and furniture quickly barricaded the square. And none too soon. Both sides commenced shelling as if on some secret signal, the Rebs from east of town and the Yanks from the west.

Ben and Danny stacked a few more things on the pile growing in the street, ducking their heads and running bent down, although the Reb cannons seemed to be shelling the next street over instead of the square.

"Still finding their range," remarked a tobacco-chewing soldier. Then he spit.

Ben and Danny only returned to the basement kitchen when a shell exploded near the other end of the barricade, and the soldier told them they had to clear out. They could hear more shells bursting into houses as they ran back around the store and into the kitchen, slamming the door behind them.

Danny put his arms around Mavis's neck and talked softly into her ear, calming the restless cow. Ben lay back down on the cot in the corner. The booming cannons filled his ears, rumbling continuously across the summer morning. Ben closed his eyes in the shadowy stillness of the kitchen.

Despite the several hours of sleep he'd gotten, he was still tired. The kitchen was cool and sort of peaceful despite the noise outside. But, of course, a body couldn't sleep with a battle going on.

He'd just close his eyes and figure out a way to find his brother. Maybe a message sent with that sergeant in the square. Maybe he could deliver some of Mrs. Hupert's bread to the Union boys and ask around himself—if anybody'd seen the . . . seen the 106th . . . ? Ben lost his train of thought, suddenly jerking on the cot.

No, he wouldn't fall asleep. He wouldn't. He'd ask around to see if anybody'd seen . . . what? . . . oh yeah, the tin clicker. Where'd he put that clicker, anyroad? He could see Captain in a sunny field full of daisies and buttercups, running toward him, leading a whole herd of stampeding cows. He could see. . . .

As it turned out, it was the *end* of the noise that woke Ben.

"Did you hear that?"

"What?" Ben asked, starting awake.

"They're not shooting. I can't believe it went on for two hours and it's finally over. You slept through the whole thing."

"I wasn't asleep," Ben defended himself, running fingers through his hair to flatten the sleep hump it sometimes got. "I was just resting my eyes."

"And snoring," Danny announced. "You snore when you sleep on your back."

Ben didn't answer, and they both sat listening to the silence for what seemed like a long time.

"Who won, anyroad? That's what I want to know," Danny demanded.

Ben didn't answer. Why did Danny expect him to know who won when they'd both been in the basement kitchen together the whole time? It had to have been the Yanks.

But what if the Rebs had won?

How would he find Reuben if everybody in town was taken prisoner? What did Rebs do with a town when they won it, anyroad? It was a strange idea, really, that anybody could "win" a whole town, like a prize at the county fair.

Ben pulled the blue cap and the gray cap from his flour sack. He stuck the blue hat on his head, then pushed it off and put on the gray hat.

He pushed that off, too. He turned to Danny, wrinkling up his nose.

The kitchen smelled like pungent, day-old straw in a barn stall. Ben left the caps on the cot and rose, taking a step toward the pump. "I swan, this kitchen smells like—"

Ben put his foot dead center in a cow plop.

"You gotta clean up after that cow," he grunted, hopping the rest of the way to the pump.

"The widow's nephew came by while you were napping and said the Confederates were bringing in a wagon train over a mile long." Danny gave a low, appreciative whistle. "Said there were over one hundred supply wagons they stole off the Yankees in Maryland." Danny shook his head sadly. "I bet the Rebs won, with so many wagons."

"Supply wagons don't win battles," Ben answered, using the stove's coal shovel to scoop up Mavis's droppings. Captain sniffed curiously at the shovel. The dog trotted over to Mavis and touched noses with the cow, as if greeting a good old friend. Too bad Captain couldn't be the one to clean up after her.

"Besides, it doesn't matter who won and who didn't, you're still the one who promised to clean up after that dadblame cow."

"I think the cannons scared her," Danny offered, as if that explained the mess. "But you're wrong about the Rebs. I bet they did win. I was upstairs, watching out on the square for a spell, and I seen some Yanks with Reb prisoners, and *then* I seen some Rebs with Yank prisoners. Whaddaya make of that?"

"I make that both armies are taking prisoners," Ben said shortly. He was totally fed up with Danny. Bring a cow home and expect somebody else to clean up after it. That was Danny Seldomridge all over.

The kitchen door opened and Mrs. Hupert bustled in with a pot of sweet-smelling stew. She looked calmer, now that the shooting had stopped.

"My nephew came through during the barrage with a fat old squirrel he'd shot on the next street over. So I boiled it up for you boys. You need something more substantial than bread in those stomachs."

Danny clapped his hands together happily and pulled bowls and spoons down off a wall-hung shelf. Ben wasn't sure it was such a good idea to sit down and eat again. The guns had stopped. He had to get moving. This hadn't been the Big One, he was sure of it. It hadn't been a proper battle at all, where men stood in lines and shot at each other. There'd only been cavalry in the square, and Reuben wouldn't be with the mounted troops, despite the horse he rode as an officer. He'd be with the foot soldiers of the 106th, and Ben was nigh unto positive they weren't here. Captain seemed to know it, too, pacing restlessly from stove to table and back again, ready to move on.

"We gotta eat," Danny said simply, cutting into a baked potato so the fragrant steam filled Ben's nostrils. Stew and potatoes did sound good.

"Fergus—that's my nephew," said the widow, putting a kettle on for tea. "He said the squirrel was just standing there, sort of stunned, right after the cannon barrage started. The tree was swaying and the ground was shaking and the critter was still as a rock. Didn't know whether to go up or down. So Fergus shot him, bless the boy. I swan, some soldiers are like that, too. Can't decide whether to go forward or back, so they just stand there until somebody shoots 'em."

Ben was surprised at his own appetite. Despite his keenness to get moving, he ate two full bowls to Danny's one. They gave the lickings in the pot to Captain. Evening was coming on, and Mrs. Hupert lit a single lantern. "Well, now, you boys have seen a real battle. You can go home and brag on it. And that's what you should do. You should go back home."

Ben shook his head firmly. "That wasn't the big battle everybody's been talking about. You heard that sergeant when the shelling started. It's just the Reb cavalry. I'm not turning back. Not without my brother. Not without Reuben." Captain raised his head from the spot where he lay beside Ben's chair. The dog's tail could be heard all around the quiet room, *whump-whump*ing against the chair leg at the sound of Reuben's name.

"How're ya gonna find one man in the middle of two armies?" Mrs. Hupert protested.

"I'll find him all right."

Mrs. Hupert shrugged in resignation. "But you, at least, will stop this foolishness, won't you, Daniel Seldomridge? Why, your mama would skin me alive if she ever got wind I had ahold of you and didn't keep you safe."

"I'm going with Ben," Danny said in a voice that showed his mind was made up. "Ben needs me."

"No." Ben spoke so quickly, his voice squeaked. He tried it again, more slowly and deeply this time. "No, Danny, the widow's right. You should stay here with Mavis and patch up the store."

Danny's face drew in on itself and his shoulders hunched forward. His voice was whiny, but his eyes didn't flicker. "I came this far, and I'm coming the rest of the way. I'll follow behind you if I have to, Ben. I done it before. And I'll do it again. You know I will."

Ben sighed. There was no arguing with Danny.

Fergus Hupert knocked lightly on the door. Mrs. Hupert spoke to Fergus in huddled whispers, before coming back, hands on hips, to pass on her nephew's scouting report: "The Rebs have pulled out. Fergus thinks they're heading up the road to the north. Leastwise, one thing is sure, they aren't heading south to Virginia, to fight on their own home ground."

So that was the way of it. The Rebs had pulled out of Hanover, but they were still all over Pennsylvania. The Big Battle was coming, Ben could feel it, the way you could feel in the summer air when a thunderstorm was coming.

Ben's mind flashed back to Jim and Curtis. He didn't want to think of his new friends as being part of the same army that had sent a cannonball right over his head trying to kill him. But, of course, they were. They were the enemy. He had to stop thinking of Jim and Curtis as friends. He just had to.

For a while, Ben could hear the distant rumble of wagon wheels as J. E. B. Stuart's men rattled past town with what Fergus said were 125 stolen Union supply wagons. When everything was finally quiet, Ben took a few supplies from the store shelves upstairs. He packed a jar of peach preserves and a couple of cans of brown beans, and Danny took two of Aunt Mavis's best quilts from the bedding chest. He said he needed them to make a tent, but Ben suspected they were to soften the ride when he ended up on Mavis's bony backside again.

There was no question about Mavis coming along anymore. Danny was practically in love with the dadblamed cow, and Ben found he didn't really mind having her around.

Both boys put their shoulders to it and pushed the heavy chiffarobe up against the wall with the cannon hole in it before they left. A soldier at the barricade had carted away the cannonball from where it lay beside the back wall. It was hard to believe a cannonball could roll along so soft and easylike that it wouldn't even dent the pressed-tin wainscoting on the wall where it came to rest. But that was the way of it.

It was dusk now. The shadows lengthened and the crickets started in on their nightly concert. A good time to leave.

"Where are we going?" Danny asked as they slipped out of the store, heading for the northwest side of town on the Abbotstown Road.

That was just like Danny. Always asking questions that didn't have answers.

"North, if that's where the Reb cavalry's going," Ben mumbled. "I 'spect the Rebs'll find the Union Army soon enough. Well then, so will we. Don't ask stupid questions."

An old man, smoking a pipe that smelled like roasting hickory nuts, sat in a rocking chair on a porch they were passing, rocking peacefully as if there'd been no battle at all just a few hours earlier.

"Hey, mister," Danny hailed.

"Sshhh," Ben warned.

But Danny paid no attention. "Hey, mister," he repeated. "Is there gonna be another battle around here?"

The old man nodded his head and kept rocking. "Oh, this wadn't a battle. This wadn't no more than a skirmish today. But there's sure to be a battle, lads. There always is when armies come together. This was just a coupla companies looking for General Robert E. Lee. Passing through, you might say." His voice sounded as creaky as his rocking chair. "They wadn't ready to make their stand in a flyspeck town like Hanover. Them generals like to have their big battles where they got high ground and cover and a way to get reinforcements." His white hair stood out in the late evening gloom.

"Yeah, well, where's the big battle gonna be?" Danny asked bluntly.

"Not thinking of joining up, are you, lads?" the old man asked. "Even with these old eyes and this poor light, I can see you're too young to be away from your mamas."

Ben cringed at the sudden thought of his ma wondering where he was. "No." He spoke up quickly. "We're not lookin' to join up, sir."

"I might be," Danny interrupted, but he whispered the words to Ben alone.

"We're lookin' for my brother. He's with the 106th Pennsylvania. Company A."

"Do tell?" The man on the porch stroked his whiskery chin. "Thing is, nobody knows if Robert E. Lee will stand and fight hereabouts. In Chambersburg maybe. Or Harrisburg. Could be he'll head south soon, out of harm's way. Hard to say."

"Well, thank you kindly," Ben said shortly, shoving against Danny to get his cousin moving again. Mavis tried to crop some weeds growing at the side of the road. Captain had already disappeared into the gathering darkness ahead.

"If I was you," the old man continued. "And I was lookin' for the main Union army. . . . " He paused and seemed to be considering the matter. Or maybe he was just sucking on his white clay pipe. Ben couldn't tell. "I believe," he said slowly, "I'd head west along the Hanover Road. Not *on* the road, mind you. Too many soldiers in blue and gray around here these days. Might run into some who weren't so friendly. Either kind."

The old man stopped and pulled on his pipe. Ben figured that was all he had to say.

"Thanks," he called again. "Bye now." He turned and began walking away, finally spotting Captain as the dog emerged from the darkness up ahead like a welcome beacon to lead the way. But the old man called after them, and Ben heard his words clearly. He remembered them later.

"If I was you boys," the old man called, "I'd go to that

crossroads town about fifteen miles over where the roads all come together. Somebody there is bound to know which way the armies are moving. They get all the news, what with so many turnpikes passing through. You just might run into an army or two yourselves. If you stay near the Hanover Pike, you can't miss this crossroads I told you about. Town by the name of Gettysburg."

CHAPTER 10

July 1

Ben woke with a start. Captain was nowhere in sight. Mavis grazed quietly on whatever grass she could reach from the tree where Danny had tied her. They were in the woods about five miles west of Hanover, and Ben had been sound asleep until that noise woke him.

"What was that?" The three words sounded loud here under the tall maples and shaggy-barked locusts.

"What was what?" Danny asked blearily, rubbing his eyes and sitting up. "How'd morning get here so quick!"

"I heard something." Ben's voice dropped to a whisper. "Somebody's coming."

They hadn't gone nearly as far as Ben wanted last night. Danny went on and on about wanting to "pitch" his quilt tent and get some sleep, and Ben finally gave in. He couldn't argue against sleep. The idea of staying awake and walking all night again made his head hurt.

They'd looked for a branch to hang the quilts on, but there was nothing low enough that wasn't covered with pine needles or leaves. Finally, they'd laid the quilts on the moss under a big, old, black walnut tree. Ben couldn't remember the last time he'd fallen asleep so fast. But he'd come fully awake in a blink when he heard that footstep.

Captain suddenly appeared in the small daylit clearing, leading a boy just a little older than Ben himself. The boy wore Union blue and carried a haversack with a brass buckle stamped with the letters U.S. He also carried a long rifle with a polished wood stock. This soldier must have gotten separated from his unit during yesterday's skirmish in Hanover.

The boy stopped in his tracks when he caught sight of Ben and Danny. His eyes got wide behind a pair of thick, round glasses, and he kept sticking his tongue out to wet his lips. But he didn't speak. There was something very familiar about this soldier, but try as he might, Ben couldn't place him.

"Howdy," Danny said, tipping the Union cap he'd pulled out of his pocket and quickly put on his head. "Where're you headin'?"

Danny acted like it was the most natural thing in the world to run into a soldier in the woods on a fine July morning. Ben wondered if his cousin had any idea of the thing looming up on them—the battle, the war, whatever you called it. Couldn't Danny feel it? It was starting to make the hair prickle on the back of Ben's neck.

Captain trotted up to Ben, still wrapped in his quilt, and Ben tried to fend off the dog's tongue.

The soldier spoke finally, but he didn't answer Danny's question. "I didn't think I'd run into anybody out here." The woods surrounding them shimmered with the deep green of full summer. The clearing was quiet except for some mourning doves and a woodpecker drilling into the black walnut tree overhead.

"We're on our way to Gettysburg." Danny broke the silence, rising to give the stranger a cheerful grin and the offer of a handshake. "My name's Danny, and this here is Ben. We're cousins."

The boy didn't shake the hand Danny offered him. Instead, he looked at his feet, scuffing his dusty but new-looking brogans in the grass. "What's your name?" Danny wasn't about to give up on this one-sided conversation. "We come all the way from Lancaster, over the other side of the river."

This made the boy look up and grin. "Me, too. You going to join up?"

Ben shook his head. "We're looking for my brother. He's with the 106th Pennsylvania."

"You actually 'spect to find Reuben when practically the whole Army of the Potomac is comin' here, and the Rebs to boot? What makes you think you can find one man out of fifty thousand?"

Ben blinked. The soldier knew Reuben. "How did ya know my brother's name?"

"Don't you know me, Ben?" The boy in the Union uniform suddenly reached up and pulled off his cap. Curly reddish-brown hair spilled out in every direction. The boy bent over and juggled a pretend pair of dice in one hand, as if he were shooting a quick game of chuck-a-luck.

"Henry Owen? I don't believe it!" Ben rose and stuck out his hand. "What in tarnation you doing out here, Henry? I thought you joined the home guard."

Henry, laughing, took Ben's hand in his own, pumping it up and down. "I did, Ben. I joined up to fight. But those Lancaster Fencibles just sit around worrying and digging holes to hide in. I figured if that was all the action I'd see in the home guard, I'd head out and find me the real fighting."

"Then that *was* you I saw in Columbia at the bridge. I thought it was. You were pushing barrels with some other men. But I didn't see you any more after that."

"How did you get across the river?" Danny asked suspiciously.

"That was some fire, wasn't it?" Henry enthused, slapping Ben on the back. "I had to stick around to watch those Rebs scurry outta the way when we fired that thing up. You could see 'em at the other end when we was pouring out the coal oil. But they couldn't stop us. We showed them!"

Henry sounded proud, as if he'd stopped old Bobby Lee's army all by himself.

Danny stepped up to Henry, planting himself in front of the boy in uniform. Danny didn't take well to being ignored. "I asked you how you got across the river," he demanded.

Henry looked at Danny with mild surprise. Henry was big for his age. Danny was small for his. It looked to Ben like an angry ant confronting a grasshopper.

"Same way you did, I suppose," Henry answered calmly. "I borrowed a boat and rowed across."

Danny's shoulders slumped, and he turned sadly to Ben. "How come we didn't think of that?"

"I did think of it," Ben shot back, "but we couldn't take your dadblamed cow in a rowboat now, could we?" He turned back to Henry. "You want somethin' to eat? We mainly got beans, but you're welcome to share if you've a mind."

"Where'd you get that gun?" Danny asked before Henry could answer.

"This?" Henry glanced at his shoulder, as if he'd forgotten he carried a gun. "I got this off a fella in Wrightsville after he . . ." Henry hesitated, but then continued matter-of-factly, "he took a Reb bullet in the gut. It was early in the day, and we were fightin' a holding action on the west shore, trying to keep the Rebs off the bridge. I had my pa's old possum gun, the one with the cracked stock. This fella beside me had been bragging on his new gun before he got himself shot."

Henry paused, twisting his cap in his hand. He shook his head, as if a swarm of gnats were bothering him, and then continued. "After he got hit, I could see he didn't need it anymore. So I took it."

Henry, Ben, and Danny all sat Indian-style, legs crossed under them, passing around a cold can of beans. Each would take a spoonful and pass the can on. It sort of lay in their stomachs in a cold lump, but it was food. Besides, Ben was so interested in what Henry had to say, he hardly tasted the beans.

"But your unit? The home guard?" Ben asked. "Won't they call you a deserter? I thought they needed troops in Lancaster County."

"Troops!" Henry snorted, spraying bean juice on Ben's sleeve. "Old granddaddies and college boys from Franklin and Marshall aren't troops. There were no real soldiers. I'm going to fight with the *real* soldiers, and see me a real battle. I'm on my way to join up with General Meade right now. Him and the whole Army of the Potomac."

Henry stood suddenly, giving his tin spoon a lick and jamming it back under the lid of his haversack. He pulled out a derby hat, much like Reuben's, except it was brown instead of black. It looked brand-new.

"I got me this hat so I'll stand out from all them other

soldiers," he told Ben, adjusting the felt derby on his head so he looked like a dandy.

"You're just copying Reuben," Danny said, giving Mavis a good all-over scratching as he spoke. "That's what *he* always wears."

"Then I'll be in good company," shot back Henry with a wink. Ben couldn't believe what he was hearing. Why, this Henry was like a whole different fella from the Henry Owen Ben had known in Lancaster. This Henry was confident and sort of grown-up.

Captain had his nose buried in the bean can, licking out the last drops. It wasn't much of a breakfast for the big dog, but it would have to do.

"I gotta keep moving." Henry sat forward and looked back over his shoulder. "There's gonna be a big one. Everybody says so. Sergeant Mick, from the home guard, got wounded and sent home from Antietam. Sarge only has one arm left. But he could feel it in his bones, he said. He could feel a big battle coming. He said it was like knowing rain was on the way. A certain ache. A little twinge. He was right about Chancellorsville. He was right about Antietam. That's where he lost his arm. And if he's right this time, I'm gonna be there to see it."

"He sent you?" Ben asked. Excitement roiled in his stomach. His feeling was right then. Something was coming. Something big. And they were almost there.

Wherever *there* was.

Henry shook his head. "Are you crazy? Sarge forbid me to even think about it. Said it was a dumb thing to want to see a big one, and I'd be sorry if I ever did."

"But you're here," Danny said, stating the obvious.

Henry grinned. "So are you. Anybody give *you* permission to come?"

Danny actually looked at his feet and scuffed them in the soft forest dirt. "Not exactly," he mumbled.

Henry shook his head vigorously again. "You shouldn't come this way. You're not soldiers. You're just kids."

"I'm twelve," Ben said, mighty peeved that Henry, who wouldn't be fifteen for another month yet, should say such a thing. "You better watch who you're calling a kid."

Henry nodded a quick apology. "Sorry, Ben. But I gotta hurry. Word is," Henry lowered his voice conspiratorially, "troops are massing near Gettysburg."

"Well, that's where we're headed, too." Ben knew he sounded peeved, and he didn't try to hide it. "We've been on the road, day and night, nigh unto three days now. We're in quite a hurry ourselves. We could all go together."

"If the three of us was to show up, they'd see three kids and send us away. You didn't even recognize me in this uniform, remember? They'll take me if I go alone." Henry straightened his belt and touched the polished walnut stock of his scavenged Enfield rifle. "But I gotta hurry. I don't want to miss any of it."

Ben shrugged. "Have it your way, Henry. But if you see Reuben before I do, tell him I'm coming. Tell him to keep his head down. I'll find him."

"I'll do that," Henry called over his shoulder, marching away in a quickstep rhythm that looked strange out here in the middle of the woods.

"I'm still hungry," Danny whined. Ben knelt and opened his flour sack, taking out half a loaf of bread. He broke it in half and handed a piece to Danny. He broke his own piece and gave half to Captain. Ben wondered if Henry had it right. Maybe he should join up when his brother went home and take Reuben's place. That would be fair, wouldn't it? Henry seemed so sure fighting was the right thing to do.

Ben watched Danny squat beside Mavis and milk a cupful into his tin cup. A thin spray was about all the milk Mavis had left. All this walking and cannon fire probably wasn't good for a cow. Danny gulped down the milk without offering any to Ben.

Ben shrugged and chewed on his piece of crusty brown bread. He didn't care if Danny hogged the milk. Ben swigged several mouthfuls of water from his canteen. Danny was a year younger. He needed milk more.

"Come on," Ben said, brushing crumbs off his pants and handing the rest of his bread to Captain. "We need to get movin'."

They set out through the woods, following a narrow

deer path that was almost invisible in the underbrush. It was cool and shady in the early-morning woods and full of noises. Possums and chipmunks scurried through the laurel and tulip poplar trees. Chickadees called *tsick-dee-dee-dee* from the branches of maple and box-elder trees, and squirrels chittered as they dashed up the closest trunk. An occasional white-tailed deer, startled by their presence, raised its flag of a tail in warning and crashed through the bushes, away from the needle-carpeted path.

The dog took off along the westward path as if he was tired of waiting around for plodding cows and two-legged humans. The whole lot of 'em went too slow for Cap.

Ben whistled Captain back, trying to keep him in sight. If he just kept an eye on the yellow hound, he felt sure the dog would warn him of any strangers.

Not that it seemed likely anybody else was out here.

But there could be soldiers. They'd run into Henry, after all. They had to be getting close to the armies now. Maybe they were surrounded by soldiers. Union soldiers. Confederate soldiers. The back of Ben's neck itched, and he suddenly wondered if some unseen sniper had him in his sights.

He almost yelped out loud when Captain padded silently up from behind him and touched his cold, wet muzzle to the back of Ben's hand. Ben covered the gasp that slipped out with a quick cough. The fool dog was always circling around out of sight, and then showing up out of nowhere and surprising him.

They walked on at a steady pace. Ben guessed they'd needed that extra sleep under the black walnut last night. But he couldn't waste any more time. They'd stay off the road to avoid any armies that might be marching by, but they had to get to Gettysburg as quick as they could.

Ben pushed on, ignoring Danny's complaints about skipping lunch. He barely took time to go two steps off the path to relieve himself. The morning soon disappeared, and the afternoon ticked past. Ben fingered the pocket watch in his pants, pulling it out and snapping it open.

Five o'clock. It still said five o'clock. It always said five o'clock now.

Ben sighed and snapped the watch shut, slipping it back in his pocket. It wasn't five o'clock, of course. But whatever time it was, they had come a long way. Danny was quiet for once, leading Mavis by her rope halter, murmuring softly to the cow every now and then. This had to be the farthest they'd ever gone without Danny opening his mouth to ask some dumb question Ben couldn't answer. They'd probably come a good eight miles by the time they finally recognized the noises they'd been hearing since noon.

It was definitely gunfire. And not just snipers either. Lots of gunfire.

Ben had been fixing to call a halt for supper, or maybe

even for the night, but now he wanted to press on. In fact, he wanted to run.

He took off at a fast jog along the shady, pine-needle-covered path, and hadn't gone more than a hundred yards when he stubbed his foot on a jutting rock, which left him hopping along and then limping. Finally, Ben gave up, stopped and bent over to rub his throbbing toe. It was in this bent-over position that he saw the blood, trampled, but still visible, on the narrow path.

"Hold up," Ben ordered.

"Do you think we're coming up on the war soon?" Danny asked eagerly. His cousin hadn't seen the blood yet. Danny was more interested in the faraway pops and booms of rifles and artillery. If this was another skirmish, it sounded like a big one.

"Look." Ben knelt down and tested the blood with the tip of his finger. He expected it to be dry as dust. But it left a small, red smudge on his fingertip. It was fresh.

"Somebody passed this way, bleeding. Not long ago, by the look of it."

Ben looked up at Danny, who gaped at him, open-mouthed. "But the shooting's way over yonder. How'd blood get all the way over here?"

Ben shrugged. "I think we should follow this trail. Somebody might need help." Maybe Reuben. "Maybe we can find out what's happening up ahead." He waved a hand vaguely westward.

"You don't know how to track," Danny pointed out. "And it's too dark under all these trees to follow a trail, anyroad."

But Captain was already circling Ben, fanning out, nose to ground, then giving an excited bark and plunging through a thick tangle of rhododendron, heading north into a stand of oak and sugar maple.

Thick woods were all around them, but this particular stand of trees seemed even closer together and more forbidding. The shadows in there were deep. Ben figured Captain would disappear completely in another few seconds.

Ignoring Danny's shout of protest, Ben plunged after the big, yellow dog, crashing through a row of young fir trees as high as his shoulders, trying to keep the dog's pale coat in sight. He'd been thinking he'd sneak up on whoever was leaving the trail of blood, but he was making so much noise trying to keep up with Captain, Ben figured any sharpshooters hiding out in these woods would be able to plug him by sound alone, without ever laying eyes on him.

He could hear Danny behind him, yelling at him. "You're going the wrong way, Ben! That's not west!"

But Ben didn't care. His imagination, like his dog, ran ahead of him. What if he found Reuben, right here, right now? It was crazy. It was impossible. Aunt Mavis was always talking about a "higher plan." On the surface, it looked like he was just following an old, yellow dog. But Ben felt sure there was more to it.

Ben heard Danny, a ways back, muttering darkly and following the trail of trampled weeds and broken branches Ben was making. Mavis clumped along close behind Danny. Now Ben could smell something, too. Something besides the woodsy scent of pine and cedar. It was bacon. The sizzling, tangy smell of hickory-smoked bacon. It made Ben's mouth water as he ran.

Maybe the fool dog was just looking for a handout. How could blood and bacon go together?

Ben wheezed along, trying to catch his breath. He lost sight of Captain, then spotted him again, running up ahead. He couldn't hear Danny and Mavis anymore. They'd fallen too far behind. He felt like he'd run near on a mile, crashing through bushes and barely dodging the tall pines whose trunks loomed like overgrown fence posts all around him. They'd been zigzagging from one bush to the next, until Ben no longer had any idea where he was.

The sound of distant artillery was fainter now.

But there was another sound.

Ben stopped, leaning on his knees, doubled over, trying to catch his breath. He could hear a voice over his own labored breathing.

The voice was singing, trumpeting the words of "Battle Hymn of the Republic" at full volume. "Glory, glory hallelujah, glory, glory hallelujah."

Ben straightened up and craned his neck, but caught no glimpse of Captain. He began walking, slowly, cautiously, in the direction of the rich baritone voice, now starting in on the verse about "his terrible swift sword."

Ben could see the light of a clearing ahead. The smell of bacon was so delicious, it was like a finger hooked in his nose, pulling him forward almost against his will. He stepped on a twig that cracked sharply. Ben stopped and listened, holding his breath.

The singing stopped, too. Now he could clearly hear someone speaking.

"Lookee here, Petey boy. It's a big old yellar hound dog. Tail's just awaggin' to beat the band. I think he's hungry. Are you hungry, ole fellar? Is that why you come to visit us?"

Ben let out a relieved breath. The man hadn't heard him. It was the arrival of Captain that had made the person in the clearing stop singing. Ben inched forward.

"He looks like a right friendly dog to me, Vern." Ben stopped short. The second voice was high and reedy, sort of pinched sounding. Ben darted his head out from behind the fat, twisted trunk of an ancient oak, and tried to take in the whole scene with one glance.

Two men, sure enough. Both wore blue. One sat on a camp stool, mashing something up in a dented tin cup. The other lay full-length on the ground, his head pillowed on a fallen tree. The top of his right leg was wrapped in a strip of blue-checked cloth—probably an old shirt. The wrapping was soaked with blood. Captain stood next to the man on the ground, licking his face.

Ben drew back to consider his next move. A dead twig, right at elbow height, broke off as he moved. Ben froze. For a moment, it was so quiet, he thought he could hear Captain's tongue slurping against the wounded man's skin.

"Whoever you are, come on out." The singing man's voice was deep and menacing now. "Drop your gun where I can see it. I'd hate to have to shoot you right at dinner-time."

CHAPTER 11

Blood & Bacon

Ben pawed frantically through his bag, searching for the Union cap. He grabbed the blue wool hat and stepped from behind the tree into a small clearing. Lifting the cap, he waved it.

"I'm not a Rebel," he yelled. "I'm a Yank. Like you." His voice broke on the word "you." It was hard to speak when your heart was pounding in your throat.

"Come on out here, where we can see you, boy." The older man, who wore a red bandana around his neck and had a reddish-brown mustache that hung down past his chin, gestured at Ben with the business end of his rifle.

"I ain't gonna shoot you, lessen I hafta."

Ben stepped forward, both hands outstretched, palms up. "I don't have a gun, mister. I'm not really a soldier. I just have this hat." The blue cap dangled from the end of one finger. "My brother gave it to me," he finished lamely. "He's a Union soldier, just like you." Ben's voice had gotten so high, he only managed to squeak out those last words. He had been addlepated, thinking this might be Reuben.

"Calm down, boy." The older man smiled. Or maybe it just looked like a smile. It was hard to tell behind that big old droopy mustache. "Set a spell. Relax."

"Has he come for us, Vern?" The wounded man's voice sounded frightened. Ben stared at him.

"Naw, he's jus' a civilian. I bet he smelt this here bacon." The older man nodded toward the pan sitting on a rock next to the fire. He lowered his gun and leaned it against a small pile of firewood.

"I'm makin' us some hoe cakes to use up the drippings." He held out the tin cup in his hand for Ben to see. It was full of yellow cornmeal mushed up with water. Just thinking about the taste of cornmeal bread and bacon made Ben's mouth start to water. He hadn't eaten anything since that tin of beans for breakfast.

"Come on. Sit down. Name's Vernon. Vernon Watkins. And this here is Petey. Pete Dyer. I do believe we got us enough to go around. If you want some."

He winked at Ben.

Ben nodded without saying a word.

"This wouldn't be your dog, now, would it?"

Ben shook his head. "No. He's not my dog. He's my brother's dog."

Suddenly, the soldier who called himself Vern grabbed his rifle and aimed it in the direction of the woods, the spot Ben had just come from. There was a click as he cocked it.

"Who goes there?" he shouted.

Ben whirled and caught a glimpse of Danny hovering whitely in the shadows beneath the white oak. Then, Mavis trotted into camp.

The grass was long and green out in the clearing. That was the only thing on the fool cow's mind.

"Mavis! You get back here!" Danny yelled. The cow didn't even pause. Danny took two steps after her and stopped, looking at the gun in Vern's hands. "Don't shoot me, mister," Danny pleaded. "My mama would skin me alive if I was to come home shot."

At that, the older soldier began to laugh and even Pete grinned weakly. "My mama's gonna skin me, too, when she sees the mess I'm in," Pete said softly, nodding toward his crudely bandaged leg.

"I ain't gonna shoot you, boy," Vern managed between guffaws. "I'm just being careful. But that cow of yourn would make a first-rate stew, I'll wager."

Danny stiffened. "She's not an eatin' cow," he said coldly. "She's a milkin' cow. Acourse her milk's most dried up from all the traveling we been doing, but she still gives a bucketful, morning and night," Danny lied. He sat down, cross-legged, beside the fallen tree, leaning back against it. Ben had done the same. Pete didn't complain, but the expression on his face seemed to say that the slightest jiggle of the log he lay against might set him off, blubbering. The young man's breathing was fast and kind of ragged.

"You fellas come a long way?" Pete asked. He winced as he spoke. It was his leg that was wounded, but it seemed to Ben as if moving anything, even his mouth, pained him.

"We came all the way from Lancaster," Danny said proudly. "We're looking for Ben's brother." He pointed helpfully at Ben. "Captain Reuben Reynolds. 106th Pennsylvania Infantry, Company A. Do you know him?"

"Sorry, boys. We's with the 107th Pennsylvania. That's First Corps under General John Reynolds. The 106th is Second Corps. I don't believe I've ever heard of any *Captain* Reynolds."

Ben wondered if his own expression looked as miserable as Danny's crestfallen face. Vern quickly added: "Which is not to say he's not close by. There's a powerful lot of soldiers in these parts right now. We just had us quite a fight, north of a town called Gettysburg, where them Johnny boys was trying to requisition some shoes for their poor old bare feet."

"Then *that's* what we heard," Ben said. "There was gunfire and cannons over that way." Ben pointed toward the northwest. "That's the way we were heading until . . ." He paused. "Until we saw the trail of blood leading here."

"Well, there you go, Petey. I told you not to bleed so dang much," Vern said with a gentle laugh. Pete had his head back, his eyes closed.

"Right, Vern," he whispered hoarsely, and raised a hand in a sort of half salute. The hand trembled.

During all the talking, Vern had deftly fried up a batch of hoe cakes. Now he divided the cornbread cakes and thick, chewy slices of salty bacon among himself, Pete, Danny, and Ben. Pete shook his head and pushed his share away. Vern tried again, but when Pete still refused, Vern handed his friend's share to Captain, who took it carefully from the soldier's fingers, his lips just nibbling at the crumbly edges, until he had it all in his mouth. Then he gulped it down as if he hadn't eaten since before they'd left Lancaster.

"Is he hurt bad?" Danny whispered loudly to Vern.

"Bad enough," muttered Pete, with his eyes still closed. Ben didn't think the pale, dark-haired boy could be much older than sixteen. He had barely visible fuzz on his chin, but no real beard at all.

"He took shell fragments in the top of his leg," Vern explained between bites. "It was a bad time. General Reynolds hisself got shot before the fighting really got going. Over in Herbst's Woods he was, sitting on his horse when they got him. And he weren't the only general to play target for them Reb snipers. General Paul took a minié ball and lost a right good chunk of his hair. It didn't kill him, though. Some are lucky that way."

Vern was staring at Pete as he spoke.

"General Reynolds?" Ben asked breathlessly. "How bad was he hit?"

"Ben's a third or mebbe a fourth cousin of General Reynolds," Danny confided, leaning forward. "Ben's name is Ben Reynolds. You know. Like General Reynolds. Mine's Danny Seldomridge, which isn't like any general's. Anyroad, General Reynolds is a hero back in Lancaster, where he and Ben come from, and Ben's especially partial to him, being a relative and all."

Ben closed his eyes and shuddered. Why couldn't Danny ever shut up? Why did he have to tell everyone they met everything he knew?

Vern's expression had grown solemn as Danny spoke. "I'm sorry to be the one to tell you, boys, but General Reynolds is dead. He had the whole left wing with him, he did. And what did they do but shoot him right off his horse. Dirty Rebs. He shoulda been safely at the rear, like all the other generals. But no. Not him. He rode up ahead to find out what was happening . . . he really was a hero, Ben, the way he died. You should feel proud."

Ben didn't. His fists clenched and unclenched. "I can't believe it," he whispered. He felt cheated. There was no room for feeling proud.

"Can you believe this?" Pete opened his eyes. His expression had changed. He laid a hand on the bloody cloth tied around his leg. "Can you believe men's dying for slaves, which I ain't never had, and some idea about states' rights, which I don't understand?" His voice was bitter.

"That's why I left. You can only ask so much of a man." He gestured at the leg again. "I'm dying. We're all dying. That should be good enough. But no, they want more. The presidents and the generals always want more. That's why we left."

Ben noticed for the first time that Pete was sweating heavily, his white shirt drenched. Droplets stood out on his forehead and ran down into his bloodshot eyes. Ben wondered if a man could get a fever so quick from a bullet. He doubted it, but he didn't know for sure.

"Quit yer raving, Petey. You've said too much already." Vern looked upset. "These boys don't know who we are. They don't know how we got here."

Except, suddenly, Ben did know.

They were deserters—soldiers who had run away.

"Tell 'em, Vern. Go ahead. I'll tell 'em if you don't," Pete ranted, his eyes looking crazily up and down, right and left, as if he were searching for someone. "We're soldiers going home to die." His head fell back. His breathing was labored from the effort required to speak, and his eyes closed.

Vern shook his head sadly, and motioned Ben and Danny to move away from the fire. "I don't want Petey to hear this," he told them softly. "But he's right. He might just be dying, and, if he don't, he'll lose that leg for sure. He's just seventeen. I couldn't leave him in a field hospital to lie on dirty straw and beg for water with all the docs too busy to hear 'im. I've seen it happen just that way. So when the fighting swung south into town, Pete and me headed east." Vern had a hoe cake in one hand, and he stuffed it in his mouth but still kept talking. Ben could see the yellow crumbs grinding between Vern's yellowing teeth. Vern kept right on talking as he ate.

"It's not what a man wants for his friend. Petey and me, we's both from Dover, over near York. Signed up together, we did," Vern swallowed decisively and wiped a ragged, bloodstained sleeve across his lips. "Now, here we are, not all that far from home, and Petey wants to see his ma agin.

"He won't be back to the war, no matter how this little fight turns out. But I will. Once't I get him home, they'll be plenty of bullets still waiting for me." He looked down at the splotchy bloodstains on his own torn muslin shirt. Shadows from the leaves overhead splashed over the ground in the same kind of careless pattern. "If you haven't been in a fight, boys, you don't know what it's like." No one spoke for several minutes.

Then Vern broke the silence, in his old hearty voice. "Come on to Dover with us, boys. You don't want to be going to Gettysburg. It's gonna be a mean one. Might could make you pay with your lives." His voice had become urgent. "Your lives," he repeated. "What are they worth to you?"

"Mama." Pete groaned the word, half asleep, but Ben heard it clearly. "Mama. Water."

They returned to the fire. The older man knelt down beside his wounded friend and tilted a cloth-covered, blue canteen between Pete's slightly parted lips.

"You could help me get him home, if you had a mind to," Vern said, without turning around to look at them. "That dog of yourn could scout the way for us, and I got my rifle. Who knows what we'll meet up with in these woods today?"

"No." Ben tried to make the word sound both firm and sincere. He jammed the blue Union cap he'd been holding all this time back on his head as a gesture of his intention to leave. Danny pulled his own cap out of his pocket, pushing his stringy red hair back from his eyes and catching it under the brim. "We have to go," Ben said. "We can't turn back. But we won't let on to anyone that we saw you."

Ben stood up slowly, glancing at the woods. It was dark in among the trees removed from the dappled evening sunshine in the clearing. Ben hoped Vern wouldn't think of picking up his rifle and drafting them into helping him carry his wounded friend home. More than ever, he had to find Reuben. He was close now. Ben could feel it, and it made him itch to hurry forward. War or no war.

Danny picked up Mavis's frayed rope halter and followed Ben. "I hope Pete, there, makes it. And you, too, Vern. Good luck."

"Good luck your ownselves," the older man said with a

sad smile, turning and watching them leave. "You'll be the ones that need it."

Ben breathed a sigh of relief when they were out of sight of Vern's tired, sad eyes and out of hearing of Pete's feverish, labored breathing.

"Well, wasn't that something?" Danny whispered. "Genuine deserters, right in front of us. And I wasn't even scared."

Ben snorted. He snapped his fingers for Captain, but the dog seemed lost in some scent on the faint evening breeze, padding off through the bushes as if he hadn't even heard. The dog was after some squirrel, thought Ben. Captain never heeded him. He wished he still had that little tin clicker. Fool, bootlicker dog.

Ben squared his shoulders and set off through the trees, back toward the footpath. He'd gone maybe a quarter of a mile when Captain came up beside him, growling.

The fur on the dog's back stood on end. Captain's legs were stiff, his nose tilted upward, as if he were reading a warning in the humid July air. Ben stood still, peering into the deep shadows between the trees just ahead. It was coming on dusk, Ben supposed. But they had to keep going. They had to make some miles before pitching camp for the night. He felt a pull to move on. It lay on him so strong he wanted to run. But instead, he stood there, without moving, trying to fathom the cause of Captain's disquiet.

Danny came up behind him, actually bumping into Ben

before realizing they were stopped. "Hey, you said we were going to . . ." Danny began.

Captain focused on the faint trail ahead. His low warning growl turned into a snarl, and the yellow dog stalked forward, challenging the unseen watcher in the woods up ahead. The fur along his back stood straight up on end.

A tall, skinny shadow peeled away from the trees, walking quickly toward Ben.

It was a man.

Ben couldn't make out his face in the gathering gloom, but he caught a flash of something silvery bright as the shadow moved.

"Hello!" Ben called, adding almost as an afterthought, "We're civilians passing through. We mean you no harm."

"Well now, I'm right glad to hear that." The voice was low and menacing. It matched the face, which had come into focus, about twenty feet in front of Ben. Ten feet from Captain. "Cuz I'd hate to see this pretty little dog get hurt."

Ben frowned at the words. Captain was neither little nor particularly pretty. At the moment, the dust-coated dog was parked five paces in front of Ben, a continuous rumble coming from his throat. His tail was down, twitching slightly at the tip.

The stranger was another soldier, like Vern and Pete, and Henry that morning. Only this time, the soldier wore a gray uniform and a slouching gray cap. He had long, black hair, pulled back and tied with a length of rawhide, as well as at least a week's growth of coarse beard. The whiskers straggled across his chin and cheeks like they weren't sure they wanted to be there. His eyes were almost as black as his hair, and they shifted constantly, from Ben to Captain to Danny to Mavis to the trees. The glint of silver flashed in his hand. He balanced a hunting knife loosely in his long fingers.

"Ain't you boys a little young, even for Yanks?" he sneered.

Ben wanted to whip out his gray cap and trade it for the blue one on his head. But it was way too late for hat tricks. His stomach twisted sharply. Ben wet his lips.

He reached up and slowly pulled the cap from his head, twisting it in his hands, trying to appear calm despite the prickle at the nape of his neck and Captain's constant, warning growl.

"We're civilians," Danny said, catching up after feeding Mavis a fistful of clover. He was oblivious to the danger Ben was sensing. "We're from Lancaster. I'm Danny. He's Ben. That there dog is Captain, and this," he raised the cow's rope lead and turned his head slightly, "is Mavis."

The Reb laughed, but it wasn't a friendly sound. It was angry. He cut the laugh off quickly and asked Ben: "You got bacon? Bacon and biscuits, mebbe? I smelled me some bacon cooking."

"No, sir," Ben answered. He didn't want to tell the Reb about Vern and Pete. "We smelled it, too, but we couldn't find nothin'. We got some beans and a little bread. That's all."

"Back that way, we ran into some de—ooph." Danny doubled over as Ben's fist shot back, punching him in the stomach.

"Back that way," Ben pointed at an angle away from the clearing. "We run into a lot of Reb soldiers. In Hanover."

"Are they still there?" The Reb sounded worried. "Who'd you see? Who was there?"

"J. E. B. Stuart, I think," Ben said. "Anyroad, folks said it was him."

"Aw, old Jeb can't sit still." The soldier seemed to be talking to himself. "He'll be long gone by now."

His tone was distinctly sour as he glowered at Ben and Danny. "What you kids doing out here alone with that cow?" He licked his lips and smiled wickedly. "Ya know, beef tops bacon any day of the week for fillin' a man's belly."

"Mavis is a *milk* cow," Danny asserted indignantly. "*Not* an eatin' cow."

The knife twitched menacingly in the Reb's hand. Ben noticed, for the first time, that the soldier had dried blood on his fingers and fresh powder burns on his ragged, gray jacket. But he didn't have a gun.

"What're you doing out here, anyroad?" Danny challenged. "I bet you're a deserter, too."

Ben wished desperately that he'd punched his cousin

harder. Hard enough to knock him out. Ben knew instinctively that Danny's statement was exactly the wrong thing to say.

"I'm with Company C, 13th Virginia Cavalry, if it's any of your business," the Reb responded, sauntering a few surly steps closer. "I was right there in Hanover, like you said, with Jeb's troops. Shell went off over my head, and I lost my senses for a spell. But I was there, all right."

He was lying. Ben was sure of it. This soldier standing in front of him was looking him right in the eye and lying. Why else had he asked if the Rebs were still in Hanover if he'd been there himself? Why else was he coming from the direction of Gettysburg?

The Reb looked around, as if the surroundings made his point obvious. "This is Pennsylvania. Close enough to home. Brandy Station last month. Now this. I cain't do another battle. Not so soon. Not without my horse. All I'm interested in now is a good meal and gettin' myself home. I got a bellyful of this war. A bellyful." He moved toward Mavis. "Now I'm goin' to get me a bellyful of fresh beef."

"Told you he was a deserter," Danny squealed.

"Shut up," Ben whispered.

The Reb edged closer and closer, tossing his knife from hand to hand. "You boys don't mind sharing that cow with me, do ya? It's for a good cause."

"Stay away from Mavis," Danny squawked, stumbling

backward, grabbing a flap of Mavis's skin and pulling himself up onto the unprotesting cow's back. Mavis nosed along the forest floor, looking for more clover.

Captain turned and circled round behind the cow. The dog disappeared, as usual, into the shadows. Fool dog. Ben stepped squarely in front of the cow. He was reaching into his flour sack, saying, "The cow goes with us, mister. But I can give you our other food, like these beans . . ."

"You going for your pistol, boy?" The words came out so softly, it took Ben by surprise when the Reb lunged at him, knocking him down, grabbing a handful of Ben's thick hair with his left hand and pulling Ben's head high, exposing his neck. The blade hung in midair, poised over Ben's throat.

Ben knew he should fight back. He should struggle and knock the knife out of the Reb's hand. But his arms and legs seemed to be paralyzed, lying unresponsive on the leafy ground as he tried to get them to move. The rich sounds and smells of the forest came to Ben with such clarity, he could hear a katydid call and taste the bittersweet mint of pine needles on his tongue.

The seconds crawled by, the knife hanging like a blazing stroke of lightning, searching for a place to jolt to earth. It didn't move. Somewhere behind them, Danny whimpered. "No. Don't. Don't do Ben."

The knife began to move downward.

Without a sound, in a blur too swift to really see, a flash of yellow hit the upraised arm, sending the knife sailing into the shadows, clamping down on the wrist with a terrible strength. The Reb hollered something—a swear word Ben had never heard before—and rolled off, thrashing and cursing, trying to pry his wrist away from the dog's stubborn jaws. He tried to kick and punch and swing the big, yellow dog bodily off the ground, but Captain's steady pressure kept the Reb so off-balance, he flailed and screamed in vain. Ben wondered fleetingly if this was what a Rebel yell sounded like up close. He scrambled to his feet.

"Call off your dang dog. Call it off!" the Reb yelled.

"Can't," Ben answered, surprised by the calm assurance in his own voice. "It's not *my* dog." For the first time since he'd started on this journey, the words gave him a curious sense of satisfaction.

The Reb tried moving farther and farther away. Captain hung on to his arm like a burr on wool.

"Clear outta here, and he'll turn you loose," Ben called. The Reb was backing away so fast, Ben wasn't sure he'd even heard him.

Danny slid off Mavis's back and stood beside Ben, his voice small and a bit apologetic. "I would have given him Mavis," he said. "I wouldn't have let him slice you up, Ben. I'd have said, 'Here, you stinky old Reb, here's my cow, and I hope you choke on her. Choke on her and die.' That's what I would have said."

Ben surprised himself by reaching out an arm and putting it around Danny's trembling shoulders. "Thanks, Dan," he said softly. "But we're in this together. Nobody's eating Mavis. Not today, leastwise."

CHAPTER 12

July 2

Ben slept so soundly that night, it was as if he were in his own bed at home with Reuben just across the room and Captain curled up on the braided rug in the middle. When he awoke, he was startled to find himself still in the woods. He blinked at Danny. His cousin's face was half hidden by the quilt, lying with his head pillowed on Mavis's curved neck. Danny didn't need three pillows anymore. "Congesting sleep vapors" weren't a problem when you slept in the woods with a cow.

The tip of Captain's nose rested inches from the tip of Ben's. The dog's breath was slightly sour. Not bad. More like lived-in. Ben had to cross his eyes to look at the peacefully sleeping animal beside him.

When Captain hadn't come back by the time they pitched camp last night, Ben wondered if the dog had wrestled that Reb all the way to the Mason-Dixon Line. Ben rolled over from his side to his back, and the dog's eyes opened. Captain reached out a long tongue and slurped it across Ben's lips, making him splutter and twist away. The dog stood up, shook himself, and sniffed the length of Ben's body as if checking to see that all the parts were still there. Ben reached out a hand and touched Captain's velvety ear. He'd never seen Captain do this particular trick with Reuben.

"Leave off," he gruffed, sitting up, yawning and stretching. What he really wanted to do was to take Captain in his arms, hug the dog tightly, and say, "Thank you for saving my life." What he did instead was to cup the square muzzle in one hand and pull the big, yellow head close.

"I know you haven't forgotten Reuben," he whispered. "Neither have I. You want to be with him, and that's what I want, too."

Trouble was, it was a lie. Ben wanted Captain the same way he wanted to keep the pocket watch that, by rights, belonged to Reuben; the same way he wanted the war to be over and life to get back to normal.

Ben stood up and shook himself all over. The dog sat, watching him curiously. They had all slept much later than Ben had planned. Eyeing the sun through the trees, Ben calculated that it was midmorning already. Maybe nine. Maybe ten. Maybe eleven. He wasn't good at telling time by the sun.

He woke Danny by bending over and whistling loudly in his ear. Danny jumped so quickly and so high that the top of his head rammed into Ben's jaw. Mavis turned to examine these unruly calves and mooed her concern. The cow slowly rose, back end first, taking her good old time about it, the way she always did. Captain barked, wagged his tail, and pranced around the three of them, as if he didn't want to be left out of the fun. The dog's spirits were high, despite the encounter with the Reb the day before.

Ben delved into his flour sack and pulled out a tin of fancy biscuits from England and the paper sack of pork jerky. He pulled out four flat sticks. Danny got enough milk from Mavis to fill Ben's cup once for each of them. Ben shared his cup with Captain. It was a strange breakfast, quite chewy in parts, but it tasted perfectly delicious according to Danny, and Ben saw no reason to disagree.

While each boy chewed his way slowly down a single stick of the tough jerky, Captain gulped two strips without chewing at all.

They still had a piece to go before they reached the town of Gettysburg, which Ben expected to find as empty as Hanover had been when they'd first arrived. They'd heard no artillery last night, no shots to wake them up this morning. Nothing. Whatever soldiers were fighting yesterday had no doubt moved on. But they couldn't have gone far. Ben was sure he'd find the Union Army and Reuben. If not today, then maybe tomorrow.

They folded up their quilts, laying them over Mavis's back, and started out, swinging close enough this time so they could actually see the hard-packed dirt surface of the Hanover Pike. Like yesterday, the road was empty of horses, wagons, and soldiers. There wasn't even a civilian in sight.

Ben wondered how many other deserters lurked in these woods. He hoped they didn't meet any more—not Rebs or Yanks.

Ben thought about his mother as he walked. Would she understand that he'd only left to find help, to find someone who could do the things Pa used to do before he signed on for the home guard and was sent to Fort Curtin in Harrisburg? The night the telegram came, saying Pa was dead, was the worst night of Ben's life.

He'd run up to Reuben's studio and hid behind an oilcloth backdrop of a gentleman's parlor. He'd wanted to disappear into that picture, into a life where none of it— the war, Pa's death, Reuben's going off to fight—had ever happened.

How could a strong man like Pa die before he even got into battle? It wasn't a bloody wound that took Pa down. No. It was little red spots.

Ma had gone into her room and not come out for a whole night and day. They closed the shop, of course. Henry and his mother came up and hung the "Closed" sign and draped the door in black cloth. After his night in the studio, Ben spent most of the next day sitting in front of his mother's bedroom door, waiting. Not thinking too much. Not feeling. Because if he let himself, all he could feel was—guilt.

Guilt for not being what Pa had wanted him to be. Guilt for not being more broken up about Pa's passing. Maybe Pa wouldn't have gone off and enlisted at Camp Curtin if he and Ben had been closer. Maybe Pa's dying was all his fault. Now Ma really needed somebody to help her. She needed a man. And Ben could only think of one thing to do—go find Reuben.

That had happened a month ago—June 2, right around the time the Rebel invasion had begun in Pennsylvania. It seemed like years ago, now.

That's when Ben began to form his plan to find his brother and bring him home to Ma. The Union couldn't take everyone from a family. It wouldn't be fair.

Ben snapped back to the present with the first pop of rifle fire. Somewhere ahead, somebody was shooting. But Ben kept walking.

Other rifles joined in, sounding for all the world like a pan of corn, *pop-pop-popp*ing on the stove. Then a cannon thundered. Its reverberating wave of sound made Ben's eardrums thrum.

They picked up their pace as they began to pass buildings. Sheds and small barns. Paddocks and fenced fields. They were on the eastern edge of what had to be Gettysburg, with houses just in front of them, most shuttered or with the shades pulled down despite the fierce July heat. It had gone strangely quiet after that first, distant volley.

They climbed a steep incline with a farm on the right. Whitewashed barn. Split-rail fences. Corn stalks shoulder high in the fields. They crossed a rocky creek, easily wading across the shallow current, the cool water splashing against their ankles.

Another cannon shell burst in the distance and both boys ducked into a dilapidated shed in an unfenced backyard. The dog and the cow came with them.

"I thought the skirmish was yesterday," Danny whispered, clearly confused. "I thought the fighting would be over."

Ben shook his head. The thought that came to him was almost too terrible to consider. What if yesterday's fighting had been only a beginning? "Chancellorsville lasted five days," he said out loud.

Rays of sunlight stretched through gaps between the boards of the shed, striping the plain, dirt floor beneath their feet. Dust motes danced in each beam.

"So, what do we do now?" Danny demanded.

Ben thought before he spoke. "We walk into town as if we belong there." His plan didn't sound as good when he said it right out loud to Danny as it had in his head. But he didn't have another plan. So he went on. "We'll look for your pa's cousin, the one you told me about. Find his house. Mebbe stay there tonight."

"But if they're still fighting, how do we know who holds the town?"

"Doesn't matter who," Ben said, patting his flour sack with its caps from two opposing armies. "We go in bareheaded and, if anybody asks, we say we live here. Neither Yanks nor Rebs should know the difference. They haven't been here long enough to know who lives here and who doesn't."

Danny nodded. But he kept asking questions. Danny always had more questions. When he got nervous, they never stopped.

"What'll we say about Mavis?"

"What do you mean, 'what'll we say'? She's a cow. That's all. We were sent to fetch her for your cousin Travis. That's why we're out here. There's a baby who needs the milk." Ben made it up as he went along. He was surprised at how easy it was.

"What if they want to eat her?"

Ben snorted out his exasperation. "What if they want to eat *you,* Danny? We won't let them. That's all."

Ben pushed open the shed door. The cannons and rifles had started again, sometimes sounding close, sometimes far away. Ben hoped all the soldiers would be so busy with their battle, none would be left over to hang around in town. Battles weren't fought house-to-house in town, after all. Battles were fought with long lines of men strung out across a field, marching straight at each other, firing their guns. All the books about war said so.

And if there *were* any soldiers in town, surely they'd be Bluecoats.

But they weren't going to be that lucky.

Hatless, they walked over to what looked like a main street. There was a metal signpost on the corner, with the words BALTIMORE STREET stamped on it. Ben wanted to look around, but he didn't. They needed to look like any ordinary boys and dog and cow, who often took walks together and wouldn't let a bit of cannon fire ruin their routine. Ben had Captain on his rope, and the dog heeled smartly at his side. Danny walked next to Mavis, one hand on the Jersey's halter and the other draped around her neck.

Two Graycoat soldiers, guns on their shoulders, stopped Ben and Danny before they went more than a dozen paces.

Rebs. The Rebs held the town of Gettysburg. Not the Yanks.

Ben felt a tickle of sweat roll from his forehead down his nose.

"Don't you boys know enough to keep your heads down when there's shooting going on?" one Reb drawled. "What are you doing out in the street, anyway?"

"Oh, we're going straight home," Danny piped up enthusiastically. "Right on this street. We live right on this street."

"Where's your house?" asked the other soldier.

"Our house?" Danny sounded puzzled. "Oh." Now he got it. He looked up one side of the street. He looked down the other. He looked at Ben. "I don't know," he said.

Ben closed his eyes wearily. This wasn't going well.

"You don't know where you live?" the first Reb asked incredulously. "Are you addlepated?" Ben was having trouble concentrating. Cannons boomed somewhere just to the south of town now, making his stomach flutter and twang. Gun reports rang out in volleys, first from one direction, and then from somewhere else.

"We're bringing this cow from the farm out east by the hill," Ben began a trifle uncertainly.

"The Benner farm?" the first Reb asked, and Ben nodded, his brain still scrambling for a better excuse.

"Yes. The Benner farm. Old Mister Benner wanted it taken to Travis Seldomridge, who paid for it, and needs it bad now, what with all the troops here and shortages and all."

Ben watched the first Rebel carefully as he spoke. Apparently, he was saying the right things. "He needs it for his baby," Ben added.

The Reb nodded his head. Captain was busily sniffing his boots.

"Yeah," Danny said, making the story far more complicated that it had to be. "This here is Ben Benner. Mister Benner's boy. I'm Danny Seldomridge, and Travis is my pa's cousin on his pa's side. So we came into town together to deliver this milkin' cow. That's what she is. Not an eatin' cow. And we're getting paid to do it, too. Two bits. Each."

This was too much. Ben elbowed Danny to try and make him stop. The soldiers would never believe all these elaborate lies. But when he looked back up at them, both were grinning.

"We stayed over at the farm, and now I just can't remember which house it is when we come in from this direction," Danny continued. "There's too much shooting to think straight."

"That's the truth, little brother." The second Reb gestured up the street toward the town square. "Go up there and get your bearings. There's townspeople helping with the wounded up there. All around here, as a matter of fact. Some of 'em's almost nice enough to be Virginians."

Captain wagged his tail enthusiastically, as if Virginians were just the critters he'd been hoping to meet. Ben's mind flashed back to the Rebel in the woods with the menacing knife. He'd said he was from Virginia, hadn't he? No, that wasn't right. He was *with* the 13th Virginia Cavalry. But he was *from* Maryland. Mebbe real Virginians wouldn't come lunging at a body to try and stick a knife in him.

"You wait here," Danny said, turning to dart up the street. "I'll find it."

"Watch yourselves, boys. There's a right lot of lead flying around out here. Best keep your heads down and get inside quick as you can," the first Reb said as the pair of

Graycoats continued on their patrol. Ben stood alone in the middle of Baltimore Street, with one bony, brown cow and one big, yellow dog. He thought he caught the movement of lace curtains as folks in the houses along the street stared out at the strange sight. A minié ball whistled high overhead. As Ben watched, it fell spent to the dirt, not more than one hundred yards past where he stood.

The minié ball came from somewhere south of town, where a battle was raging, from the sounds of it. This was no cavalry skirmish. No quick clash between units on the move.

This was the battle everyone had been talking about since the Rebs first came into Pennsylvania, almost a full month ago. This was two massive armies, hunkered down to beat on each other till one or the other hollered "uncle."

Ben knew with a desperate certainty that he had failed.

He hadn't gotten to Reuben first.

The battle had.

Crouching down, Ben turned and ran, Captain ahead of him, Mavis trotting along behind, down the street toward the square, following Danny.

CHAPTER 13

The Crossroads Town

The house, when they found it, was like all the others: brick, three floors high, stone front steps up to a formal, black-painted door with a brass knocker at eye level. Only the number 11, painted in scrolled, white numerals above the knocker, marked this as the house of Danny's cousin Travis.

Eleven was the same as the number of letters in "Seldomridge." Eleven letters. It was the trick that finally helped Danny remember how to find the house, after asking several people in the square.

"Go ahead. Knock," Danny urged.

"Me? He's *your* cousin," Ben objected.

"I don't remember ever meeting him. Maybe at Grandpa Seldomridge's funeral, but I was only five. And there were so many folks there. I don't really recall."

Grimly, Ben stepped up to the door. They couldn't stay out here in the street. Stray shots from the fighting outside town splintered bricks all around them. It wasn't safe. Ben just hoped Cousin Travis wasn't afraid to answer his door.

Ben knocked. The boom of a cannon made the glass rattle in the windows. Captain whined.

He knocked again, harder. Finally, the door opened a crack.

"No room for wounded here," said a gravelly voice. "Try next door at the church. Every one of our beds is full. Every one of our couches and chairs, too."

"We don't have wounded." Danny stepped forward, so that he stood shoulder-to-shoulder beside Ben. "We only have a cow. And you're my cousin."

At that, the door opened a bit wider. A short, heavy-set, balding man with wisps of gray hair behind his ears and in them stared at them with a faint air of curiosity. "Is that cow provisions from the Confederate Army? It's about time. We could sure use some help with feeding all these mouths."

"It's me, Cousin Travis. It's Danny Seldomridge. Mavis and Elliott's boy." Danny danced anxiously from foot to foot as he prattled on. "You remember me, don't you? And this here is my cousin Ben, on my ma's side." He pointed as he spoke, jabbing the air with a nervous finger. "And Ben's brother's dog, Captain. The cow is Mavis. She's really mine more than Ben's"—he nodded at Ben, but didn't even pause for breath—" 'cause he can't milk too good, and he didn't want to bring her with us across the river."

"What river?" Cousin Travis was clearly puzzled by the whole conversation.

Ben didn't blame him.

"The Susquehanna, acourse." Danny skittered back down the stairs and grabbed the cow's rope halter where he'd hooked it over the finial of the porch rail. He appeared to be fixin' to lead Mavis up the stairs and into the house.

Cousin Travis began to close the door.

Ben figured he'd better speak up, or they'd never get any farther than the front stoop. "We're looking for a place to stay the night, until I can find my brother, Captain Reuben Reynolds. He's with the 106th Pennsylvania, Company A." Ben paused for a minute, half waiting for the astonished-looking man in the brown canvas apron to say, "Oh, yes. Reuben Reynolds. Why, I know him well. Saw him just yesterday." But, of course, he said no such thing. Ben had to accept the fact that Reuben wouldn't be here in town. He'd be with the 106th and the rest of the Union troops, where the fighting was.

Ben continued. "My uncle Elliott, from Hanover, is your cousin. Leastwise, that's what Danny tells me. So we thought . . . we hoped," he amended, "you might let us stay. We won't be any trouble. Got our own sleeping gear, and food, and we can work, if you've got chores that need doing."

"Elliott is your uncle?" Cousin Travis asked suspiciously.

"Look. Right here." Danny pulled a velvet case from his jacket pocket. He clicked it open to reveal two tintypes.

On the right, Aunt Mavis, looking as stern as she did in real life. On the left, Uncle Elliott, with a face like Danny's only longer and thinner and not so full of mischief. Uncle Elliott's thin lips were hidden by a walrus mustache that covered his whole mouth. By comparison, Cousin Travis had a pencil-thin mustache and a tickle of pepper gray hair on the tip of his chin.

"See," Danny continued. "There's my ma and pa. You must know them. You do, don't you?"

"Well, don't that just cap the climax! You really are El's boy. Don't stand out there on the stoop and get shot. Get in here, boys, before someone uses you for a target. We got no room. But we'll make some. I swan, I never expected little Danny Seldomridge to show up at my doorstep in the middle of a battle." Cousin Travis paused and his voice got stern. "No, Danny. Just a minute there, lad. I don't mind your cousin Ben, or even the dog, but I *won't* have a cow in this house, unless it's cooked and on my dinner plate."

"She's a real good cow. She don't take up much space," Danny argued. His voice was tinged with desperation. "I can't leave her tied up on the street. Please, Cousin Travis."

"Take her around back," Travis directed. "I got an empty shed back there."

Danny looked at Ben, who nodded. "It'll be fine," Ben assured him. "I'll come with you." Danny sighed, shrugged, and turned to lead the cow down the narrow passageway between Travis's house and the house next door. "Come back around front after you tie her up," Travis called after them. "If you use the back door and go through the kitchen, you might make Mae's bread fall."

Another volley of cannon fire boomed up from the south. Ben figured every loaf of bread in town must have fallen hours ago. But he wasn't going to argue.

"Mavis'll be fine out here," Ben told Danny, trying to sound reassuring. He hated to admit it, but he understood how Danny was feeling. It felt wrong to leave the old, brown cow out in the shed. It only felt right when all four of them were together.

"I don't know why we can't take her inside," Danny grumbled. "She came inside my house and she didn't hurt anything."

"And if your ma'd been home?" Ben grinned at the thought as they settled Mavis in one cobwebby stall of what was really a small plank-and-fieldstone barn behind the house. "If Aunt Mavis had seen this cow in her kitchen, the cow wouldn'ta been the only critter chopped up for meat pie. She'd have chopped us up, too."

Danny grunted his reluctant agreement.

Ben actually had to grab his cousin by the hand and yank him away from Mavis. Captain sniffed all around the stall before following them, lifting a leg in one corner. Now it was marked as theirs.

Ben and Danny hurried back to the front of the house

and entered the parlor right behind Captain. It was dark and shadowy inside after the bright sunshine on the street. The air was stifling and smelled like fresh baked bread. But underneath, it smelled peculiar, like a sickroom. Sounds of battle drifted through the closed and shuttered windows. Ben heard a splintering thud outside, as if a stray minié ball had just buried itself in a nearby brick.

The sick smell tickled Ben's nose, making him sneeze. Captain sneezed, too, snorting and shaking his head. It was a rotten-sweet odor that made you want to choke. But that would be most impolite.

"There are five wounded Rebs here," Travis explained, as if he knew exactly what Ben was thinking. "Two in the parlor on the couches. One in the dining room on a cot, and two upstairs in Freddie's bedroom."

"Why've you got Rebs?" Danny asked with surprise. "I thought you were Yankee people, like us."

"We're Christian people," Travis replied. "And these are wounded men. We have to do what we can to help them."

A boy of about six or seven appeared in the arched doorway as if he'd been summoned. "Freddie's sleeping in with us, and the girls are still in their own bedroom," Travis explained as he guided Ben into the parlor. "If they send more wounded, Bessie and Judith will have to move in with us, too. Mighty crowded, that's what it is. Acourse, the Reb officers are using the church next door as a hospital, so we're right handy to that. Men lying on every pew over there. On the floor, too. Even on the altar. They got one doc, sometimes two, and this is close for them to get over. Some of these Gray boys seem near as young as you two." He looked at Ben and Danny but didn't really seem to see them.

"You'll have to sleep on the kitchen floor tonight. We got a rug in the attic we can put down under your bedrolls. But, for now, I'm gonna take you up on that offer to help out. Danny can tote bread next door. My wife, Mae, and my girls have been baking for hours. Too many hungry mouths in this town.

"And, Ben, you can tote water for me. Pump's in the kitchen. All these men need water. Think you can handle that?"

"Yes, sir." Ben nodded, wondering how they could all be so busy with ordinary chores like baking and carrying water when a battle was going on south of town, what seemed like right on their doorstep. It puzzled him so much, in fact, that he asked Cousin Travis about it. "But what about the fighting? What are we going to do about that?"

This time, the older man looked at Ben with an expression of weary sadness. "Nothing we can do, boy. It's like a fire. Gotta burn itself out. Now, get to drawing that water. Some of these Gray boys will be gone by tonight, but we'll take proper care of 'em while they're with us."

"Gone? Are the Rebs moving out?"

"Right now, around here, the only thing gone means is dead. That's what I mean, boy. Some of these Graycoats—the ones with the fevers mostly—will likely be dead by tonight. So don't keep 'em waiting."

Ben felt as hot as if he were the one with a fever. He knew people died in a war. Look at Pa. Didn't even need bullets to kill 'em. Cold or heat or marching or measles . . . they could all do it. But he never bargained on being the last one to see soldiers before they left this life. That should be a preacher, or their mothers, or anybody besides Ben Herr Reynolds.

Ben took the tin bucket and wooden scoop Travis handed him. It was funny, the way the smell of baking bread mingled with the sour stink of sickness to make it hard to decide if it smelled good or bad. He pumped the water, gratefully taking the slice of bread and apple butter Travis's plump wife offered him. Danny was sitting on a bench at the long trestle table, telling two girls, both with short, round bodies and full-cheeked, round faces, about his adventures with Mavis and the Confederates. The brown-haired girls both had their long hair caught back behind their necks in black, netlike snoods. They had to be Travis's daughters, Bess and Judith. They were giggling as they listened.

"I rode her all the way across the Susquehanna," Danny bragged. "And she was as fast and brave as any horse. She's the best cow anybody ever had. We were in the woods when . . ."

Ben stopped listening. The *pop-pop* of distant shooting seemed so far away from these stuffy-smelling sickrooms. He wondered where Reuben was, right this minute. Was he near the shooting? In the middle of it? He couldn't be too close, or Captain would be whining at the door. Instead, the dog was wandering from room to room as well, checking everything out. Ben carried a wooden bucket of water from room to room, giving each Reb as many dipperfuls as he wanted. They were all quiet men. Only an occasional moan. But each one thanked him. Some couldn't sit up, and Ben had to prop up their heads and steady the dipper in their shaking hands. He spilled a whole scooperful down one man's neck, but the soldier didn't seem to notice. When Ben tried to apologize, the man said it felt good on his skin. Ben picked the soldier's gray blanket from the floor where the man had kicked it off, and placed it carefully back over him. The sweating, shivering soldier thanked him for that, too.

Trudging upstairs with the slopping, half-full bucket, Ben wondered, for about the hundredth time since he'd started on this journey, why these men were his enemy. They didn't act like an enemy. He didn't hate them the way you were supposed to hate an enemy. Some he pitied. Some he admired. Some he downright *liked*, like Jim and Curtis, back what seemed like a million years ago on the river.

Ben turned down the hall and opened the first door at

the top of the stairs. Obviously Travis and Mae's room. A wide, spool bed stood in the middle of the room. A chiffarobe and a round, pedestal table holding a white pitcher and bowl stood on either side of it. A highboy dresser had been shoved aside to make room for a mound of pillows, wrapped in a quilt. That had to be where little Freddie slept.

There was a small, high window in the dormer, open to the hot July day. Through it, Ben could hear sounds of the distant battle, and he winced at the thought that Reuben might be out there. The boom of cannons made the window glass rattle and the whitewashed walls creak.

The room across the way had a big, four-poster bed with a lacy coverlet. Obviously where Bessie and Judith slept. They were lucky. They didn't have a brother out in the thick of this. They could probably sleep without tossing and turning, worrying what to do.

Ben sighed wearily and opened the door at the end of the hall. The sickroom stench came at him much stronger than it had been downstairs. It was almost as if he had caught a skunk in a corner, and it had just let loose at him.

There was another smell here, too, but Ben couldn't quite place it. It was raw and angry, and it frightened him. Two bodies lay on the double bed in the middle of the darkened room. All the room's shutters were pulled tight, but Ben could make out one man lying flat and the other propped up against pillows. They both looked old. Ben suddenly wondered if it was just a matter of bed space that kept these two soldiers from being downstairs with the others.

The hot air in the small room under the eaves clung to Ben like a heavy blanket. He waited a moment for his eyes to adjust to the gloom, brightened only by golden threads of sunlight sneaking in through the tilted louvers of the shutters. A double sleigh bed with a high, carved walnut headboard and a curving footboard sat with its head against one wall, looking like a horse-drawn sleigh gone aground.

"Who's there?" a weak voice called. It was the lump on the right under the yellow-and-green plaid coverlet. The voice sounded oddly familiar.

"It's just me," Ben said, feeling stupid. These men didn't know who "me" was. "It's just the boy with the water."

"Water?" the voice croaked. "Quick, bring it here."

Ben came forward, set the bucket on the wide, unvarnished plank floor, and scooped out a dipperful. He offered it, tentatively, to the man who had called for it. He still couldn't quite make out the face. But the figure in the bed made no attempt to reach for the long-handled dipper, so Ben had to move closer.

Ben bent over and lifted the blond head gently, bringing the scoop of water right up to the man's lips. He could see a pair of feverish eyes, staring up at him. He looked down and smiled, trying to be friendly, trying to bring the face into focus, despite the shadowy surroundings.

"It's you." The voice was matter-of-fact, but faint. "You got here after all."

It was all Ben could do to keep from flinging the scoop in the air, drenching the bed. It was so hot in this suffocating room. Ben's head swam. He blinked away the sweat stinging his eyes.

"Yeah. It's me all right. Here. Drink this." Ben was vaguely surprised that his voice sounded so gruff. He tilted the scoop until a trickle of water ran into the soldier's open mouth. This couldn't be real. Ben felt as if the real him, the boy who'd left Lancaster only five days earlier, was standing back, watching a stranger moving mechanically, doing what had to be done. His throat knotted up with pity.

"Hey, Curtis," Ben whispered when he could find his voice. "How's Jim?" It was a dumb thing to ask. But Curtis didn't seem to notice.

"Jim's fine," Curtis rasped. The Reb boy's lips moved into what could have been a smile if his face hadn't looked so wretched. He gestured with a finger toward the still figure beside him. "This ain't him, if that's what you're thinkin'. Not old Jim. He didn't step hisself in front of a cannonball, like me."

Ben nodded, unsure what to say next.

"I still got your clicker." Curtis opened his right hand, which had been clenched on top of the coverlet. "See."

"Hey, you really do. You got it, all right."

"Do you still have that yellow dog a'yourn?"

For the first time since he began this journey, Ben did not protest having Captain called his. "You want me to bring Captain up here?" It was the only thing Ben could think to say.

Curtis shook his head, barely moving it on the pillow. But the movement still made him wince. "You better give Nate here some water. He ain't said nothing for quite a spell. I think he's in a bad way."

Ben looked over at the other man in the bed. The one lying out flat. He wasn't an old man at all. He was probably no more than eighteen or nineteen, but the pinched, white expression on his face made him look about a hundred. His eyes were open and unblinking, and the tiniest string of bloody drool hung from the corner of his lip.

Ben carried the bucket around the bed and spoke to the lump Curtis had called Nate.

"Hey, Nate. Try some of this cool water. It'll make you feel better. Cool you off a piece. And I'll go get you both some food, too."

There was no response. No movement of any kind.

"Shake him, Ben. Might be he's sleeping real sound. He was up most of the night with the pain."

Ben reached down gingerly and shook one thin shoulder. No response. Gently, he took both shoulders and shook a little harder, calling urgently, "Nate! Hey, Nate! Wake up."

Ben let go of the boy and stood up, shaking his head worriedly. "He won't wake up, Curtis. I even pinched his arm a little. I never saw anybody sleep like that before. Something's wrong. Mighty wrong."

"Naw," Curtis drawled the word with that musical Southern slowness that made time seem unimportant. "Ain't nothing wrong, Ben. Nate just died, is all. I thought it might happen soon, the way he carried on last night. Nate was eighteen. But he died. Ain't that funny?" Curtis sounded as if he'd seen and done everything the world had to offer and was about worn out from it all.

Cousin Travis was tromping noisily down the hall, coming to see what was keeping Ben. "Other chores to do, boy," he called out before he even got to the room. He stood in the open doorway, sniffing audibly. "Which one died?" he asked matter-of-factly, as if he'd smelled death in his house before.

"This one," Ben pointed to the body on the left as Travis stood looking at the bed. Ben gave the name. "Nate died."

Cousin Travis didn't bow his head or pause for even a second. He bustled over and put a hand over the dead soldier's staring eyes, closing his eyelids. "Yeah, well, let's get the lad moved out. We'll take him next door to the church. How's the other one doing?"

Captain nosed through the door that Travis had left ajar. He trotted over to Curtis and laid his muzzle on the bed, not touching the wounded boy, just looking at him.

The dog watched Curtis intently. Captain's nose twitched, as if he could read everything that had happened to Curtis by the smells lingering on the Reb's body.

"How's that one doing?" Travis repeated.

It bothered Ben that Danny's older cousin didn't use the Rebs' names. They weren't just enemy soldiers. They were people. One of them was a person he knew.

"He's not doing too good. His name is Curtis, and Danny and me know him. Him and his brother Jim. They pulled us out of the Susquehanna when we were near to drowning. Curtis is feeling real poorly. Can't we get him that doctor you were talking about? Or some kind of medicine for the pain?"

"The doctor's already seen him today." Travis spoke in short, pointed sentences, as if he really didn't want to talk about this. "There's no medicine to spare. It smells like the start of gangrene. Can't you smell it? They both got hit early in yesterday's fighting. Hit where they couldn't amputate. Shell fragments too deep to dig out. The first signs were here by noon today. The one you called Nate went fast. He was lucky."

Travis was saying these things right in front of Curtis! As if the young Reb wasn't even here. Ben glanced at Curtis. His eyes were closed, his breathing shallow but regular. He looked to be sleeping, despite the noise of their talking and the smell of the dead man lying next to him. "What about the soldiers downstairs?" Ben asked.

Travis understood Ben's unspoken question.

"Amputated arms and legs. One of them, the bullet went through the side of his stomach and came back out."

"What about Curtis?"

"Fragments still in him. Not certain yet, but there's no medicine to cure it if he's got the gangrene. Already, he can't seem to eat. Drinks all the time. Doctor says it doesn't look good."

"But he's only fifteen and a half," Ben protested. "And he's got a brother."

"Sshh. Keep your voice down, son. The Reb's sleeping. All we can do is let him sleep."

"But I *know* him." Ben spoke more softly this time, his voice catching on something rough in his throat. He stared down at the neat coverlet. It hid so much pain and hurt. "I know him," Ben whispered.

Curtis's hand lay limp and open, the small tin frog clicker still in his palm. Captain lay down on the floor beside the bed. "We can't just let him die."

"Wouldn't matter if he was old Abe Lincoln himself." Travis spoke more gently and put a comforting hand on Ben's shoulder. "If he's gonna die, we can't stop him."

Suddenly, Ben knew he had to find Reuben, and right away. Battle or no battle. Reuben would know what to do.

CHAPTER 14

July 3

The shooting and the sounds of battle went on till after dark. Ben helped Travis carry Nate's body out. Some of the injured men in the church next door screamed and others moaned and called for water or morphine or death. Ben was relieved he didn't have to go in. They left the corpse, wrapped in a stained muslin sheet, on the front steps of the big stone church building.

But the sound of the voices stayed with him, playing through his head again and again as he and Danny bedded down on a rug on the kitchen floor. It was after midnight, and he still couldn't go to sleep. He couldn't even go outside to look for Reuben, to knock on doors and tent flaps and ask around. Travis said a civilian wandering around between enemy lines tonight would likely find himself shot for his trouble.

Ben's head ached from trying to put it all in order. What did Nate die for? And had he minded dying for it, whatever it was? Ben silently ticked off reasons on his fingers. To free the slaves. To preserve the Union. To protect the

North. The reasons sounded noble, but they didn't feel real. None of 'em seemed worth dying over.

Danny was already asleep, making those little whistling snores Ben was finally getting used to. Captain was stretched out between them. Ben curled his fingers, scrunching them into his palm harder and harder, until his knuckles stretched white in the faint moonlight coming through the kitchen window. Curtis had been young and alive and grinning at him just four days ago, and now he looked old with all the life draining out of him; alone in a bed in a stranger's house. A bed another soldier had just died in. Ben wondered if Curtis cared one way or the other about things like the Confederacy and the Union. Maybe he was like the Bluecoat deserters they'd met in the woods. Maybe he cared more about staying alive than anything else.

Ben shut his eyes. At this rate, he'd be awake all night, wound up too tight to sleep. But when he opened his eyes again, it was daylight and the kitchen smelled of buttermilk biscuits and sugar-cured ham. It made him feel almost cheerful as he got up, rolled up his bedroll, and nudged Danny with his finger. There was even the sound of a robin chirping in the sassafras tree in the small backyard. Except for not being in his own bed, over the store back home, Ben could have sworn things were back to normal.

"We got three more wounded coming."

Travis came through the swinging door from the dining

room. "We'll put them in the kitchen here, on the rug. Danny, you and Ben will have to shift down to Claude Adams's house, on the south end of town. He's got a few sheep in his barn, so that'll be a better place for that cow of yourn, anyroad. You can't keep it here and feed it the cornmeal we need ourselves. It's a cow, Danny. Just a cow. Not a person."

"Sorry." Danny hung his head, but Ben could see his cousin's freckled face under the shock of red hair that covered his eyes. Danny might be sorry about being caught, but he wasn't sorry about stealing the cornmeal.

"Is the battle over, now?" Danny changed the subject as he folded up his quilt. "Are they done fighting?"

"Hard to say." Travis was smoking a white clay pipe, and the fragrance of tobacco helped cover the smells of blood and mustard plasters. "They've been at it for two days now. Not many battles last longer than two days. But I can't rightly make out who won. Not from the talk up in the square leastwise. They fought all over yesterday—the hill, the orchard, the railroad cut, up by the cemetery. But I can't tell who won what. Trouble is, the Confederates still hold the town. General Meade can't exactly pull back and leave the Rebs in charge of a Pennsylvania town, now can he?"

Travis tapped his pipe against the palm of his hand. "Both armies are still in place this morning. No one's moving yet. So I don't know, Danny. Mebbe they won't fight today. But I don't think they're done. Not by a mile."

"Have you heard who's out there doing the fighting?" Ben asked hopefully. "Is the 106th Pennsylvania out there?" Even though he figured it *was* here, faced with the reality of knowing for sure, he didn't know what he'd do. Would he rush out between the two squatting armies and pull Reuben clean away?

"I don't rightly know." Travis folded his pipe into a square of soft leather that buttoned where the corners came together. He stuck the packet into his front vest pocket. "With the town held by Rebs, there's not much news of our side's doings. Not news a body can trust, any-road. We just keep hearing the cannons and the rifle fire. Might not know who's doing the shooting, Ben, till the shooting's done."

The women, their faces dripping with perspiration from working at the blazing cookstove, were too busy serving out food on plates to bother about talk of shooting and war. "You boys take these plates around to the soldiers," bossed Travis's oldest daughter, Judith, who couldn't have been much more than twelve herself. "Bess pumped the water, and you can carry that around, too."

Ben volunteered to take breakfast to Curtis, upstairs, and wasn't surprised to find Captain already in the room with the wounded Reb, lying beside the bed. The dog whined softly and stood up when Ben entered. His tail thumped against the bed frame and he shifted from paw to paw without ever leaving his spot beside Curtis.

"Hey Curtis! You ready for ham and biscuits? Fresh cherry preserves, too," Ben offered, trying to sound cheerful.

Curtis's eyes fluttered open. Just since yesterday, they seemed to have sunk into his head. The stench was almost unbearable in the warm, closed-up room. With no gunfire outside, Ben moved to open a window. He felt like he had to do something, anything, to help. "Let's get some fresh air in here," Ben said. "It'll make you feel better."

"No," Curtis said weakly. "Better leave the windows shut. I'm cold."

"Uh . . . do you want another blanket then?" How could anyone feel cold in this hot, stuffy room?

Instead of answering, Curtis clicked the tin frog and Captain leapt nimbly onto the high bed, careful not to land on the injured boy. The dog settled down beside the Southern boy's blanket-swathed body, licking a concerned tongue over Curtis's ear and cheek. Curtis actually laughed a little, but the laugh turned into a cough so violent, Ben could see the bloody spittle flying out of his friend's mouth. Without a word, Ben scooped a dipperful of water out of the bucket he was carrying and held it to Curtis's lips. The young soldier swallowed gratefully.

"This old yellow dog keeps me warm when I get to shaking," Curtis rasped. "He visited me three or four times last night." Ben hadn't felt Captain get up even once. Maybe he'd slept sounder than he thought.

"I wish my Ripley was more like him. More a dog like yourn."

He thought about protesting that Cap wasn't his dog. But it was beginning to feel like a lie.

"Listen." Curtis's voice was low now. "I want you to know, Yank, you can have this here clicker back after I . . ." He paused. "After I don't need it no more. Jim won't want it when he comes to get me after the fighting's over. 'Sides, I figure you weren't so keen to trade it to me back by the river. I could tell." When Ben started to protest, Curtis cut him off. "Wisht we could all go back to that day. Not far back. Just a little ways. Now that was a good day."

Curtis sounded as though he wasn't much counting on having any good days left. Ben didn't know what to say. His lips and his cheeks felt stiff and wet, and he realized, with a start, that he was crying. That was just what Curtis needed. Some kid without a scratch on him standing here, blubbering like a baby.

Captain put his muzzle on Curtis's shoulder and seemed to study the Reb's gaunt face. He turned to look at Ben and thumped his tail against the coverlet. Ben didn't know what the dog was trying to tell him, but, somehow, he felt a little better. He sniffed as quietly as he could manage and rubbed the back of his hand across his runny nose.

Curtis's eyelids had fallen shut again. He was no more interested in eating breakfast than he was in flinging the windows open to the outside. Curiosity had been working on Ben since yesterday, and he gently lifted an edge of the blanket to see the wound. The rotting stink came at him like a fist. Ben hadn't much noticed it before, but there was a faint whistling sound coming out of the hole in Curtis's belly each time it rose and fell, the wound wrapped in a jumble of so many cloth bandages that it made skinny Curtis look almost fat. There were dark stains on the white of the bandages, in a spotty pattern, dots and lines spidering down the sides. Stains on the bedsheet, too. It could be blood. It could be coal oil. It could be brown molasses. To Ben's eyes, it was just dark spots. Curtis groaned and twisted and a new spot appeared, popping up against the white, and Ben understood that his friend was still bleeding. That the bandages underneath the top bandage weren't just spotted, but soaked through with blood.

Ben set the white plate with its border of tiny, pink roses on the wide plank floor, but Captain didn't make any move toward the food. The dog lay with his head on Curtis's shoulder.

He looked steadily at Ben. "Food's there when you're ready for it," Ben offered. Captain thumped his tail softly on the coverlet.

Ben ducked out of the room before that blubbery feeling could catch him again.

By noon, the chores were done and the new wounded had arrived. Only when Travis's wife did a round of dressing changes, first on the new soldiers, then on the old, did Captain get up again. Mae came in to work on Curtis last, and Captain headed off downstairs. The dog sat on Ben's feet as he rolled out dough for molasses cookies. Judith and Bess sat with him at the big kitchen table, doing the same thing. It seemed silly to make cookies in the middle of a war, surrounded by wounded men. But Mae said that was exactly what a wounded man needed when home seemed a million miles away.

Danny had already gone to get Mavis out of the shed behind the house and take her down to the Adams place, on the southernmost edge of town. Mr. Adams had a real barn and some barley feed. Danny milked the cow and gave what he got to Travis for the wounded before he set off trudging down the hard-packed dirt street, leading the cow by her halter. At least he didn't try riding her this time.

"Better get on your way, too, Ben," Travis said gruffly. "I don't like the way it feels out there. Too quiet. Like they's waiting for some kind of signal to start again. And you don't want to be outside when that signal comes."

Ben nodded, stood up, and whistled softly for Captain to follow. "You know, I thought that dog a'yourn might decide to stay with that young fella upstairs. Seemed right attached to the Reb boy. But I can see he knows who he belongs to. Guess he just automatically follows wherever you go."

"I guess," Ben agreed, not meeting Travis's eyes.

◆ ◆ ◆

Ben trotted down the street with Captain at his heels. It was only five blocks to the Adams house, a big, three-story stone house with a bank barn beside it. Ben heard Danny's voice as soon as he arrived. His cousin was arguing with Mr. Adams in the open barn doorway.

"I gotta stay in the barn. Mavis doesn't sleep good without me. She doesn't like all the shooting. You'll see. I'll be fine out here in the barn."

"You'll be fine in the house, young man, and we'll have no more argument. Cows in the barn. People in the house. I promised Travis I'd watch out for you two boys, and that's just what I mean to do. Your Jersey and my Dorsets will keep each other company. They're in the bottom half of the barn, behind the stone foundation. They'll be safe enough. But I want you in the house, both of you. I've got a bad feeling about today."

Ben looked up at the bright, blue sky, strung across with puffy, white clouds. It didn't look like a fighting day. It looked more like a sittin'-tight day, Ben thought. After all, it had been pretty quiet so far. Just a bit of firing, far in the distance.

"The gout's troubling my toe something fierce," Mr. Adams continued as he limped toward the house. "Could mean rain. Could mean another battle. Gout came on hard yesterday, but it didn't rain. I just don't know what it means anymore."

Claude Adams pulled a gold pocket watch out of his plain, black wool vest, snapped it open and clucked his tongue. "Near unto one o'clock. Lots of chores still need doing, and Travis said you two could handle them." Mr. Adams called to Ben, "You, young fella, put your dog in the barn and get on inside."

Ben shook his head. He fingered the broken watch in his own pocket. "Captain's my brother's dog, Mr. Adams," he explained, trying to sound as polite as he knew how. "He's staying with me until we find Reuben. In the barn or in the house. Doesn't matter. But he's with me."

Mr. Adams looked as though he was about to argue when Danny spoke up. "I'll put Mavis in the barn, with your sheep, and Captain can come in the house with Ben."

Before Mr. Adams could open his mouth to object, Danny added, "I'll skim the butterfat off the next milking and you can have a glass or two tonight. Butterfat from Mavis is as thick and sweet as whipped cream. It'll taste mighty nice on that cherry cobbler I smell baking."

Mr. Adams licked his lips. His muttonchop sideburns fairly quivered with the smacking sounds he made. Danny had done it again, thought Ben. Gotten his way and made Ben smile to boot.

"All right. Dog in the house. Cow in the barn. People in the house. No more arguments. Understood?"

Captain advanced, tail wagging cheerfully, and stuck his nose against Mr. Adams's black wool pants, sniffing up one side and down the other. The dog seemed to agree that the matter was settled.

There were five other people in the house. Six if you counted the Confederate sniper hiding in the attic, gun resting on the sill of the third floor dormer window facing south. Nobody seemed to want to talk about him, but he had to be fed, just like the others.

The others were Mrs. Adams, the Adams's five-year-old twin girls, Betsy and Bonnie, their baby, Annabel, and old Mr. Hobbes, the neighbor on the farm to the south, beyond the town limits. Mr. Hobbes had left home when bullets started whining down the rows between his cornstalks. It wasn't really his farm. He was a hired hand who lived in an outbuilding. And he didn't fancy no Reb saber stuck through his gullet. Leastwise, that's what he said.

Mrs. Adams stood at the kitchen counter, chopping stale wheat bread into chunks for the stew simmering on the stove as she rocked a cradle with one foot. The twins sat at the kitchen table, trying, without much success, to get Mr. Hobbes to play checkers against the pair of them.

"You can be black *or* red," they begged. "You can start first."

"I can read this here three-day-old newspaper in peace," he snapped. "If you'll just go bother somebody else."

The twins giggled and nodded, before they started wheedling the old codger all over again.

Mrs. Adams set Ben and Danny to sweeping, dusting,

and mopping, which not only was woman's work, but also, as Danny whispered, a pretty stupid thing to worry about in the middle of a war. Mrs. Adams also made each of them don a white, starched, cotton apron with embroidered daisies around the hems. Bonnie and Betsy giggled more loudly at that, but their mother soon had them helping her in the kitchen. For the first time since they'd started, Ben wished, fleetingly, that he wore a blue uniform so nobody could make him do woman's work.

It seemed as if they'd been working all day when they heard the first rumble of cannon fire. It sounded close. "It's out there somewhere between the hill at the cemetery, south of town beside the Taneytown Road, and the high ground off to the west near the seminary, out by the Hagerstown Road," Mr. Adams announced. "Must be having another go at each other after all. Best we lay low for a bit. We'll go down in the cellar, like we did yesterday."

He clicked open his pocket watch, as if it was his job to mark the time each battle started. "Three o'clock. I'll give 'em thirty minutes at this rate of fire. They can't, neither side, have much canister left after the shellings Monday and Tuesday. Bring the pinochle deck, mother. I'll get the lantern from the parlor, and we'll have us a game."

"Iffen that damn fool Reb sharpshooter"—Mr. Hobbes pointed at the attic by way of the ceiling—"don't get this damn house fired on and blown to bits with his shenanigans, I'll be hornswoggled," he grumped.

"Shush now," Mrs. Adams warned. "You'll scare the children."

Ben followed the others down the narrow, rickety, wooden steps to the cool darkness of the root cellar. Children! He certainly wasn't one of the children! Aunt Mavis had called Danny and him children the day they left home. It hadn't bothered him at all that day. Something had changed.

Ceiling-high shelves on every wall of the cellar held dusty Mason jars packed with canned peaches, pears, green beans, apple butter, and more. Bushel baskets of vegetables, radishes, beets, cucumbers, and a smattering of last year's potatoes filled every corner.

Several wooden benches stood on their sides, leaning against the stair wall. Mr. Adams pulled them down and sat them on the dirt floor side by side. Ben straddled the end of one bench, listening to the waves of sound breaking over the house. It was enough to make your head swim. The booming seemed to be all around them like the rolling thunder of a lightning storm stalled just above their roof. It sounded as if this very house might be in the middle of the battlefield, with Bluecoats and Graycoats firing at each other over the roof and through the windows.

Ben shivered and pulled Captain's shaggy head close to his own, resting his cheek on the dog's muzzle. The cold nose tickled. The dog's nose felt good—and real—in this dark cave of a basement where everything seemed strange and unreal. Captain licked him across the mouth, then got up and trotted over to the bushel baskets in the corner. Ben knew the dog smelled the turnips and was fixin' to get himself a good, long chew. A sudden memory of the lump of chewed turnip on the back steps the night he left Lancaster filled Ben's head. He wondered how Ma was doing on her own. He wondered if she missed him half as much as he missed her right this minute.

The others played pinochle. The twins dug a hole in the dirt floor along one wall using a garden spade. They filled it with water and began making sticky mud pies the size of their five-year-old hands. Then they took them around like waitresses in a busy tavern.

"Thanks," Ben said absently as one of the girls handed him a mud pie. He was lost in the thunder of the barrage. Over and over it rumbled, shaking the heavy timbers above their heads. It was so loud, he couldn't hear the thoughts in his own head. He could only listen to the cannon fire booming inside his chest.

"Aren't you gonna eat it," one of the twins demanded, bringing her lips close to yell in his ear. She stamped her small, bare foot. "It's yummy good."

Ben nodded without thinking and raised the mud pie to his lips. His head tingled with the constant explosions. *BOOM-BOOM-BOOM.*

The fighting was much closer to town than it had been yesterday. It felt like it was right on top of them.

"Eat it," the girl yelled, and Ben put one edge of the sticky pie up to his lips. He bit down.

"Blaah!" Ben spit the muddy morsel out violently and let the pie fall from his hands onto the dirt floor from whence it came. Bonnie twittered with delight. She clapped her hands and ran to Betsy, yelling, "He ate it, he ate it!"

The girls had delivered a dozen more mud pies, all of which Ben had managed to refrain from nibbling on, while the yellow dog turned several unwashed turnips to pulp. Ben had no idea how long they'd been down here. Hours? Minutes? It felt like days. Captain still had a chunk of turnip hanging in a slobbery, white bite from his black lips when he stood up suddenly and barked.

"Keep that dog quiet," warned Mrs. Adams, ignoring the constant roar of the bombardment. "He'll wake the baby."

Ben didn't reply. Something new was happening outside, Ben was sure of it. He stood up, as did Mr. Adams. He couldn't put his finger on what was different, but something had changed.

"Thank God," Mrs. Adams said softly. "They've finally stopped."

That was it exactly. The sudden quiet, after all that noise, sounded like a noise itself. A great clap of quiet.

Mr. Adams clicked open his watch and tilted it toward the lantern's glow. "Five o'clock. Two hours of bombardment. I wouldn't have believed it possible."

Ben pulled out his own watch and clicked it open. Five o'clock. He held it close to his ear, trying to hear if it had somehow started ticking again. But he couldn't hear a thing.

"But the shelling hasn't stopped," Danny protested, rubbing his ears. "I still hear it."

Ben, too, heard a ringing. A reverberation of volley after volley after endless volley still pounded between his ears, even if it no longer sounded outside them. But the ceiling above had stopped rattling.

"Do you think they're all dead out there?" Danny asked.

Ben hated his cousin for asking right out loud exactly what he'd been worrying about.

"No," Mr. Adams replied. "Deaf mebbe, but not dead."

Ben followed Captain cautiously up the stairs, ignoring Mr. Adams when he said Ben should wait below with the women and children. The acrid smell of spent gunpowder stung his nose and eyes when he opened the kitchen door.

How could it be so quiet? There was no bird sound. No crickets. No breeze. But Reuben must be out there. Amid the angry cannons—and now the silence! His brother had to be alive. He had to. Ben had come too far to allow himself to think anything else.

He caught his breath, wanting to fling open the back door and run toward the battlefield. Instead, he ran to the kitchen stairs and took them two at a time until he reached the attic. He pushed the door open quietly, wondering if the Reb sharpshooter would hear and turn and cut him down on the spot. He didn't care. He had to know what was happening.

The attic was shadowy, but Ben could clearly see the stool pulled up to the open dormer window, and the bearded soldier sitting on it, gun propped on the sill. The Graycoat turned, but didn't fire. He looked to be near as old as Mr. Hobbes, with a straggly gray mustache and a three-day growth of grizzled beard.

He saluted Ben in a friendly way, waving him over to the window like he had something he wanted to show him. The man's face was a mask of amazement.

"Lookee there, boy."

He pointed, and Ben's eyes followed his finger. There was a huge, roiling cloud of gray smoke, laying like a thick fog across the wheatfields, making it impossible to spot Blue or Gray or anything at all. High above the pall of battle smoke, the sky was still blue. But the land between the armies was a black swamp of smoke and death.

Ben squinted, straining his eyes to see the battlefield. The glint of a trumpet. The flutter of a flag.

Was that a flash of dark blue down there—the colors of the 106th? Or was it his imagination? Ben rubbed a hand across his eyes.

"Ain't never seen any barrage the like of it before," the Reb said proudly. "Bet them damn Yanks are turning tail and running."

Ben, however, could hear the pops of scattered gunfire in the silence. "Then who's doing that shooting?" Ben asked the Reb, genuinely puzzled.

But before the Graycoat sniper could answer, Captain growled, one sharp sound as a minié ball whined through the open window and into the sharpshooter's neck, piercing his throat so it fountained blood on the floor and the window and the dog and Ben.

Ben had been standing so close beside the Reb, he could smell the man's cornbread breath. Both of them had been too busy gaping at the distant battlefield to worry about a bullet. But now the Reb's body sprawled against Ben and then slid silently to the floor.

Ben knew the answer to his unanswered question. The Rebs and the Yanks were both still down there. Both still shooting. Shooting at this window.

CHAPTER 15

He Has Loosed the Fateful Lightning

Danny pounded up the stairs and burst through the attic door, singing.

"Glory, glory, hallelujah,

Beat them Graycoats, yippee, who-ha,

Drive 'em back down south, and they better shut their mouth,

No how Rebs are marching on."

Danny liked to make up his own words. He actually stumbled over the Graycoat's sprawled body before he noticed it.

"Wh-what . . . ?" Danny stuttered, but before Ben could tell him to get down, another bullet whizzed past his ear, just missing Danny behind him, and burying itself in a roof beam on the other side of the attic.

"Get down! Quick!" Ben ducked below the windowsill as he spoke, pulling Danny with him.

"Why are they shooting at us?" Danny whined. "What did *we* do?"

"It's our own soldiers shooting at this window. They

think there's a Reb sniper up here," Ben whispered. He doubted anyone outside was close enough to hear him, but he didn't want to take any chances.

"But they got him—they got the Reb." Danny gestured at the body on the floor. "Why're they still shooting at *us*?"

"We could be Rebs, too, for all they know," Ben hissed. "They just know somebody's been shooting at 'em from up here."

"What're we gonna do?" Danny asked, bending even lower beside Ben on the dusty attic floorboards.

"We're gonna get back downstairs," Ben instructed, crawling toward the attic door. "Right now."

"But I didn't get to look outside," Danny complained, bumping into Ben's feet with his hands. "What's out there, Ben? Did you see? Are there Reb bodies everywhere? Did you see the 106th and Reuben with his gun?"

"I saw smoke. That's it. Lots of cannon smoke. Maybe a mile long and as high as a house. It's like a big ole dirty cloud laying right on the field. You can't see anything else for the smoke."

"But . . ." Danny began to protest.

"Downstairs. Now." Ben pushed his shoulder against the door, lunging out onto the top step. He turned and pulled Danny through, slamming the door behind them.

They were back in the cellar before the hour was up—all of them.

Mr. Adams and Mr. Hobbes went up to examine the body in the attic and drag it down, rolled in a braided rug. They left it outside the front door. "It's nigh onto ninety degrees," Mr. Adams said reasonably when his wife urged him to leave the dead Confederate where he was. "If he stays in this house for long, the smell will drive us all out."

Thanks to Ben and Danny, the two older men knew to stay clear of the window. Even so, Mr. Adams scolded Ben for going up to the attic without his say-so. "You young 'uns never think to keep your heads down," he said.

Before the retreat to the cellar, Captain yawned, stretched, and lay down right in the middle of the kitchen floor on the polished oak floorboards. Everybody was forced to step over him, but nobody said a word.

The people in this house walked around sort of hunched over, Ben noticed, with their arms drawn up close to their sides, as if they were all trying to make themselves smaller. Smaller targets. There was only time for a bit of bread and jam and a quick cup of chamomile tea before it began again. The sound of rifle fire, of scattered cannon bursts, and a sort of roar, like thousands of screaming, shouting voices, assaulted their ears and drove them back into the cellar. It sounded like the famous Rebel yell—but bigger. The whole Reb army surely couldn't make that much noise. Captain whined at the sound of it, and Ben covered his ears. Danny ran out to the outhouse and back so fast, Ben wondered if he'd even had time to pull his pants down.

Mrs. Adams brought a loaf pan full of fresh-baked bread down to the root cellar. It smelled nice and yeasty, but the pieces looked squished and misshapen. The loaf, just out of the oven before the cannon barrage began, deflated in its pan on the table. When the white dish towel was pulled back, the airy, rounded loaf-top was flatter than a dinner plate. The squat, compressed loaf didn't even peek over the edge of the pan. Like the people, it seemed to be trying to make itself smaller.

It was torture to wait in that dark cellar for it all to end. It seemed to go on and on, until Ben wondered how anything could still be standing out there.

He pulled out the broken pocket watch and studied it in the light of the oil lamp Mr. Adams kept on the bench beside him. Ben hadn't thought about home much since the night he'd left. Now, he couldn't seem to think of much else. He missed Pa. He missed Ma. He missed Reuben most of all, and he didn't know anymore if he hoped Reuben was right here in Gettysburg or a million miles away.

Ben turned the watch over slowly in his hands. He had an idea.

Mrs. Adams had her sewing basket on the floor beside her feet. She was leaning over a square of needlework, holding it close to the lantern as she plied the cloth with deft stitches.

Ben moved closer, standing in front of her, the watch hidden in his clenched fist.

"Uh, excuse me, ma'am," Ben began. Mrs. Adams looked up, but her fingers didn't slow. "I was wondering if you might have a straight pin I could borrow?"

Mrs. Adams clucked her tongue. "Now, don't be so shy, Benjamin. Show me what needs mending, and I'll have it done quicker than butter melts in July."

Ben shifted to his other foot. He wondered if she'd drop a stitch soon. It looked like she could ply her stitches blindfolded.

"Ah, no, ma'am. It's not for sewing. I need to scratch a name on this watch." He opened his sweaty palm and the gold case shone in the lamplight. "So I can put it on Captain's collar." Ben pointed at the yellow dog, who sat hunched over in the far corner with his back to the rest of the cellar, his tail thumping every now and then on the dirt floor.

He couldn't see the dog's jaws. But Ben knew they were slobbery with the pulp of another well-chewed turnip.

"I need to make sure folks will know who he belongs to if he wanders off, like he does. It's so loud out there . . ." Ben let the sentence trail off. He swallowed hard and began again. "I don't want Captain getting himself lost in all the confusion."

"And you'd use a fine gold watch for that?" Mrs. Adams

asked, her voice loud with disbelief. Mr. Adams and Mr. Hobbes stopped playing pinochle on the opposite bench and looked over at her. Ben could feel the heat rising in his cheeks.

"Oh, never mind." He mumbled, and turned to go, adding, "It's broke, anyroad."

Mrs. Adams caught his elbow and pulled him back.

"Now don't go gettin' riled. I swan, boy, you're as bad as a grown man. Why didn't you say it was broke when you asked for the pin?" She was fishing in her basket with both hands, having finally laid aside her cross-stitch hoop. The words on the cloth read, GOD BLESS THIS . . .

Ben wondered fleetingly if the next word would be "Cellar."

"Here now. Will this do?" Mrs. Adams held up a packet of pins and extracted one. "Hold your hand flat, or I'll prick you with it."

"Thank you kindly." Ben took the pin in his hand, carefully pinching it between two fingers. He moved to the other side of the lantern and sat down on the bench with Mrs. Adams.

He needed good light for this.

Ben scratched the dog's name at the top of the gold case. C-A-P-T-A-I-N.

He went over the letters again and again. The gold was soft and easy to scratch. And there was plenty of room left.

Ben bent closer to the lantern and scratched tiny words

underneath Captain's name. "Belongs to R. Reynolds, Lanc., PA." He looked at his handiwork. There was still room at the bottom of the case. But what else was there to say?

The dog's pink nose smeared the gold finish as Captain came sniffing around to see what Ben was up to.

"Get away," Ben said softly, putting the watch on the bench and cupping the fuzzy snout with one hand. He studied the dog's eyes. Dang if they didn't look to be studying Ben right back.

Suddenly he knew what else to put on the watchcase.

He picked it up and scratched intently, making the letters as small as he could. Cap sat at his feet, watching him. When he was done, he slipped the strap of the watch fob under Captain's brown leather collar, buttoning the ends together securely. The watch thumped against the dog's broad chest. Captain tried to tilt his head enough to sniff at it, but it was impossible.

"What did you put on it?" Danny came up beside Ben and straddled the tip end of the bench, making it rock. Mrs. Adams gave a shrill little "oh my," but she didn't drop a stitch.

"See for yourself," Ben offered, moving over enough so Danny could see the watchcase clearly. Danny read the words aloud, making each word sound solemn and important:

"*CAPTAIN*

Belongs to R. Reynolds

Lanc., PA.

OR

B. Reynolds

"That's some smart thinking, Ben." Danny straightened up and let the watch drop back against Captain's chest. "He can't get lost now, no matter if he runs off or not. Everybody'll know he's your dog."

"He's not my . . ." Ben started the familiar denial, but stopped himself in mid-sentence. Instead, he said, "Thanks, Danny. That's what I'm counting on."

Captain barked.

Someone was pounding on the front door, making them all jump. Captain bounded for the cellar steps, scrambling up them and pushing against the door at the top. Everyone else followed, not shoving exactly, but bumping into each other in their hurry.

Mr. Adams looked at his watch. "Six o'clock," he proclaimed.

"In the morning?" Danny asked, echoing Ben's own thoughts. He felt as if they'd been down in the cellar half the day and the night besides.

"Don't be daft, boy." Mr. Adams tucked away his watch as if the matter were settled, and opened the basement door.

It wasn't until Ben saw the gloomy light filtering through the dining room curtains that he realized they'd only been down below for about an hour this second time.

The sun was fixing to go down, but it was still only Wednesday. The fighting following the barrage lasted little more than an hour. There was a grayness outside, and gritty dust lightly coated the windows. The battle smoke must have grown and expanded until it covered the whole town. Maybe the whole county. Maybe the whole world.

The pounding again.

Captain barked at the front door until Mr. Adams shoved the dog aside with his foot and opened it. "Travis! What are you doing all the way down here? They're still shooting, aren't they? It isn't safe." Ben could hear scattered rifle fire, but it was far away and sporadic.

"Let me in. I'll tell you what we heard up in the square," Cousin Travis urged, glancing fearfully back over his shoulder.

When everyone was seated around the long trestle table in the kitchen, with Ben and Danny sitting on opposite ends of the benches, Travis bent forward and began.

"I've been to the square. Word is, the Rebs charged the Union line. Thousands of 'em tramped over the Codoris' farm and met our boys head-on. General Robert E. Lee was right there, they say, watching it all from Spangler's woods. And it was an eyeful. Our boys met the Rebs at the stone wall between Frey farm and Codori's fields. Broke the Gray line and made 'em duck for cover."

"Was it the 106th?" Ben asked, fresh worry washing over him like a bucket of cold water.

"Don't know, son." Travis's voice was kind. "All I know is, the Rebs came on, thousands of 'em, wave after wave, but they couldn't break our line. The Union held." Travis slapped his palm hard against the table to emphasize his words. His face was wide with pride, his mustache trembling against his lips. He took a deep breath and went on.

"There was one fella who said he seen it all. Don't know how. He wasn't *in* the battle, mind. But he said the bodies were so thick in Codori's field, you could walk right over them without ever setting foot on the ground. That's what he said, anyroad."

"You believe him?" Claude Adams sounded doubtful.

"The Rebs are talking about pulling out. Heading south. I heard two officers talking about it over to the church."

For the first time that day, Mr. Adams smiled.

"And our boys? Did we lose many of our boys?"

Travis nodded his head sadly. "Plenty. Either dead or wounded. Just like the Rebs."

Ben turned and looked out the kitchen window. It shouldn't be dark yet. But it was. The cloud of smoke from the battle hid the sun.

"Some of us will be going out with wagons after midnight if the armies allow us to pick up wounded. Theirs and ours." Travis's voice had become businesslike. "If you want to come, Claude, meet us on the Baltimore Pike, just south of town, around midnight. Are you in?"

Mr. Adams nodded. "I've got a body by my front stoop, Travis, even as we sit here. A Reb sharpshooter camped in our attic, and he took a bullet through the neck. I'll bring him along in the spring wagon and drop him wherever they're piling the Rebs."

Travis nodded. "I saw the carpet roll by the door. I figured it might be that." He got up to leave. Danny couldn't contain himself any longer. He stood up, too. "They jus' about got Ben and me, Cousin Travis," he burst out, "up there in the attic. We went up to see what was happening and almost got shot."

Travis frowned and Mr. Adams cleared his throat noisily to warn Danny away from the subject. "They weren't supposed to up there." He looked at Danny pointedly.

For once in his life, Ben noted with satisfaction, Danny seemed to take the hint. He sat back down.

"We won't get a lot done in the dark, but we can make a start. We'll have to wait till the Union boys give us the signal," Travis continued. "Can't do too much till the Rebs leave, but I've been sitting on my hands, helpless, for three full days, now." Travis's businesslike voice had disappeared and his face clouded over. "I gotta do whatever I can for our boys."

"How's Curtis?" Ben asked softly.

"Who?" Travis looked at Ben blankly.

"The Reb in your son's bedroom. The real sick one. Remember?"

"Yes. Yes, of course." Travis had the good grace to look sheepish for forgetting. "That boy's not so good, son. Not good at all, I'm sorry to say. I can't think what would happen on a long, rough wagon ride back to Virginia, iffen his brother comes to take him. Won't do him any good, that's for sure. I left Judith sitting with him. It seems to help him rest easier to have a girl rocking and doing needlework there in the room with 'im."

Curtis wasn't alone. Ben hoped Jim would find his brother soon and take him home, despite what Travis said. That was what Ben had to do. All at once it came to him, clear as day. No matter how he found him, he had to find Reuben tonight and take him home.

"I'm coming with you," Ben told Travis.

"Me, too! Me, too!" Danny squealed, jumping up and down.

"You're both of you too young," Travis began, but Ben interrupted him. The calmness in his voice surprised him, considering the way his heart was pounding. This was what he had come for. This was what he had to do.

"Danny's only eleven. Mebbe he's too young," Ben said quietly. "But I'm twelve. I came all this way to find my brother." Ben's voice cracked as he added, "I'm going."

"You'll never find your brother on that battlefield, if that's what you're thinking," Travis told him. "Be patient, Ben. Wait until morning. Claude and I will help you make inquiries then."

"Thank you, sir." Ben's voice sounded as deep and assured as Pa's. He buttoned the top button of his shirt, the way Pa always did when he wanted to look official. "But I *will* go with you tonight. I'll take Captain. If Reuben's on that battlefield, my dog . . ." Ben stopped, choking on the words. Where had that come from, that word "my"? Ben began again, shakily. "If Reuben's here, Captain will find him."

The big, yellow dog whacked his tail against the table leg at the sound of his name. His eyes were half closed, as if he were half asleep. Or in a trance. Looking for Reuben, Ben thought. That's what he's doing. Cap can feel him, too.

"All right, Ben. You can come, as long as you stick close and do as you're told."

Ben nodded.

"I'm going out to see Mavis," Danny announced sullenly, and the grown-ups seemed willing to let him. Ben didn't try to stop him either. Danny wasn't his responsibility anymore. The fool cow neither. He had one thing to worry about, one thing to do. Reuben.

The hours before it was time to go were the longest hours Ben had ever lived through. Ben sat at the Adams's dining room window, keeping his face invisible behind the drawn lace curtains, staring out at the newly falling rain. A hard summer rain that had burst from the sky as if it couldn't stand waiting anymore either. Ben stared past the raindrops sliding down the glass until his eyes began to ache. But there was nothing to see.

Mr. Adams looked at his watch so many times, Ben figured he might soon wear it out. Mrs. Adams fixed a pot of butter beans with a little salt pork, but Ben's stomach was too twisted to eat anything.

He wouldn't be dead. Not Reuben. Pa was gone, and that was enough for one family to sacrifice. It wouldn't be fair for God to ask for more. It wouldn't be right.

At 11:30, Mr. Adams hitched up the one scrawny mule no one had gotten around to eating yet. Danny refused to go back into the house. He insisted on sleeping in the barn with the battle-skittish cow. Nobody felt like fighting him about it. Nobody felt like fighting about anything tonight. There'd been enough fighting this day to last the little town a hundred years. It seemed to Ben that no one should ever say a cross word here again, or the whole place would shatter and crack like a mirror too close to the fire.

Ben thought about putting on his Union cap, but, in the end, he left it tucked in his flour sack in the parlor of the Adams's house. He didn't want some wounded Reb to see that cap and feel afraid.

They took two lanterns, one apiece, and put Captain on the seat between them. The wagon creaked down the dirt road so loudly that any Reb with a mind to call "halt" could have found them easily. But nobody did. They saw no one.

Not until the Baltimore Pike, where they met Travis and the others in buggies and wagons, and even a pony cart pulled by a skittish goat.

"Everybody here, then?" Travis shouted, standing on the seat of his flatbed wagon. There was a general grunt of assent. "You all want to watch careful-like—even on the road—that you don't run over no one. On Monday, up at Herr's Ridge, I pert near fell over a man I mistook for a lump of sod. No telling what it'll look like out there tonight. We're looking for the ones who's calling out, calling for help. Tomorrow we can go back for the other bodies." The men in the wagons sat silent, listening. No one spoke. No one asked questions. No one even coughed.

"The army'll be out, too, and we don't want them shooting us for Rebs. So tie these black scarves on your arms. Hold your lanterns high. And for God's sake, no souvenirs. We don't have time for such foolishness."

Distant lightning lit the bottom of black clouds, and thunder rolled like the echo of cannons. The rain had briefly stopped, but now its drops splattered down, slowly at first, then faster and faster. Captain turned his head from side to side on the front bench of the open, spring wagon, sitting between Mr. Adams and Ben. The dog's nose was as busy as a telegraph office, taking messages and sorting through them.

"Look smart now!" Travis shouted, pulling up the collar of his canvas jacket as he slid back down onto the seat.

The ragtag wagon train rumbled slowly south. "With this rain, some are liable to drown in a puddle if they're too weak to lift their heads." The rain pelted them, but Ben hardly felt it.

This was it, then. Captain would sniff out Reuben, wherever he was, and Ben would be able to tell his brother everything. Reuben would be out here helping the wounded, directing his men. In another couple of days, they'd all be back in Lancaster, and Ma would be so happy to see Reuben, she'd smile again. She'd fall into Reuben's strong arms, sobbing, and Reuben would know just what to do. His brother would take over at the store. Ben would go back to sucking on marzipan fruit and swinging on the rope over that wide, flat spot in the Conestoga Creek where he and Henry liked to go and have breath-holding contests. The world would wake up from this nightmare, and so would he.

But something niggled at Ben. Something he couldn't quite manage to dismiss. He pushed his dripping hair back from his forehead. What if it didn't turn out the way he wanted? What if he didn't find Reuben? What if he had to go home alone and face Ma with nothing but a red-faced apology for not bringing her what she needed? And there was something else, too. Something even worse.

What if he did find his brother—his brother's body?

Ben hunched his shoulders, lowering his head against the steady rain. It came hard and fast now, as if it was determined to wash away all traces of the day. Something whispered in Ben's ear. Or maybe it was just the warm breath of Captain, who'd turned to look at him. Nothing will ever be the same, the whisper seemed to say. Everything's changed. Grow up. Face it.

CHAPTER 16

July 4

The field smelled like a mud bog with just a hint of sulfur even the hard rain couldn't wash away. It might have been the rain or the cries of the wounded, but it sounded like the trampled ground itself was moaning. As soon as the wagon splashed to a stop, the big, yellow dog jumped off and ran, tail up, barking deep woofs into the rainy night. He seemed to know exactly where he was going.

Ben clambered down and, lantern held high, turned to the left to follow Captain's barking.

"Pennsylvania companies left and middle," a deep voice shouted in the darkness. "Ohio and New York to the right."

The field, in the circle of flickering light cast by his lantern, was all puddles and lumps. Some of the lumps were stubble, but the lump beside Ben's foot was a dead Reb, his mouth hanging open and filled with rainwater that dribbled over his lips and washed down his beardless chin. Maybe the soldier was too young to grow a beard, but he looked like a wizened old man to Ben. His eyes were

open, staring lifelessly up into the rain with water streaming down his cheeks as if he were crying. Ben swallowed
against the hard knot in his throat. He stepped over the
body and set out after Captain.

"Hey now! Hold up there, young man," Mr. Adams
called after him.

But Ben didn't stop. He stumbled and tripped over one
body and then another. He accidentally kicked against an
arm, and the arm rolled away. It had just been lying there,
shot off. He hadn't really kicked it off. But his stomach
roiled and wrenched just the same. He could taste hot
vomit on his tongue, but he swallowed hard instead of
bending to throw up. There was no place to do it, anyway,
without hitting a body. And that was unthinkable.

Ben stumbled over an outstretched leg and heard the
leg's owner groan.

"Sorry," Ben mumbled, and dodged on, determined
not to lose sight of the dog who ran ahead of him, just at
the edge of the circle of rain lit by the lantern's watery
beam. He held the lantern high over his head and saw
Captain at the outer edge of the light, nose high, searching for a scent in the rain-washed darkness.

"Captain!" Ben whistled softly and the dog paused,
looking back at him with eyes that glowed yellow in the
lantern light. The swinging watch, fastened to the dog's
collar, gleamed like a third eye below the two real ones.
Cap barked and ran on. Ben had no choice but to follow,

doing his best not to step on anyone. Bodies were every-where. He'd never touched a dead body before yesterday, when he'd helped move the corpse of the boy, Nate, who'd been lying in the bed next to Curtis.

There was the Reb soldier in the attic, too. He'd fallen dead against Ben when he'd been shot. But Ben felt oddly disconnected from that, like it didn't count. Now, there were bodies at every step. Some called out—the ones who were still alive. But Ben hurried by them. He didn't have time to stop now. Later, he'd have to pray for God to for-give him.

Some men lay at preposterous, twisted angles, as though someone had wrung the life right out of them and then tossed them aside.

One man—Ben couldn't tell in the rain if he wore a blue coat or a gray—crawled toward him, pulling himself along slowly and painfully through the mud, arm over arm.

Ben paused a moment, squinting at the cursing, pant-ing specter. The soldier crawled into the light, and Ben could see he had no feet. He had only bloody stumps drag-ging along behind him.

Ben ignored the man's curses and hurried on. He had to. Travis and the others weren't far behind. They'd find this wounded apparition.

There were lanterns flicking like fireflies through the darkness. Lots of them. Both civilians and Union soldiers, methodically checking for life, stacking the dead, carrying off anyone with a pulse for treatment by an army surgeon.

"Reuben!" Ben called out his brother's name. He could almost feel his brother's presence. He couldn't let himself think any further than that. Reuben might be out here right this minute, tending to the wounded. It would be just like Reuben—always thinking of the other guy.

"Reuben Reynolds?" Ben shouted. "Are you here?"

There were answering groans and cries for help, a sad sea of voices rising to sweep him away. But none of the voices sounded like Reuben.

Suddenly, Ben heard a howl, a chilling, heartbroken wail directly in front of him. The noise stopped, then started again.

It was Captain.

A tingle of foreboding raced down Ben's spine.

"Captain?" he called.

The only answer was the wild howling, crying into the rain.

Ben's steps slowed. He lowered the lantern, afraid he would see what he was afraid to see. Each step was an effort. He was swimming through black-strap molasses, and the night only got darker and heavier with every step.

Captain was just ahead, his eyes yellow flames in the light of the lantern. The dog sat beside a prone body, one paw resting on the soldier's back. Ben knelt down beside the still form and felt a quick wave of relief. There was no derby on the streaming strands of wet hair. This wasn't Reuben. Captain was wrong. He had to be wrong.

Ben knelt down and reached out to turn the body over. The round glasses on the soldier's nose reflected the lantern light, just as Captain's eyes had done. They gave the face a cold, accusing look. Crushed in the hand that had been trapped under the body was a battered felt derby.

Ben fell, more than sat. Mud squeezed through the seams of his wool pants, cold and clammy on his bottom. All the noises of this awful night faded away. He reached out to touch the face that somehow didn't quite look like Reuben. He brushed a piece of wet leaf off one cheek, then felt along the neck, searching for the pulse he knew wasn't there. His hand continued downward, over the jacket, pausing at each gold button. Reuben's chest was broad and strong. This chest seemed skinny and sunken. Could Reuben have gotten so thin? Further down, Ben's fingers passed a hole—a hole the size of a cantaloupe. His fingers stretched out and explored the gaping wound. Was this where his brother's life had been kept, here in this hole in his chest? His fingers came out slightly sticky with blood that had stopped flowing hours ago.

"Reuben," Ben whispered. "Don't leave me."

Ben wiped his sticky hand against the wet, blue wool of the soldier's jacket and felt a square of something hard sticking in the jacket pocket. His fingers trembled as they reached to pull it out. It was a tintype. Its silver case shone in the glow of the lantern. A picture of their mother. It had to be. Reuben always carried it.

Ben clicked the case open, his eyes blurring with tears. There she was. Rain splattered across the glass oval, washing across her beloved face, so familiar he. . . .

Ben blinked and looked harder. He moved the picture down beside the lantern so he could see it more clearly.

There she was all right . . . Henry Owen's mother? Mrs. Owen stared back at him with her white lace collar framing her unsmiling face.

Ben tilted the picture back and forth as if he could somehow force it to explain itself. What was Reuben doing with Henry's mother's picture?

Ben's head shot up and he leaned forward, pulling the lantern with him. There was Henry's big old mole, there on his chin, the one Ben always teased him about with the black hair growing out of it. The sunken cheeks, the staring eyes. They didn't really look like Henry, but they weren't Reuben's. This was his neighbor, Henry Owen. Only fourteen years old. By the end of the summer, fifteen.

But not now. He'd never reach fifteen now.

Ben held the lantern closer. Ben hadn't noticed it at first, but Reuben's derby was black with a black silk band. This derby was brown, with a thin leather cord around the brim.

Captain whimpered softly beside him and looked at Ben accusingly.

Ben could feel the rain running down his neck, dripping off his ears and the ends of his hair. He felt like he might drown out here. His shoulders were shaking, his breathing ragged.

He stood up unsteadily, pulling the derby out of Henry's stiff, clutching hand and punching out the collapsed top into smooth roundness. He put it on his own head.

Ben could taste salty tears on his tongue, mixing with the rain. He hadn't even known he was crying. He bent down and tried to close Henry's eyelids over his staring, empty eyes, but they wouldn't stay down. Captain licked Ben squarely across the nose as he bent over Henry, and Ben dropped back to his knees. He threw his arms around the dog's neck, pulling Captain close, sobbing into the dog's thick familiar fur. The only normal thing left in the whole wide world was this dog.

With effort, Ben pushed Captain away.

"What about Reuben!" He rasped out the words, sharp and stinging. The dog cowered back under Ben's sudden, unexpected anger.

"You made me want you for my own," Ben was shouting now. "You liked me." Ben reared back. He felt like he was falling. "All the way here, you were the only smart one, the only one I could trust. Danny talked too much. Mavis was . . ." Ben hiccuped at a momentary loss for the right word. "Mavis was a cow. But you . . . you were Reuben's dog." Ben swallowed hard, but he couldn't get the sour taste out of his mouth. The taste of his own betrayal. "I shouldn't have wanted you . . . get away from me . . ."

Ben struck out so swiftly with his open palm, Captain didn't have time to dodge. The dog took the sharp slap across his muzzle, barely flinching. He didn't growl. He didn't slink away. He just stood there, watching Ben.

"Get away." Ben's voice held no expression. "Go."

Captain turned and slowly walked away. Ben didn't even watch which way the dog went. His eyes filled with fresh tears, blurring the night and turning the lantern into a fuzzy rainbow of colors.

He sat by Henry's body without moving. He sat in the dark and the rain, not even feeling it. He could hear Mr. Adams and Cousin Travis calling his name, but he didn't answer. His voice didn't work anymore. Henry was gone. Pa was gone. Reuben was somewhere, maybe dead or dying. And now he'd sent Captain away. Each thought was like a knife, stabbing at his insides. Ben cradled himself in his arms, swaying back and forth, trying to rock the pain away, the way Ma used to when he was little. He hummed a tuneless song and began to sing, his tongue so thick with crying he could barely form the words.

"Mine eyes have seen . . .

the coming . . . of the Lord,

Trampling out the vintage . . . where the wrath is stored . . ."

He was getting the words wrong, but he didn't care. Ben had never understood the words, anyroad. But now his friend Henry lay before him, trampled by a terrible, wrathful God.

Ben sat there, humming and rocking, until Mr. Adams found him. He had insisted he was old enough to help tonight, and here he sat like some little kid, useless and blubbering.

Mr. Adams didn't scold him. He simply scooped Ben up in his arms and carried him wordlessly back to the wagon.

CHAPTER 17

Mine Eyes Have
Seen the Glory

It had stopped raining that gray morning, but it began
again around noon. The drops running down the win-
dowpanes somehow comforted Ben. He couldn't allow
himself tears.

But the sky could cry.

It wasn't long after the rain started that someone
knocked on the front door. Travis's wife, Mae, bustled past
Ben and came back into the parlor leading a tall, dripping
Graycoat. Ben was momentarily startled by the new-
comer's resemblance to Reuben. But it wasn't Reuben. It
was a Confederate. The enemy.

"Will you please take Sergeant Evans upstairs to see his
brother?" Mae asked Ben. "The rest of us are real busy,"
she continued pointedly. "You're the only one jus' sittin'.
Come on now. He wants to see the boy in Freddie's room.
You remember him, don't you?"

" 'Course I remember," Ben said, the words low and
toneless.

"Howdy, boy." The Rebel soldier swept off his

wide-brimmed straw hat, splattering rainwater and re-vealing dark, exhausted eyes. It was Jim. Curtis's brother Jim. "Didn't rightly think I'd ever be seeing you again," he said gruffly.

"I'm not *really* Confederate," Ben blurted, realizing he was no longer wearing the gray cap Jim had first seen him in. He was still wearing Henry's brown felt derby. "I live right here in Pennsylvania."

Jim nodded. "I knew that a long time ago," he said, smiling at Ben. "No self-respectin' Southern boy would ever saddle hisself with a dog, a cow, and a freckled-faced kid like Danny. How're your troops doing these days?"

"Captain ran off," Ben answered vaguely. "Danny and Mavis are down the street." He couldn't explain more. If he didn't talk, the hurt inside him settled down to a dull ache.

"Well, what about Curtis?" Jim asked. For the first time that day, Ben was jarred out of thinking about his own misery. He hadn't been up to see Curtis since Friday morning. They'd been down at the Adams's house all the rest of that terrible day. Today was Saturday, wasn't it? Ben could hardly recall. It didn't seem like the same week as when it had all started. It didn't seem like the same lifetime.

Before Ben could answer, Travis entered the room, head half-bowed. "My wife told me you were back, sir." Travis sounded wary, but sympathetic. "You'd best hurry upstairs." Travis shook his head, his eyes full of pity. "While there's still time."

Jim followed Travis's pointing finger to the stairs. He took them two at a time. Ben sprang up and followed close behind, calling, "I'll show you," at Jim's back.

"Curtis is at the end of the hall," Ben added, but Jim seemed to know where he was going. He covered the distance in three long strides, bursting into the room so noisily, he should have woken the dead. But Curtis didn't even open his eyes. The young Reb's breathing was labored and sweat stood out on his forehead, although he shivered under a heavy load of blankets. Two jasmine-scented candles burned—one on the dresser, one on the bedside table—not quite masking the sour, sickroom smell.

"Curtis." Jim knelt beside the bed, taking both of his brother's limp hands in his. The tin frog clicker clattered to the floor, but Jim paid no attention. "I'm here, Curtis. I'm right here."

A stab of envy shot through Ben. If only he could hear those words from Reuben. He'd give anything for that. Curtis and Jim were lucky.

"Jim? That you?" Curtis's pale eyelashes fluttered, and he raised his eyelids with what appeared to be considerable effort.

"It's me, little brother." Jim's voice was shaking. "I'm right here." He squeezed Curtis's hands gently.

"I've been hoping you'd come." Curtis's voice was creaky and old sounding. It didn't sound like the voice of any other boy Ben had ever known.

"Did we win, Jim? Can we go home now?"

"We're going, little brother. Ma'll be so glad to see you, she'll bake you a sweet-potato pie." Ben couldn't see Jim's face, bent as it was toward his brother.

Curtis's pale face had a faraway look. "You be good to Riley, Jim. I shoulda brung my old tick hound with me, like Ben did his dog. Remember, Jim? The one we run into over at the river? He was a good ole dog."

There was a stirring on the far side of the high-backed bed. Captain's square muzzle appeared over the edge of the bed and moved up to nuzzle Curtis's hand. All this time Ben had been downstairs feeling sorry for himself, Captain must have been up here with Curtis.

Ben hadn't even noticed the yellow dog. He'd been too wrapped up in his own misery.

"Riley," Curtis breathed, choking on the words. "You stayed with me. I knew you would."

Curtis moved his hands weakly to cradle Captain's head.

The door creaked open, and Ben turned to see Travis creeping quietly into the room. It was like an official decree that time was up. The lump in Ben's throat felt as if it were swelling, getting bigger and bigger. It felt like it might burst out of his neck any minute now, and land, like a rock, on the uneven plank floorboards. Curtis was dying. Here. Now. Right in front of him. And there was nothing Ben could do about it.

It was like a sunset. Coming and coming, so that it seemed to take forever to get there, but then, when the sun went down, it was over in a blink.

Ben held out his hand to hold Travis back.

Curtis, summoning strength from somewhere Ben couldn't imagine, reached for Jim's hand and pulled it across to rest on Captain's head. "You take care of each other, Jim. You and Riley." Jim's long frame was stiff as he knelt there beside Curtis's bed. He nodded, but didn't speak.

His nod was interrupted by a gurgle in Curtis's throat and a spasm along the length of his body. Curtis's eyelids flew open, staring at the ceiling. His lips parted and a dribble of white spittle ran out. A noise like a sigh came from those cracked lips, and then the only noise was Jim's sobbing. Jim leaned forward and gathered his brother's shattered body close. Captain raised his head and let loose with a long, melancholy howl.

"Curtis. Curtis." Jim repeated the name again and again as he rocked back and forth.

"Excuse me—I'm sorry—but there's another Confederate soldier downstairs, looking for you," Travis said softly. "He asked me to tell you that your unit's leaving. In fact, all of Gordon's infantry is pulling out. He wanted to know what to tell your lieutenant."

Jim lifted his head and looked at Travis, then at Ben. His eyes fell on the tin clicker on the floor, and he picked it up and held it in his open palm, staring at it. Then he reached out to Ben, offering it to him.

Ben stepped forward and took it.

Jim rose stiffly and reached down to scoop Curtis's lifeless body off the bed. He draped one old wool blanket over the half-naked boy and brushed past Ben and Travis, marching slowly down the hall to the stairs.

"I'm takin' my brother home," he said to no one in particular.

Captain followed Jim, like a mourner in a funeral procession.

Ben fell in behind the dog.

"We're all real sorry about your brother," Travis called after them. "He was a nice, polite boy, even if he was a Reb. He didn't deserve to die this way."

Jim paused and turned around. He seemed to hold Curtis tighter, raising him up, until Jim's hand could touch the brim of his straw hat, which was pressed down tightly over his forehead. He touched the brim, saluting them.

"Nobody deserves to die like this, mister. No one deserves to go so young . . ." He paused, gathering himself. ". . . or so hard." He started down the hallway, then stopped. "Curtis always wanted to come up north and see how things were up here. He told me once that Pennsylvania was a whole different shade of green from our Georgia. He liked it here . . . you people tended him fine. I'm beholden to you."

Jim turned and started on his way again, Curtis cradled like a baby against his chest.

"Best call your dog back, boy, or he might follow us all the way to Georgia. Use that clicker."

The clicker was clenched so tightly in Ben's fist, the metal edges cut into his palm.

The dog was starting down the steps behind Jim. Soon, Captain would be out the door, and Ben wouldn't have to wrestle anymore with loving a dog that wasn't his. The responsibility would be gone, out the door, right along with the Rebs.

Ben loosened his grip on the clicker and pushed on the smooth, round bubble of the frog's back.

Click. Click.

Captain's head swung around, and the dog hesitated. He was halfway down the stairs. His tail was between his legs, his gait slow and sorrowful. His brown eyes met Ben's.

Ben crouched down, held out a hand, and gave a soft whistle. "Come on back, Cap. Stay here with me."

Captain's tail swung up and began to swish back and forth. The dog turned and bounded up the stairs. He came so swiftly, he bowled Ben right over. Ben's arms closed around Captain's neck.

"Fool bootlicker dog. Do you forgive me?"

Captain licked Ben's chin and cheeks, his ears, and forehead, and even his neck. It was all the reply Ben needed.

CHAPTER 18

July 5

There were folks on the narrow market streets again, but the ladies carried handkerchiefs soaked in rose water over their noses and half the men carried burning sticks of camphor. Anything to mask the awful smell that was bringing every greenbottle fly in the world for a closer look at the stunned countryside around Gettysburg.

Some even carried smelling salts for those who came out unprepared.

The horses and mules were the worst. Their bloated carcasses seemed to be everywhere, shot—or sometimes crushed under the cannons they had been hauling. Those that weren't dead could be found here and there, still hitched to a team of corpses. The few living horses stood dazed as they flicked their tails at the flies that buzzed in their nostrils and walked boldly across their eyes.

Some of the mules gnawed at gaping wounds on their own hindquarters and squealed like pigs if you tried to approach them. It sounded, thought Ben, like they were convinced men weren't to be trusted. With good reason.

One horse charged past their wagon as Ben and Cousin Travis headed out to help with the burying. The back of the wagon was loaded with powdery chloride of lime that had just arrived from York. The sorrel mare charging past them up Emmittsburg Pike had blood running from both nostrils, but it went by so fast, Ben couldn't spot any wounds.

"Shouldn't we try to catch that one?"

Travis shrugged and kept driving straight ahead. "It'll stop all by itself, pert soon, from the looks of it."

Two hollow-eyed, blue-coated soldiers walked past them, carrying a limp body on their crossed rifles. Ben started to jump down to help, but Travis caught his arm.

"Leave 'em be. Must be a wounded mate, if they're carrying him like that. We're detailed to the dead, not the wounded. They know where they're going, and so do we. This is too big a thing to go running off in every direction, Ben. We gotta focus on what we've been asked to do, and nothing else, hard as that might be."

They drove past a burial detail in the woods beside the road. The trees here looked like winter trees, naked, with all the leaves shot away. Travis reined in his horse for a moment and removed his battered hat. Ben took off the brown derby he was wearing and stared at the soldiers in the burial detail, their jackets off, their sleeves rolled up, as they dug hole after hole. First, they scooped out a shallow trench, then they rolled a body into it. The corpses were laid out in a neat row, stiff as logs. When one was rolled under, the dirt from the new hole was used to cover the body.

Nobody even thought about trying to take the bodies to the town's only proper cemetery, up on the hill. It seemed like every field and clearing as far as the eye could see had been drafted for cemetery duty.

Travis flicked the reins. "Just hope they're planting them boys deep enough that the next good rain doesn't float 'em away."

By the time they reached the spot chosen for disposal of animals, a dozen carcasses towered together in a mass of jutting legs and swollen bellies. Ben swatted at the swarms of flies that seemed to be massing for a battle of their own over the rotting flesh. He was glad he had one of Travis's big, white cotton kerchiefs tied over his nose and mouth.

"Simon!" Travis waved to a white-bearded man who stood, hands on hips and a red bandana tied over his nose and mouth, surveying the carnage. "I brought the lime that just came in. Looked like a whole line of supply wagons are headed our way on the York Road."

"Let's hope." The old man came over and gravely shook Travis's hand. "Good to see you made it through, Travis. There were a coupla times there I wasn't so sure our little town was gonna be left standin'. They say there's over twenty thousand wounded, some of 'em Rebs that were left behind. We already sent out telegrams, asking for food and blankets. And we need all kinds of medical supplies, too, like alcohol and creosote and nitric acid. You name it. We need it."

"So where do you want this load of lime?"

"Leave it be for now. Once we get twenty carcasses or so piled, we'll start a fire. Then it'll just be a matter of adding more bodies till we're down to nothing but ash. We'll send some fellas to lime all the spots where the bodies was layin'. It's gonna be a long day."

Ben knew now what the white-bearded old man meant by "a long day." Travis's neighbor wasn't given to exaggerating. By the time they stopped for lunch, Ben's back ached and his hands were blistered from hauling and hitching the ropes that moved the unwieldy animal corpses.

Danny had disappeared so early that morning, he'd been spared any part of this disgusting, backbreaking work. Leave it to Danny to get out of work. And it appeared that Captain had disappeared right along with him. Ben figured the dog, at least, had an excuse. All this blood and rot out here would drive a dog's sensitive nose crazy. Danny was crazy on his own hook.

But Ben stayed to help. He didn't feel right turning his back on the people who'd taken them in. He owed something to Travis and his family, and Mr. Adams, too. Every pair of hands was needed for this cleanup, and more besides.

There were only about two thousand folks living in the town of Gettysburg, and now, suddenly, in the space of just a few days, they were faced with the prospect of more than twenty times that number of dead to bury and wounded to nurse. There were hundreds of animal corpses, too, stiffening and bloating in the July sun. So much to be done. And not enough time or strength or supplies to go around.

Travis said they needed every volunteer piling into town from York and Hanover and even Lancaster. Some had already arrived with more coming every hour, hundreds pouring into little Gettysburg along with wives and mothers looking for their men to bury or take home. Ben couldn't imagine where they were going to put everybody.

The out-of-town undertakers had arrived first and thrown up their own row of square, white tents to do their embalming. It was quite a boom in the undertaking business, Ben expected, what with all the folks who wanted their husbands and fathers and sons shipped home for burial.

Most searchers were like Ben, though. Just had no idea whether the men they were looking for were dead or alive, already under the bloody ground, or moved on to fight in the next battle. When he found the time, Ben planned to search every hospital and house where the wounded were kept until he found Reuben. Or at least until he found out what had happened to his brother.

One of the men stacking carcasses had told him the

106th Pennsylvania had been in Gettysburg the first day, but after that, he wasn't sure.

It gave Ben hope.

Captain returned while Ben was heaving a rope around a mule that lay on its back with its hind legs straight up in the air. The dog ghosted out from behind a stand of minié ball–riddled poplar trees. The sweat dripping in Ben's eyes stung as he tried to blink it away.

When he turned away from the trussed carcass, the unexpected sight of Captain startled him. He stumbled backward against the board-hard belly of the dead mule and heard a pop as the dry skin of the corpse split somewhere along its swollen belly. A cloud of noxious gas whooshed out with so much force that Ben could hear it. And smell it. Ben reached to press the kerchief against his nose as he threw himself forward, away from the horrible stench. He fell to his knees, gagging. Ben hadn't had much for breakfast—a piece of toast and a single slice of fried pork—but his stomach twisted and heaved, and a strangled sound escaped his throat. Ben didn't want to throw up. He was pretty sure that if he started, he wouldn't be able to stop.

Captain stretched his muzzle forward and licked Ben's sweaty forehead. The cool tongue trailed down over Ben's ear. It felt surprisingly good, like the cool cloths his mother put on his forehead when he was in bed with some fever.

"I thought mebbe you'd run off again," Ben said gruffly, straightening up and reaching to run his fingers through the yellow dog's thick fur. His fingers lingered on the watch, still attached to Cap's collar. "I was a mite worried when you disappeared this morning. It's not like before. Dogs have been shot around here for dragging off arms and legs after the amputations. You better watch yourself."

Ben moved over to the shade of a maple tree that had somehow managed to hold on to most of its leaves, despite the fusillade of rifle fire that stripped its companions. He plopped down, crossing his legs, and pulled Captain close.

"Now I'm not saying I think you'd do such a thing. Personally, I think you're way too smart for that. But being as how you *are* a dog, it's not safe. That's all I'm saying. And what would Reuben say if I let his dadblame bootlicker dog get shot *after* the fighting?"

Ben let his arms go around the dog's neck and buried his face in Captain's fur, jerking down the kerchief and taking deep breaths of the rich, doggie smell. It was the finest perfume compared to the whole rest of this stinkin' day.

Ben leaned back against the tree and closed his eyes. He wondered where Danny was, right this minute. It was just like Danny to weasel out of work so he could go hunting battle relics. 'Course, mebbe Danny was the smart one. There were dozens of souvenir hunters out here already. Ben had seen several corpses with turned-out pockets and slit-off belt buckles. Once, he'd even heard what sounded like distant cannon fire. Travis had assured him it wasn't the Rebs coming back, just pesky souvenir hunters digging up a live shell.

The haze lying over the fields today wasn't rifle smoke. It was the choking gray debris of a dozen bonfires from other groups like Ben's that were burning animal flesh. Yesterday, the smell of death was pungent. Today it was old and stale. Ben sneezed and pulled out a second kerchief he had jammed in his back pocket. He blew his nose and looked down at the white square of cloth in horror. The stuff in his nose was black from all the smoke and gunpowder he'd been breathing. Ben wadded up the kerchief and hastily pushed it back into his pocket.

Captain's arrival on the scene was the only thing making it bearable to stay. The dog kept right at Ben's heels, everywhere he went. Ben could swear Cap was studying him as he worked, patiently trotting by his side, following him with those unreadable brown eyes. It was almost as if the dog was looking for a way to tell him something. Ben didn't know what, and he didn't have time to wonder about it.

The carcasses seemed endless. It was clear that one day of hauling the corpses away wouldn't do it. Ben was too numb to think and too tired to care.

"There's a man coming up the Emmittsburg Pike from Maryland in one of those photography wagons." Travis sat down beside Ben on the gnarled root of an ancient maple tree after they'd worked together wrestling a dead gray mare onto the pile. "I hear he's needing some help from a boy who knows about cameras and such."

It was getting toward evening, and some of the men in their detail had taken Travis's wagon and were spreading chloride of lime wherever sticks poked up out of the ground to show where carcasses had been.

Ben feared he might pass out if he had to touch just one more dead horse, with its mouth wide open and its bug eyes staring. Instead of getting used to it, as Travis had assured him he would, Ben had found it harder and harder each time they dragged another corpse to the crackling fire.

"I told the fella what told me about this photographer that I had a boy working with me whose brother had his own studio back in Lancaster, and that most likely this boy knew a good bit about the picture-taking trade. That boy would be you, of course."

Travis had taken pity on him and was trying to help him. But Ben couldn't muster the strength even to nod his head. He just listened.

"The photographer goes by the name of Gardner. Alexander Gardner, out of Washington, D.C. I haven't rightly heard of him before. Still, I thought it might be something worth your time, Ben. This Gardner fella has a couple more photographers with him—O'Sullivan and Gibson, I think their names were. Anyroad, you're to go down to the Rose farm tomorrow morning to help them out. You're to do that 'stead of coming back here with me, you hear?" Travis patted Ben's slumped shoulder.

"What did you say the man's name was?" Ben was surprised to hear that his voice still sounded almost normal. His throat felt raspy and raw from all the smoke.

"Alexander Gardner," Travis repeated. "They say he took photographs at Antietam in '62."

"Well, the only photographer I ever heard of besides my brother is Mathew Brady."

"Yeah, he'd be the famous one, all right. They say this Gardner fella used to work for him. All I know is, they're down to the Rose farm today taking pictures of the dead soldiers. So you go on down there in the morning and give them a hand."

"Thanks." Ben couldn't think of anything else to say. He'd often watched Reuben posing people in front of painted backdrops in his little studio above the store. He'd seen his brother cautioning them to sit perfectly still, carefully arranging each one on a chair or a couch.

Surely dead people couldn't be much of a problem that way. They'd pose right where they were and never move a muscle, from now till forever. It was when you wanted 'em to move you'd have the problem.

Ben started to laugh. He quickly covered his mouth with his hand to stifle the unseemly sound. A man working the pile of burning carcasses, stabbing at it with a pike, was singing, "Mine eyes have seen the glory of the coming of the Lord," for what must be about the one hundredth time. Hearing it only made Ben laugh harder. His whole body was shaking with helpless laughter as he looked across the smoky, blighted field. Glory, glory? Not from what Ben had seen.

He smothered his face in Captain's fur, staying that way till he could hardly breathe. He had to make this fit of laughter go away. It wasn't manly. There was probably something seriously wrong with a fella who'd start laughing after a day of hauling and trussing the bodies of dead horses and mules. Ben felt like he might fall over and roll on the ground, laughing and laughing, until he laughed himself into one of those shallow trenches where the Union soldiers were putting the bodies.

What was the matter with him, anyroad?

Ben sighed. He took a deep breath and got up to help spread the mounds of hot ash across the field.

He hoped Danny was having a better day than he was.

He had to be.

What could possibly be worse than this?

CHAPTER 19

Ben, on His Own Hook

Danny found something worse. He lay in the same bed Curtis had been in only the day before, his head swathed in a white bandage. His right arm was in a sling, and his right cheek had a jagged little cut on it, like a tiny streak of red lightning. And those were just the parts Ben could see above the covers. There was a bandaged leg hidden from sight under the drape of the white muslin sheet.

It turned out Danny had paid a high price for the stack of battlefield souvenirs beside the bed. Of course, it could have been worse. He could be dead.

Ben looked at the brass infantry belt buckle, the tattered piece of a Confederate flag, and the pocket knife with its ivory handle. He should have dragged Danny along to work with him on the carcasses yesterday. Ben felt a twinge of guilt. He'd given up watching out for his cousin for just one day, and look what happened.

"If I hadna gotten explodicated, I coulda found lots more relics," Danny assured Ben when the morphine finally took hold and he stopped thrashing around in pain. "They're all over the place."

"I'll give you a relic, young man," Travis's wife scolded as she bustled into the room just in time to hear Danny's bragging. "I'll give you a relic right across your britches if I ever catch you sneaking off to rob those dead soldiers' graves again. The very idea. It's a mercy you weren't killed instead of a broken bone and a few cuts."

"We didn't rob any graves," Danny protested, wincing as Mae Seldomridge checked his bandages and adjusted his pillows. "We just took what was laying around in plain sight."

"Well, I hope you learned something, young man." Her hand swept over Danny's body, indicating his many bandages. "I swan, if that shell had exploded straight at you, 'stead of alongside of you, how would I have explained it to your dear mother? Just look at you, lying here with a busted arm, a gash in your head, and a slice out of your thigh to boot.

"You're not going out there again, you hear me? You're staying right here in this bed, Daniel Stewart Seldomridge, if I have to rip up another one of my poor bedsheets and tie you to the posts."

Danny rolled his eyes, but he didn't answer back.

"Now Ben here has to go out to try to find his brother. It's a good family thing to do, entirely different from your gallivanting." She pulled a scribbled list of names out of her apron pocket. "Ben's been working hard on the cleanup with Travis—Ben, I don't mind helping." She handed Ben the list. "Here are the places I know that have Union wounded. Mainly people's homes, churches, and school buildings. They're all over. That's not to say there aren't more than's on this list, but these are the ones I've heard were doing hospital duty like us. Your chores are caught up, and you've got time before it gets full dark. Take the porch lantern with you. Knock on a few doors. And good luck to you, Benjamin Herr Reynolds. May God go by your side." She turned from Danny and planted a kiss lightly on Ben's cheek.

Her voice softened and her eyes crinkled into a smile as she spoke to Ben, the same gentle, coaxing way she had when she was tending to the wounded. Ben didn't know why. She didn't need to be extra nice to him. He wasn't wounded.

Ben glanced down at the penciled list of names and sighed. He was really too tired to tramp all the way from the McCreary house on Chambersburg Pike to the Catholic church on West High Street. And wounded were everywhere, just like Danny's precious relics. They were holed up in mills, tollhouses, farmsteads, barns, taverns, stores, even in the seminary building up on the ridge. And that was just the beginning. They were gathered by the hundreds into tents called field hospitals.

And tomorrow morning, he had to be up early to meet that photographer fella at the Rose farm.

Still, this was what he'd come for, even if he had no better chance of finding Reuben in this bulging-with-people town than of finding a four-leaf clover in a dandelion patch. He knew he had to look.

Ben whistled Captain to his side as he methodically began knocking on doors and wandering between church pews that had been turned into makeshift cots. It wasn't long before the places started to jumble in his mind. It was as if the whole town was one giant hospital, with beds in every living room and operating rooms behind every church pulpit. Ben stopped one place to dip out water for a groaning private whose lips were cracked and parched like a man crossing the hottest desert. At another place, he found a blanket for a soldier shivering so hard in the muggy July night that his teeth chattered.

And at each place, Ben asked his question.

"Have you seen Captain Reuben Reynolds of the 106th Pennsylvania, Company A?"

Again and again, he asked. He stopped at tents and warehouses, schoolrooms and barns. Again and again, people shook their heads and shrugged their shoulders or stared at him in such a pitying way, he quickly hurried on. As the evening wore on, maybe a dozen or so took the time to say, "Sorry, son," and pat him on the shoulder.

Ben bent down beside Captain in the darkening street. He pulled out a match and lit the lantern, putting it down on the hard-packed road, so that its glow made a yellow pool in the dirt. Ben took Captain's head in both hands, tilting it so the dog had to look right into his eyes.

"You could find him, Cap. I know you could."

Suddenly, Ben straightened up. Of course. That was it. His voice cracked like a whip.

"Go. Find Reuben. Find Reuben, Cap. Find him."

The dog looked up at Ben once, as if to acknowledge the order. Then Captain trotted down the street as if he knew right where he was going. Ben picked up the lantern to follow, but a hoarse voice called to him from the porch across the street. A single candle flickered on the wide porch rail, but Ben couldn't make out the person calling to him.

"Cudya help me here, boy?"

"Whaddaya need, mister?" Ben called, anxious not to lose sight of Captain.

"I don't want to shout out for the whole town to hear. I need . . ." The man paused. ". . . some help."

Ben turned, wearily, whistling for Captain to come back. He trudged up the steps to the wide covered porch and was just bending down to see what this wounded soldier wanted when he heard shots.

"What was that?" Ben stopped, staring into the summer night, windows dimly glowing across the street. Full darkness had descended and the candle on the porch rail threw dancing shadows onto the uneven plank floor of the narrow porch.

The man on the porch didn't answer. Instead he said, "I can't reach my pot." The soldier gestured to a white porcelain chamber pot a few feet from his cot. "The missus put it just a mite too far over last time. I hate to bother her 'bout it, when she's got so many of us to tend and all, but I can't get up."

The soldier gestured toward the blanket, which lay perfectly flat. There were no long wrinkles where the man's legs should be. It took Ben a second to realize what this meant. There were no wrinkles because there were no legs.

Ben hastily grabbed the pot and handed it to the soldier. "I thought I heard shots," Ben said. "Just a minute ago. Didn't you hear rifle fire?"

"Oh, that." The soldier dismissed the sharp reports with a wave of his hand. "Don't be feared a Rebs, boy. Our boys're shooting a different kind of varmint round here tonight."

"What do you mean?" Ben looked around the porch for Captain, but the dog was nowhere in sight. The lantern didn't cast enough light into the street to see if the yellow hound was waiting for him there. More'n likely, the dog had gone his own way, like he always did. But Cap would return when he was good and ready. He'd return and lead Ben to Reuben. Please God, let him find Reuben tonight.

"Gunshots round here mean those mangy curs what keeps stealing them amputated limbs are at it agin. Some of the sentries have started pickin' 'em off now 'stead of shootin' over their heads to scare 'em off. And rightly so. I can't bear thinkin' 'bout some mangy mutt chewing on *my* legs. I'll tell you what, boy . . ."

But Ben didn't hear the rest. A fire boiled up in his belly. They couldn't be shooting at Captain! Ben bolted down the steps and began to sprint down the street as fast as his tired legs would carry him. Far ahead, he saw a lantern. A silhouette. A man with a gun. Bending down. Bending over something in the road.

Ben ran blindly forward. He ran smack dab into the dark form of a Union soldier, who caught and held him, shaking him slightly as he asked, "What ails you, boy? Is somebody chasin' you? Why're you running out here in the dark with folks as jumpy as ticks on a griddle? Somebody less steady than me just might decide to shoot you first and ask who you are later."

The sentry held Ben's shoulders, steadying him. Ben tried to get the words out, but they caught in his throat. He was choking on the thing he had to know, fighting for breath as his eyes fell on the lump of black and white fur in the middle of the street. Black and white. Not yellow.

Ben's breathing slowed with relief, and he wheezed out two words.

"My dog . . ."

The soldier grimaced and turned to stare, along with Ben, at the narrow face of the dog in the street, a neatly placed bullet hole right between its two sightless eyes.

"You're not telling me that's *your* dog, boy, out here at night, nosing through the sawbones' leavings? It looked like a stray to me. A boy like you has no business bringing a dog out . . ."

Ben found his voice, interrupting the sentry. "No, no, it's not *that* dog. My dog is a big, yellow hound with a squarish muzzle, brown eyes, short, floppy ears, and sort of a pinkish-black nose. He's my brother's dog, really." Ben waved a hand toward the side of the brick church that housed a temporary surgery. He could see the pile of legs, some still wearing shoes, and arms, some still wearing the bloody remnants of shirt sleeves.

In the morning, a squad of soldiers would load the severed limbs into a wagon and take them out to bury them, strangely separated from the bodies they'd come here with. It was sort of a grim joke around Gettysburg that a man could get himself buried all over town, if he just took it one piece at a time.

"My dog's helping me look for my brother, Reuben. Captain Reuben Reynolds of the 106th Pennsylvania Volunteers, Company A. He came this way just a few minutes ago. Not my brother. My dog, I mean. Looking for Reuben. Did you see my dog?"

"Well, I don't rightly know about your brother, son, but I believe I did see your dog, messing with that pack of dogs that was just by here. I got this one." The grim-faced soldier stretched out his leg and nudged the slumped body with the toe of his muddy boot. "The others mostly got away, but I'm pert sure I winged a couple. I did see a big old, yellow hound on the street with 'em. Mighta winged him, too. It was too quick to say for sure. I'm rightly sorry if he was your dog, son, but I had no way to know that." He sounded angry now, as if the sudden pang of guilt plaguing him was Ben's fault.

"Where did the dogs run off to after you shot at them?"

"Don't rightly know." The soldier kept a wad of something pouched in his cheek and now began chewing on it. He spat a noisy stream of tobacco juice just to the side of the dead dog's body. "But the ones we wing don't get far. You might find your dog curled up close by here, under a tree or up against a fence. That's where they go to . . ."

The soldier stopped short of finishing. But Ben knew exactly what he'd been about to say.

"Where they go to die?" Ben's voice had gone high on him, like a girl's. But Captain still wore the watch with its scratched message of ownership. Surely someone would find the dog and come looking for Ben.

He was suddenly angry with himself and his stupid plan. No one in Gettysburg would know the name R. Reynolds, or B. Reynolds, either. Ben wanted to scream. He wanted to yell. He wanted to hit somebody. Instead, he swallowed hard and asked softly, "You really think you shot my dog?"

"Like I told you, son, I don't rightly know. I heard a

couple of 'em yelping. Couldn't say which ones." He put a hand on Ben's shoulder. People kept doing that, as if it would help somehow. But it didn't.

"Tell you what. If your dog's waiting for you at home, you'll know I didn't shoot him. And if he isn't, well . . . alls I can say, boy, is if you find him, don't bring him out at night no more. This is a right fidgety town after the battle and all. It don't take much." The soldier started to raise his gun, then quietly lowered it as he stared at something over Ben's shoulder.

"Ben?"

The voice behind Ben was so unexpected, it sent a shiver down his spine.

Ben turned slowly, trying to sort out what it was he was feeling. Eagerness? Relief? Sorrow? Fear? Was it possible to feel so many things all at once?

"Oh, Ben, Ben. It *is* you. I've been looking for you everywhere."

CHAPTER 20

July 6

Ben fell into his mother's arms like some little baby, without a shred of pride or a moment's hesitation.

"Thank God you're safe."

Kathleen Reynolds breathed the words softly. "Oh, Ben." She hugged him tightly. "I was so worried."

"It's all my fault." Ben stepped back so he could look into his mother's face, shadowed by darkness, but so dear he almost wanted to kiss it. It never occurred to him to ask why she was here. It seemed the most natural thing in the world. Wives and mothers were prowling the streets and fields all around town every day now, looking for their living . . . and their dead.

"I came lookin' for Reuben—I thought that would help you," Ben stammered. "But instead, I almost got Danny killed, and I didn't find Reuben anyroad. And now Captain . . ."

Ben let the words trail off, gesturing toward the sentry, who was quietly going about his business, hoisting the rear legs of the dog in the street and dragging the body around the corner of the church.

His mother reached up and smoothed back his hair. She was wearing her gray-and-white traveling dress with the mother-of-pearl buttons. Ben blinked at her and pointed at the dog.

"See that dog? That fella says he might have shot Cap, too." Ben's words came faster and faster. "Cap was only lookin' for Reuben, like I told him to. Now mebbe—"

Ben stopped. He swallowed hard, so he could speak without his voice cracking.

"I started out with a plan, Ma. A plan for what I was gonna do. But it's gone all to flinders, and I don't know how to make it right."

"Honey." His mother put a comforting arm around Ben's waist. He hadn't remembered she was so short. How fast could a fella grow in a week, anyroad? She smelled like cinnamon and vanilla. Like home.

"Look around you, Ben. Lots a folks are trying to figure how to make this terrible thing make sense. But we can't undo what's been done. All we can do is work at it, a little bit at a time, the way Cousin Travis said you did today."

She was leading him back down the block, back toward Travis's house on Baltimore Street.

"I wanted to bring Reuben home to help you. I wanted to make it better, what with Pa gone." Ben mumbled his explanation. It all sounded so stupid now.

"Seeing you safe, Ben, already makes things better for me," his mother assured him. "Besides, a person can't find much of anything in the dark. I've been looking for you since Travis told me you were out here looking for Reuben. But we're not going to find your brother tonight—or his dog, either. Things will look better in the morning. You're too tired to think straight right now, Ben Reynolds, and so am I. I've been on the road all day myself—I'm dusty and dirty. We'll both get washed up and get a good night's sleep. Then we'll work it all out in the morning."

Ben stopped so suddenly, his mother, who still had her arm around his waist, was pulled up short. Ben had been so caught up in Captain's disappearance, he hadn't thought to ask the most obvious question of all.

"Ma, what are you doing here?"

His mother actually laughed.

"I wondered when you'd get around to asking me that."

"How did you get here? Who's minding the store?"

"Whoa, Ben! One question at a time! Aunt Mavis and Uncle Elliott are minding the store. Aunt Mavis is the one who may never forgive you. She swears you kidnapped her baby, though I know better. Danny Seldomridge always had a mind of his own and wouldn't go anywhere he didn't want to go without considerable kickin' and screamin'. But you and Danny will have to explain that to your aunt."

"You've seen Danny then?"

She nodded.

"For two days, we didn't know where you were, Ben. We asked everyone if they'd seen you, and finally old Mr. Martin—you remember that strange old man down the street?—well, he said he remembered a boy and a big, yellow dog heading for the bridge at Columbia. Now, I wouldn't normally set too much store by what Mr. Martin had to say, but when he said he tried to buy the dog, and the boy—who he said was *clearly* with the dog—kept insisting it wasn't his dog, it was his brother's . . ."

His mother squeezed Ben's hand. "Then I knew he really had seen you. I suspected where you two might be headed as soon as we started getting word about the battle here. I went right to Travis's house after dropping off the supplies I'd brought over for the Patriot Daughters. We've been filling a wagon since Tuesday with bandages and such. There's been nothing else on the front page of the *Intelligencer* all week except news of the battle. Oh, Ben. I was so worried. Aunt Mavis took to her bed in a swoon when I told her Danny and you might have gone to Gettysburg to look for Reuben. Mrs. Owen and I volunteered to drive the supplies over, in hopes of finding you boys. We've been on the road since early Wednesday. Had to ferry across the Susquehanna, but I suspect you already know about the burning of the bridge. Oh Ben, I'm just so grateful you're alive."

Ben stopped walking and turned to look in his mother's

blue eyes, so much like Reuben's. Her eyes glittered with tears in the lantern light. "I know where Henry is." He paused, biting his tongue to keep from blurting out: He's dead. "But I didn't find Reuben, Ma. I tried—" Ben's mother laid a finger across his lips.

"From what the newspapers at home say, Reuben's unit was here in Gettysburg the day the fighting started. We'll find him." She urged Ben up the steps to the front door. "We won't give up."

With his hand on the doorknob, Ben turned to his mother. "I have to tell you about Henry, Ma. It's bad news."

His mother nodded. "We read the list on the court-house in Gettysburg, right after we got here. Henry's name was on it." His mother shook her head sadly. "Mrs. Owen is taking it hard. She's staying with a relative here, and I'll be meeting her in the square in the morning. You can tell her all you know about Henry tomorrow. Right now, it's getting late."

Ben opened the door. He knew he wouldn't sleep tonight with Captain missing. He wished he could stay out longer, looking for the dog, but his mother seemed determined to get him into bed, and he didn't want to fight her.

"Don't worry, Ben. We won't go home as long as we're needed," his mother assured him.

"I won't go home till we've found Cap—and Reuben," Ben said, making a promise as much to himself as to her. "I won't give up on them, Ma. I swan, I won't."

♦ ♦ ♦

Every time a dog barked in the distance, Ben fumbled Timothy O'Sullivan's tripods and glass plates, almost dropping everything as he swiveled around to search the rocks and trees for signs of Captain. His mother swore she'd spend the day searching the town for the yellow hound, otherwise Ben would have begged off this assignment. But Travis had given his word.

He'd gone to the Rose farm off the Emmittsburg Pike early that morning, only to be told the trio of photographers from Washington, D.C., had moved to a group of rock formations now known as Devil's Den. The killing ground had earned its name on the second day of the battle—the day Ben and Danny had arrived in Gettysburg. It seemed more like years ago than a few days.

It was at Devil's Den that Ben had caught up with the men.

The subjects they wanted to make into woodcut engravings for magazines and stereopticon view-cards were the slain bodies, and by the weekend after the battle, burial details had left scant pickings for the picture taker's art. Alexander Gardner, a bearded man in a wide-brimmed hat that made Ben think of a fire-and-brimstone revival preacher, was in charge, and he assigned the boys who showed up—three of them, including Ben—so that each photographer had an assistant. Ben went with Tim O'Sullivan, a tall, skinny man who took off his jacket, rolled up his sleeves, and trotted from spot to spot, looking for something in the way of an angle or lighting or composition that Ben just couldn't see.

O'Sullivan plucked at his white suspenders, like overgrown banjo strings, and whistled snatches of "Yankee Doodle Dandy" as he held up both hands, fingers spread, to frame a boulder scarred with rifle shot. Ben could hear faint shouting over by Rock Creek, where men were working round the clock to repair a small railroad bridge the Rebs had left in twisted piles of metal and jagged splinters of wood.

"I'm looking for a photograph that tells a story," O'Sullivan told Ben, pushing his thick, red hair back off his sweat-beaded forehead. "That's what people want. When we bring out our stereopticon slides of the Battle of Gettysburg, folks want to see sights that make 'em weep for the sorrow of it all, the brave boys staying at their posts till the last breath. That's why these bodies are so important."

Ben nodded. But he couldn't help thinking that most of the dozen or so bodies still scattered among the rocks hardly looked heroic. Heck, they hardly looked human.

At least he didn't have to wear that stifling bandana around his face today. The smell had faded more and more with each body buried. Now all a fella had to do was hold his breath every once in a while and keep his mouth closed against the flies.

Ben followed O'Sullivan, impressed by the man's

concentration and patience. For each shot, the photographer's head disappeared under a black cloth so that, if you looked at him from the side, he appeared to have a wooden box for a head, with an accordion-pleated leather neck and, around in the front, one staring glass eye.

Ben leaned against a makeshift stone wall, piled between two huge, gray, moss-patched boulders. A flat rock wiggled under the palm of his hand as he leaned on it, and Ben looked down at the hastily-thrown-up breastwork for the first time. It was one of many such walls slapped together during the fiercest fighting, built for protection with bullets already flying. From the way some of the wounded men at Travis's had told it, one of the worst battles of the whole three-day shebang had taken place on the second day, practically right where Ben was standing.

Ben glanced around at the field of huge boulders close beside a small brook. The field faced the high ground and gave excellent cover behind the rocks. A perfect place to make a stand.

Or maybe not so perfect.

Ben's eye fell on a stray minié ball, rolling like a loose pebble across the shifting rock under his hand. "You know, I bet there was a Confederate sharpshooter sittin' right here," Ben said aloud. "That would be a story, wouldn't it? If he was still sittin' here?" Ben looked over at O'Sullivan, who was staring at him.

"Indeed." O'Sullivan said the word so softly, Ben wasn't

sure he'd heard it right. The photographer paced down the slope, bending to examine bloated bodies. Surely these soldiers were the last ones waiting for a burial detail. It was a big job to get all of them in the ground, and it wasn't helped by the dozens of family members arriving with picks and shovels to dig up those who had just been buried. At least they were all digging elsewhere today.

Trouble was, these folks tended to *un*bury bodies, and then leave them unburied, as they hurried to find the particular bodies of their own newly buried fathers, sons, brothers, or husbands. They'd dig down a row, searching for the right body to cart to one of the busy embalming tents where they could arrange for it to be transported home.

Ben didn't understand why these frantic relatives couldn't just leave the soldiers here, where they'd fought so long and hard. It was a fitting place for them to rest. Moving them seemed wrong somehow.

"This one!" O'Sullivan shouted, motioning at Ben to come over. "Oh yes, this is definitely the one." He was pointing at the body of a young Rebel soldier. Dark hair. No beard. Probably only four or five years older than Ben himself. He almost appeared to be sleeping, lying there in the deep shade, so the sun and heat hadn't managed to swell him up as bad as the others.

"Get a blanket out of the wagon. Quick now, while we've still got this light."

"You want to cover him up?" Ben asked, puzzled. "You gonna take his picture that way?"

"Quite the opposite, my boy. I'm—we're—going to do just what you suggested."

"What did I suggest?" Ben was getting more puzzled by the minute.

But O'Sullivan shoved him toward the wagon. "A blanket and that rifle in the back," he instructed. "Get that, too. Now why wouldn't this poor unfortunate fellow have a rifle with him?" O'Sullivan was scanning the rock-strewn ground, but Ben knew the answer by looking at the pockets of the soldier's worn gray jacket.

"His pockets are slit," Ben called over his shoulder as he hustled to get the things O'Sullivan wanted. "Souvenir hunters must have been here already and taken his gun. Even his buttons are gone."

"Humph!" O'Sullivan threw his hands in the air in disgust. "What a disgraceful way to treat these valorous heroes—robbing them as they lie stilled in death. Well, we'll restore some honor to these fine fellows. And we'll start right here."

The photographer spent an hour on three different shots of the corpse where it lay before saying, "Let's move him."

O'Sullivan rolled the stiff body onto its side. "Put the blanket under him," he instructed. "Stuff it in tight there, Ben, so when I roll him back, he'll be on top of it."

Ben wrinkled his nose. He hadn't thought he needed his protective kerchief today, not since he was working on photography instead of burning dead horses. But the smell coming off this soldier was almost as bad. And the man's face was turning black. Ben shivered despite the July heat as he rolled the blanket under the corpse.

"Yes, that's it."

When the body was lying squarely on the gray wool blanket, they each took a corner and dragged it some seventy yards up the slope to the rock wall between the boulders. O'Sullivan arranged the dead soldier so he lay as if he had fallen right there, a battered old hat at his feet, and the silent rifle leaning neatly against the small fortification of rock. With the blanket rolled a little up under him, Ben had to admit, it looked for all the world like the battle was still raging and the young soldier had dropped here, mortally wounded just minutes ago.

Of course, the photographer's rifle wasn't scratched and battered like a real soldier's gun—but it was a Springfield. Foot soldiers carried Enfields and Springfields. O'Sullivan was posing the body as a sharpshooter, which meant he should really have a Sharp's breech-loading carbine. But a Springfield would have to do. At least the knapsack O'Sullivan used to prop the soldier's head up was real. The photographer had picked it up the day before, down at Rose farm. Which, thought Ben, made O'Sullivan as much of a souvenir hunter as the scavengers who turned the dead men's pockets inside out and took their money and even their letters from home.

They worked at it for a full hour, moving the camera around to two completely different spots. O'Sullivan said he needed more than one angle, so they took three shots in all.

"What do you think, my boy? This was an excellent idea of yours. You just may have the makings of a fine photographer."

"I didn't figure movin' bodies was something photographers had call to do," Ben answered shortly. It didn't seem fitting somehow, to move a man from the spot where he had fallen, mortally wounded, and pose him like a big, porcelain-headed stuffed doll.

"You never saw your brother posing people in his studio?" O'Sullivan asked with a sharp laugh. "This is exactly the same thing, Ben, the main difference being our subject holds his pose far better than any paying customer at your brother's studio *ever* did."

"Won't folks ask how you come to find this fella?" Ben asked, trying hard to understand.

"I shall call him . . ." O'Sullivan paused, but not for long. "I shall call him 'The Sharpshooter.' He was wounded at this wall by a shell fragment and lay himself down to die. He'll be a hero to the whole country. You can almost see him, can't you, composing himself like this, accepting his sad fate for the glory of the cause?"

Ben looked back down the slope to the spot where the body had actually fallen. The young man's back had been turned to the breastworks behind him, as if he were going in the other direction—running away.

Apparently, if you couldn't find a body that "told a story," you made up your own story and shoved a body around to fit. Ben was determined he'd never be that kind of photographer.

"All this lacks for absolute perfection is a faithful dog by the soldier's side," mused O'Sullivan, his head hidden beneath the camera's black veil. "Well, perhaps we'll find one of those, too, before this day is through."

Ben grunted in reply, hoping with all his heart that Captain—and Reuben—were far, far away from this bloody battlefield and this meddling photographer, safe and somehow alive in some better place.

"You don't have a dog who'd pose for us here, do you, boy?" O'Sullivan asked. "I'll wait right here if you run and fetch it, and we'll make it as famous as Abraham Lincoln himself."

Ben shook his head without meeting O'Sullivan's eyes. "No, sir," he said softly. "I don't have a dog."

CHAPTER 21

July 15

"Don't let anybody eat Mavis, Ben," Danny begged.

"Travis was funnin' you, Danny. Don't be addlepated. Nobody eats a milkin' cow."

"Are you sure, Ben? Promise me you're sure."

Ben was too nervous getting ready for this special day to mollycoddle his whining cousin. "If you're so dang worried about Mavis," Ben snapped, "get out of that bed and go take care of her on your own hook."

Ben had been stuck with the milking, feeding, and mucking out after the little Jersey since Danny's relic hunting expedition had landed him in bed.

Talk about milking.

Danny Seldomridge knew how to milk his convalescence a whole bucketful. He had Travis's wife and daughters waiting on him, Ben's mother reading to him, and Ben himself doing all his chores.

But today, Ben had a chance to meet Mathew Brady, the world-famous photographer. O'Sullivan had recommended Ben's work to the Sanitation Commission, which in turn offered his name as a battlefield guide to Brady and his assistants. It had been almost two weeks since the battle. Ben knew his ma had little hope of finding Reuben anywhere in Gettysburg after so much time. She was hoping there'd be a letter from him waiting when they got home, saying his unit had pulled out right after the battle and now they were awaiting a new assignment in Washington, D.C., or maybe escorting generals through Virginia, where things were quiet for now.

Ben had almost given up his own search, except that every time he heard a dog bark, he turned to see if maybe Captain was bringing Reuben back to him. The photography work got his mind off the lonely ache in his gut that made it hard to concentrate. At least the photography came back to him easily.

Ben had learned from O'Sullivan the bits he hadn't already learned from Reuben about the wet-plate method. He now knew how to do the whole emulsion process in the back of a small, black-draped wagon that O'Sullivan called the "portable darkroom."

Really, it was more like sitting in a steamer trunk and trying to do delicate work when you could barely see your own hands. First you poured a syrupy solution, called collodion, over a clean glass rectangle from a special box that kept the plates upright and separated. After the excess coating drained off and the surface of the glass was just slightly sticky to the touch, you plunged the plate into another bitter-smelling solution that rendered it light sensitive. Then you stuck it in a black case and rushed it to the camera. The photographer had already chosen his shot, of course, and he slid the plate right in and made an exposure—anywhere from five to ten seconds—before handing the plate back to his assistant, who ran it back to the portable darkroom where it was given a number and quickly developed.

The glass had to stay damp from beginning to end or the picture would be ruined. Other things were like that, too. Ruined if you didn't tend to them carefully and quickly. The actual wet plate process took about ten minutes. Most of the work came in choosing the shot, preparing the plates, and promptly developing each of them, one at a time.

Things were calming down a bit in Gettysburg. Not getting back to normal exactly. No one seemed to think things would ever get back to normal in this once-quiet crossroads town.

Tomorrow, the remaining twenty-five hundred Confederate prisoners would be shipped out by train to Washington, D.C. From there, they'd be sent to prison camps throughout the North.

But today, Ben would be with Mathew Brady on Seminary Ridge.

The famous photographer wanted stereo views of all the places where there'd been fighting. Round Top, the peach orchard, Culp's Hill, cemetery hill, even the Evergreen Memorial yard, with its small, iron fences around the fancier headstones and its bullet hole–pocked sign warning: "Any persons caught discharging firearms on these grounds will be prosecuted to the fullest extent of the law."

Ben approached Mathew Brady with the brown derby politely in his hand instead of on his head. He was trying hard not to stare at the famous dark-haired man in the black frock coat and vest, a small pair of wire-rimmed glasses resting on his nose, partially covering eyes that seemed to constantly dart from one thing to the next.

Brady had a small, dark goatee and a thick, dark mustache that hung below his chin and hid his upper lip completely. He looked like a teacher or a minister far more than a dashing adventurer who'd taken photographs that were published in every major magazine in the country, including *Harper's Weekly* and *Leslie's Illustrated*. Brady wasn't just a photographer. He was a wealthy man, owner of galleries in both New York and Washington.

"You must be Ben Reynolds." The voice was friendly. Mathew Brady extended a hand.

"Hello, Mr. Brady." Ben immediately liked the man's firm handshake and easygoing manner.

"I want to see anything you consider worth seeing," Brady told Ben.

♦ ♦ ♦

The first thing Ben took him to see were the trees on Culp's Hill. Maples, birches, and oaks had fallen there the second and third day of the battle, felled by a steady stream of rifle fire that cut through wood and bark like a saw blade. Many trees still standing were dying now, their leaves yellow and limp, victims of lead poisoning from the minié balls embedded in their bark. Others hung at grotesque angles, their trunks chipped and scarred, their branches bare, despite it being full summer. Ben sometimes wondered if a tree could be afraid, the way a man could. But Mr. Brady assured him that was just a youthful fancy. Trees, he said, knew nothing and feared nothing.

Brady asked lots of questions and called out lots of orders, but he never got behind the camera himself. He just ordered around his handful of assistants.

"Bad eyes," he told Ben, when he caught him staring. His hand swept past his spectacles. "Too much close work in poor light, I suspect. I like to supervise an expedition as important as this one, but I prefer keener eyes than mine for the final focusing."

Ben nodded and said nothing.

What was there to say? The keenest eye in the world could never pull this horrible battle into focus. Ben had been here in person, and he still didn't understand how such a thing could happen.

Since there were no unburied bodies left to photograph,

the Brady team concentrated on views of the battlefield itself—the breastworks on Culp's Hill, the cemetery gatehouse, the spot where General Reynolds fell in Herbst's Woods, and General Lee's farmhouse headquarters. Brady included people in the frame some of the time, to give a sense of size. One assistant in a white duster and another in a dark vest were positioned in several shots to show the enormousness of the rocks.

Brady wanted to go everywhere and see everything. Farms. Fields. Woods. Rock Creek. Even the town itself. It was sheer luck that they ran into three Reb prisoners as the team was climbing back up Seminary Ridge from a visit to the edge of town.

This was the only part of this whole photography business that reminded Ben of Reuben's studio. Brady posed those Rebs, turning them this way and that, until he had them just the way he wanted. He cautioned them not to smile. He didn't really need to, in Ben's opinion. They didn't look very happy, being prisoners and all.

The picture that took the most time, by far, was the two-plate panorama of the whole town that Brady wanted to take from the top of Seminary Ridge. You could see the newly erected Camp Letterman in the distance, a whole hospital built out of white canvas tents, row after row of them.

Ben squinted at the ribbon of Chambersburg Pike stretching away to the horizon. Not a wagon or rider in

274 • PRIVATE CAPTAIN

sight. The split-rail fences were half broken, where soldiers had grabbed the crosspieces for firewood or to build breastworks. The green fields were deserted. Most of the livestock had been moved east of the Susquehanna or north to Carlisle before the fighting had even begun. The countryside seemed to be empty.

Ben shaded his eyes with one hand and peered at a mound of freshly turned earth, almost white in the sunshine far below them. It was next to a small stand of peach trees, practically in somebody's backyard. There was a soldier buried there. The mound of dirt marked the solitary grave.

What if it was Reuben? What if he hadn't really looked long enough and hard enough? So many bodies out there in unmarked graves.

What if Ben's brother was buried here, right in front of him, and he didn't even know it?

Ben had a sudden urge to dash wildly down the hill and dig into that mound with his bare hands. He turned away from the view of town and watched Brady and his assistants pointing their lens this way and that as they searched for the perfect stereographic view. At least Mathew Brady didn't have Ben moving bodies to enhance the "drama" of the shot.

If only Captain were here. That old yellow hound would find Reuben whether he was wounded and above ground—or dead and buried under the dark sod.

Ben turned to watch Mathew Brady frame another angle from atop a broad, flat rock. But thoughts of Reuben wouldn't leave him. His brother was probably dead. Reuben and Captain both. Dying was the way of things in a battle. Ben had learned that much, anyroad.

It was no good letting himself dwell on it. Reuben was gone. Captain was gone. And by the weekend, he and Danny would be gone, too, packed up and headed home with Ben's mother. There was no use fighting it any longer.

Oh sure, he could keep refusing to leave. Cousin Travis and his wife Mae weren't complaining about having them as company, and there was certainly plenty of cleanup work left to do. But staying in Gettysburg wasn't going to make Cap and Reuben magically reappear.

They were gone. Ben had to accept it.

Brady let out a low whistle, and Ben snapped out of his reverie. He turned to look back down the hill where the photographer was pointing.

"I saw movement, but I couldn't quite make it out," Brady was telling the man hidden under the camera's black veil. "Are you sure you saw a cow? I didn't think there was a single bovine left in the whole town!"

"Oh, I saw it all right," came the slightly muffled reply. "It was a little brown Jersey, trotting out from behind that white barn over yonder. It'll be a tiny blur on the image, but there's nothing I can do about it now."

Ben felt a slow grin spreading across his face. It was a

peculiar feeling. He'd thought he'd forgotten how to smile.

That had to be Mavis.

She was practically the only cow left in town. Ben had staked her in a grassy field that morning so she could get some grazing done before he got home and fed her. Ben wasn't surprised to hear their traveling cow had pulled herself loose and set out to look around. It was just like Mavis.

The world might be going all to flinders, but Mavis could still make him smile. War. Death. Fighting everywhere. But as long as Mavis had her cud to chew, the placid old cow was content.

Ben wondered if he'd ever feel that way again. Maybe back in Lancaster. He was ready to go home.

CHAPTER 22

His Truth Is Marching On

Ben couldn't eat the salted radish Danny offered him. He couldn't even bear to look at it. It reminded him of the vegetable-eatingest dog he'd ever known.

He pushed Danny's outstretched hand away.

"Aunt Kathleen told me radishes were your favorite if they were cold from the cellar and salted up real good. Don't you like them anymore?"

"They . . ."

Ben stopped and tried again.

"I can't . . ."

Ben stopped again, turning to look his cousin squarely in the eye. "No, I guess I don't much like radishes anymore," he said simply.

Danny shrugged and popped the small, red vegetable into his own mouth, watching Ben inventory the goods in the back shed. Ben sorted methodically through the bolts of calico and boxes of wide-brimmed straw hats, the barrels of crackers and big, glass jars of milled oats. There was a whole shelf of nothing but patent medicines. Even with their corks tightly in place, the medicine bottles gave off the odors of sassafras, rhubarb, and fennel. They came in all shapes and sizes, from Hostetter's Bitters to Peruna syrup.

Ben reached for a two-gallon jar of cough drops labeled "James Smith & Sons Compound of Wild Cherry Cough Candy."

It was warm in the dusty interior of the shed, despite the late September breeze stirring outside on Lancaster's busy streets. Ben wiped sweat from his upper lip with the back of one hand. The taste of it reminded him of Captain's slurpy tongue.

He'd grown too used to having the yellow hound always turning up around the next corner, or suddenly finding it sprawled beside him on the grass. It felt wrong to be home without Captain or Reuben; working in the store again as if everything were back to normal.

That's what a man did, though.

Ben understood that now.

A man didn't go lookin' for somebody else to do what he should do himself. He did what needed to be done, and he didn't talk about how he felt. How he felt without Reuben or his dumb old bootlicker dog.

Reuben's name was now on the list of missing pinned up to the courthouse door in Penn Square. Ma and he had agreed, without ever saying it out loud, to give up looking, at least for now.

So here he stood in the storage shed by the outhouse behind Reynolds & Sons Dry Goods, sorting through sponge boots for horses and cotton lisle stockings for ladies and listening to Danny Seldomridge make as much noise as he knew how, crunching a stupid radish.

"Ya know," Danny began, after he'd done a full performance and swallowed the noisy vegetable, "my ma says we're gonna stay right here in Lancaster helpin' you until she's sure you and Aunt Kathleen can get on without us. So how long do you think that will be, Ben?" Danny bumped into Ben's careful stack of canned milk, sending several cans rolling across the plank floor.

Ben sighed and bent to pick up the cans.

"You'd have to ask your ma that. I think me and Ma are doing fine, with me working full-time in the store now." Ben hadn't returned to school, although his mother refused to let him give up on getting educated. He was studying at home in the evenings for now, and after the war they'd see about school again. Maybe even college someday, or an apprenticeship.

Mathew Brady had written to Ma, asking if Ben might come apprentice with him. His mother said he should be proud to get an offer like that from such an important man.

But Ben couldn't let himself think about it. Thinking about the future was hard these days. There was always the War, looming over every tomorrow. Battles at Vicksburg and Chickamauga just since Gettysburg.

Funny. Ben had been so sure the Pennsylvania battle had been the battle to end all battles. But it hadn't been.

Ben hoped Jim had made it back to Georgia and was, right this minute, sitting under a magnolia tree, playing with Curtis's old tick hound. It was comforting to think it. Just as it was comforting to think Cap had been scared by those gunshots in the streets of Gettysburg and fled west, or even south, and was living somewhere with a fine family that fed him turnips and radishes and let him sleep beside their beds.

Ben didn't care if the dog was living with a family of Rebs, just as long as he was alive.

Ben felt a chill down his back, even though he was sweating from the work. He could hear the distant barking of dogs. Probably the honey-dipper's wagon was rattling its smelly way up Queen Street. It was about time for the black man the children called "the honey dipper" to come around and dip out the two holes of their privy. The odor of human waste brought so many flies that even this storage shed got visits. Ben swatted at one as it circled his head. A fresh dusting of lime would take care of these Indian-summer flies.

"Did you hear that?" Danny asked. He was seated on an uncut block of soap as big as a two-bushel crate of apples.

"What?" Ben couldn't hear anything with the blasted fly darting around his head. He fanned one ear with the inventory book.

"What?" Ben repeated, but his cousin had already disappeared outside. Probably aiming to duck his lessons, Ben thought. Aunt Mavis was homeschooling Danny, too, until they rejoined Uncle Elliott at their own store in Hanover. Uncle Elliott had taken Mavis with him, which could be why Danny had reverted to his old bratty-little-kid self.

Ben cocked his head. He could hear shouting, but he couldn't make out the words. Someone whistled out on the street, and Ben thought he heard clapping out in front of the store.

Ben laid his ledger and pencil on the lid of a box of Turlington's Balsam of Life. Aunt Mavis insisted the stuff had kept Danny strong and brought him safely back to her. Ben wasn't surprised she gave all the credit to an oily elixir instead of him.

Ben swung open the shed door and rubbed his eyes for a moment in the bright September sunshine. The first leaves were just beginning to turn yellow and red for autumn. At least the trees in Lancaster *had* leaves. In Gettysburg, it had looked like September in July.

Ben walked slowly across the yard and down the narrow alley between the dry goods store and the Owen house. He'd take just a short break, and then get back to work.

He opened the gate at the end of the walk. There was a crowd on Lime Street, shouting and clapping and whistling.

He was surprised to spot his mother standing in the doorway of the store. She clutched a handkerchief and her eyes glistened in the afternoon sunshine.

Ben frowned. He hadn't actually seen Ma cry when Pa died, though he suspected she had. Nor when Reuben went missing, either. He waved at her, but she wasn't looking in his direction. She was looking down the street, over the heads of the crowd.

"What's going on?" Ben asked a little girl clinging to the edge of her mother's apron, sucking on a chunk of clear rock candy.

But the girl only ducked her head, stuffing the candy deeper into her mouth and tugging on her mother's skirt. The woman looked over and caught sight of Ben.

"Hey!" she called out, so loudly Ben jumped back a little. "Aren't you the Reynolds boy? The youngest one?"

"I'm Ben Reynolds."

Why was this woman shouting at him? Ben couldn't see the street for the milling crowd blocking the sidewalk.

He heard a dog barking again, closer now. He heard—

Ben froze. People were turning to look at him. They were smiling and nodding, gesturing him forward. Some moved aside, making a path.

That bark was so familiar. Like a ghost bark. It had haunted his dreams for months.

Someone grabbed Ben's elbow, propelling him forward. He stumbled on the uneven bricks. The crowd grew quiet.

Or maybe Ben had simply stopped hearing the noises around him.

There was a man getting out of a carriage. A single, gaunt man in the ragged uniform of a Union soldier. He held a wooden crutch in one hand and the bottom of his left pants leg was pinned up almost to the knee.

Standing in front of the house, surveying the crowd with a curious stare, was an equally gaunt yellow dog with a pinkish nose and a tail held so high, it looked like a flag waving in a triumphal parade.

The dog saw Ben moments before Ben caught sight of the dog, its quivering nose swinging round to test the familiar scents. With one chopped bark, the dog sprang forward. Ben dropped to his knees on legs that wouldn't hold him. He could hear a woman behind him burst into tears. But all he could see was the square muzzle and the brown eyes, and all he could feel was the dog's tongue working its way from his ear to his cheek to his mouth to his forehead as it crowded in close to him.

Ben could hear Captain whining a continuous, urgent sound that seemed to be trying to tell Ben everything that had happened in the two long months since they'd last been together. Ben's arms were around the dog's neck.

"Captain." He whispered the name into the thick, yellow fur where he buried his face.

When he looked up, his brother, Reuben, was looking down at him, smiling. Reuben leaned heavily on the crutch as he stood arm-in-arm with their mother. She had tears streaming down her cheeks, running right past a smile so wide, it threatened to reach the edges of the black net snood that held her long, brown hair in place.

"You'll have to call him *Private* Captain now, Ben." Reuben's voice sounded the same as it always had—strong and sure. It didn't sound like it could belong to the scarecrow of a man standing in front of Ben, his dark beard newly streaked with gray, his eyes shadowed with pain.

"He won his stripe at Satterlee Hospital up to Philly, Ben. They pinned it right there on his collar. See?" Reuben bent down a little unsteadily and twisted Captain's old leather collar, laying a finger on the yellow cloth strip safety-pinned through a buckle hole. "The doc said he'd never seen anyone make a better soldier, in or out of uniform."

Reuben straightened back up, using Captain's back to push against. "So they inducted Cap, right there in the ward, with reporters from the *Inquirer* and the *Record* and the *Ledger* looking on. Made him a private. The surgeon in charge said Cap would probably work his way up to general if he weren't leaving the service to bring me home."

Ben stood up and clasped his brother's hand, now stretched out to him. Reuben pulled him closer, enveloping him in arms that still felt strong, despite their thinness.

"I heard you came lookin' for me, little brother," Reuben whispered in Ben's ear as he embraced him. "I've spent a lot of time laid up in bed just thinking on that. Wondering what my little brother had thought when he found himself smack in the middle of the Battle of Gettysburg."

"I thought we'd lost you." Ben's voice was choked.

"Reuben!" Danny's voice danced with excitement and Ben suddenly realized his cousin was right behind him, along with Aunt Mavis and half the people of Lancaster. "I knew we'd find you. I told Ben and told him, 'Don't you worry, Ben. We'll find Reuben. Cap and me will help you.' And here you are!"

"Here I am." Reuben smiled at Danny, but his gaze remained fastened on Ben.

"And you really did find me, Ben. More than you know."

"Your brother has just told me he didn't even know his name when he woke up from that awful battle," Ma said. "He went a little out of his head after they took his—" She swallowed hard. "—leg."

Reuben put an arm around her shoulder and squeezed. She reached up and squeezed his hand, then bent and laid a hand on Captain's head. "He couldn't remember who he was, Ben. Not until this dog found him.

"Even then," she straightened up and smiled proudly at Reuben, "it took him some time to sort it all out, the good from the bad."

Reuben looked down at the dog and nodded. "I was

lucky. I had a brother who was brave enough to come looking for me and smart enough to bring along the one critter on earth who was sure to find me." Reuben smiled at Captain. "And when he found me, he had this with him."

Reuben pulled Pa's pocket watch out of his own pocket and rubbed his thumb across the case. "Remember this?"

He offered the watch to Ben, who took it reverently and tried to keep his hand from trembling as he silently read the words he'd scratched in the gold so long ago:

CAPTAIN
Belongs to R. Reynolds
Lanc., PA.
OR
B. Reynolds

The *OR* was nearly rubbed away.

"I know it must have scared you when Cap disappeared. I think he would have left you a note if he could have, Ben. He sat outside that hospital in Philly some nights and howled for you, like loneliness was just eating him up. He kept it up until the head nurse threw a shoe at him."

Ben knew his expression must have registered horror because Reuben reached out and ran a thumb across Ben's cheek. That was the first Ben knew he was crying.

"The nurse missed, acourse. No dog on earth can dodge and weave like our Cap."

The yellow hound's ears twitched at the sound of his

name, and he gazed up at Reuben, his tail thumping against Ben's leg.

"He looks glad to see you, little brother. Almost as glad as I am."

"He's your dog, Reuben." Ben tried hard to keep his voice steady. "He's none of mine."

"He's a member of this family," interjected their mother. "And that's all that needs to be said. Come into the house, now, both of you. You look done in, Reuben."

But Reuben was still staring at Ben. "I owe you, little brother."

The crowd had grown absolutely quiet, straining to hear them. Ben heard no birds singing or wagons rattling or even the wind swooshing down the street. The whole world seemed to be holding its breath.

"It's good to be home," Reuben declared, breaking the deafening silence. Children began shouting, men laughing, and women buzzing with whispers of which pies or cakes or casseroles they should bake for the Reynolds family tonight.

As Ben turned, supporting Reuben and hefting his crutch, he saw Aunt Mavis, hands on her hips, grinning at him.

She spoke to Danny loudly enough, Ben felt sure, that she wanted him to hear, too.

"Start packing, son. We'll be heading home by the end of the week."

Captain walked close beside as Ben helped his brother up the dozen broad steps into the store.

Ben was looking where he put his feet, so he couldn't see his aunt's face anymore. He could only hear her words. "Your aunt Kathleen doesn't need us here anymore, what with Ben taking charge in the store. I do believe our Ben can handle things."

"Acourse he can," Danny agreed, sounding as if he wondered how his mother could ever have doubted it. "Captain's home."

The First Thanksgiving

President Lincoln proclaimed the fourth Thursday of November as "Thanksgiving" that fall after Gettysburg. There'd been Thanksgivings before, of course. Ben had read the old story of the Pilgrims' feast in school. Around Lancaster County, all the churches would pick a Sunday in October or November to give thanks for the harvest.

But this was Thanksgiving everywhere, all over the country. All over the Union, anyroad. And it was more than just the harvest that folks had a mind to be thankful for.

Ben, himself, was thankful that Reuben was alive and home. Sure, his brother was missing a leg, but Ben hardly noticed that anymore. Reuben only told the story of how he'd lost his leg one time. But Ben still remembered every word.

"I got hit in the leg and the head on the third day of the fighting. Someone carried me to a field hospital. I don't remember who. What I mainly know is what others told me later, at Satterlee. That's where they took me. To the army's general hospital in Philadelphia. I expect they didn't quite know what to do with a man who didn't even know his own name.

"The surgeons at Satterlee never did figure out how a dog got on a hospital train. Of course, there was lots of confusion what with so many wounded. With some instinct I don't even understand, Captain knew I'd left Gettysburg on a hospital train and was determined to follow me. He must have snuck onto a train transporting the wounded from Gettysburg. However he did it, he got to Philadelphia, and followed an ambulance wagon to Satterlee. He got to the hospital's front doors and took to barking and howling and raising such a fuss, they couldn't ignore him. Tried to have him carted off, but no one could catch him. So he sat there. He just sat there for two straight days. In the rain. In the night. He never moved.

"Finally, an orderly took pity on him. Poor old dog, just sitting and waiting, day and night, at those hospital doors. He brought Cap some food and water, and on the third day of that vigil, he let the dog inside to find out what—or who—he'd been outside waiting for. I'm lucky there was an orderly with enough common sense to know a dog doesn't sit and wait for no reason. No doctor ever would have let Cap in. Army doctors don't have that much sense.

"So, Cap came into that hospital, and found his way

straight to my bed. I always said that dog has the best nose in three counties. There he stood, whining and nudging at my hand. He refused to leave when the nurses tried to chase him out. He'd run and duck under beds, and then circle back to me.

"One sawbones in particular watched the whole scene, getting madder and madder, threatening to have the dog shot if no one could catch him. Then the orderly who'd let Cap in took that doctor by the arm and pulled him over to my bed.

"I had my hand on the dog's head, and I was calling out one word: 'Captain.' It was the first thing I'd said in seven days, leastwise, that's what the doctor told me later. That Doc decided, right then and there, that Cap could stay. He said he reckoned it was the best therapy a man in my condition could have.

"And he was right. Captain was the only thing that made any sense to me. The only thing I could allow myself to remember. It was like that for a long time. Memories only came back to me gradual-like. After Cap, it was just a short step to remembering Ma and Pa and you, Ben. Whatever I did remember was enough. It brought me home."

They were heading to Harrisburg by train today.

They'd cross the Susquehanna in Harrisburg and take

292 • PRIVATE CAPTAIN

another train down to Hanover, to spend the country's first official Thanksgiving with Aunt Mavis, Uncle Elliott, and Danny. Most of the rail lines had been repaired since July. Ben hated to admit it, but he was sort of looking forward to seeing old Danny again. And he wouldn't mind seeing Mavis, either. Not Aunt Mavis.

Mavis the cow.

A little boy, sitting on his mother's lap across the aisle of the railway car, came over to pet Captain. The dog was curled up on the seat beside Ben, facing Ma and Reuben in the seat opposite.

Both brothers wore hats. Reuben wore his war-worn, black derby, while Ben wore Henry Owen's brown derby, plucked from the bloody battlefield of Gettysburg. Reuben clicked open Pa's pocket watch to check the time. The timepiece was ticking again, now that Ben had taken it back to the jeweler's and got the rusted spring replaced.

Reuben snapped the case shut and continued rubbing his thumb over the gold case, back and forth, again and again. Ma called it a nervous tic left over from the battle, although Reuben didn't seem the least bit nervous to Ben.

"Hey, mister," the child said, looking from Ben to Reuben and back again. "That's one mighty fine dog. Is it yours?"

The brothers looked at each other, and, as if on some unspoken signal, both reached up and tilted their derby hats back on their heads.

"You mean, is he *my* dog, or is he my *brother's* dog?" Reuben asked, and the child nodded. "Well, what do you say to that, Ben?"

Ben didn't hesitate for a second. "Yes," he said, ruffling his fingers through Captain's thick fur. "Yes, he is."

Marty Crisp has been fascinated by the Civil War ever since she visited Gettysburg as a young child and witnessed the one hundredth anniversary (and first reenactment) of the famous battle. Now, she researches and writes historical fiction from Lancaster, Pennsylvania, the same place that Ben, her main character, lives.

Ms. Crisp is the author of two other novels: *Buzzard Breath*, which was included on the Black-Eyed Susan Children's Choice list, and *Ratzo*.